OSBERT

OSBERT

A portrait of
Osbert Lancaster

✳

RICHARD BOSTON

COLLINS
8 Grafton Street, London W1
1989

William Collins Sons & Co. Ltd
London · Glasgow · Sydney · Auckland
Toronto · Johannesburg

British Library Cataloguing in Publication Data
Boston, Richard, *1938–*
Osbert: a portrait of Osbert Lancaster.
1. Lancaster, Osbert, 1908–1986. – Biographies
I. Title
741'.092'4

ISBN 0 00 216324 1

Quotations in the text from *All Done From Memory,*
With an Eye to the Future, Drayneflete Revealed
and *Façades and Faces,* by Osbert Lancaster,
and from *Collected Poems* and *Summoned by Bells,*
by John Betjeman, are reproduced by
permission from John Murray Ltd (Publishers).

First published in Great Britain 1989
Copyright © Richard Boston 1989

Photoset in Linotron Palatino by
Wyvern Typesetting, Bristol
Printed and bound in Great Britain by
Butler & Tanner Ltd, Frome and London

CONTENTS

Acknowledgements

First, foremost and obviously, to Osbert Lancaster, on whose published works, private papers and conversation I have drawn heavily.

Then to his many friends, acquaintances, colleagues and members of the family who have generously contributed information, comments and anecdotes, and to various others who have made useful comments and suggestions verbally or in writing. They are numerous, and to anyone whose name is missing from the following I can only apologize for what is inadvertence rather than lack of gratitude:

The Marquis of Aberdeen, Kingsley Amis, John Arlott, Lady Balfour, Nancy Banks-Smith, the late Sir John Betjeman, the late the Hon. Lady Betjeman, Drusilla Beyfus, Clive Boutle, the late Mark Boxer, Lord Caccia, Mel Calman, Moran Caplat, Sir Hugh Casson, Mary Collins, Arthur Crook, Dr Alan Forster, Walter Goetz, Professor Sir Ernst Gombrich, OM, the late Geoffrey Grigson, Lady Harrod, Clare Hastings, Clare Hollingworth, the late Philip Hope-Wallace, Mary Ingrams, Richard Ingrams, Clive James, Cara Lancaster, William Lancaster, Lady Leeper, Patrick Leigh Fermor, George Melly, John G. Murray, Simon Pembroke, John Piper, Myfanwy Piper, Denis Pitts, Anthony Powell, Lady Violet Powell, Michael Rand, Sir James Richards, Gavin Stamp, George Malcolm Thomson, Sally Vincent, the late Rex Warner.

I have received enormous help in various ways from many people, but there is one area which I can claim to be all my own work: namely, any errors of fact, judgement or grammatical construction.

The comments of Anne Boston and of Judith Eagle were invariably constructive. Like so many others I am indebted to the London

7

Library and its polite and patient staff. Also to Margaret Apps for typing at an early stage in the long gestation of this book.

One of the intractable tasks of modern life is putting a duvet into its cover. Amanda McCardie performed the literary equivalent with a chaotic pile of pages, written by hand or on a variety of typewriters and word processors on paper of all sorts of shape, size and colour. Dictatorially, considerately and charmingly, she made sure to get me to the publisher on time.

It is a breach of the writer's code to speak well of a publisher, but there are always times when you have to break ranks. From the staff of Collins I have received nothing. Nothing but courtesy, efficiency, assistance and encouragement. Awards for outstanding patience must go without delay to Philip Ziegler and his editorial successors, Ariane Goodman and Simon King, and to Ron Clark for the attention, effort and understanding he put into the visual preparation of this book.

And *un très grand merci* to Marie Claude Chapuis, who over several years controlled (up to a point) her Gallic temper and temperament, encouraged me and even put up with me.

Boundless gratitude to Anne Lancaster for her assistance and friendship. And once again to Osbert, for being Osbert.

R.B.

The present and the past are always and everywhere inseparable; scratch is a position from which one can never start, and history a meaningless fantasy if not interpreted in the light of present-day experience.

Classical Landscape with Figures

Is not the caricaturist's task exactly the same as the classical artist's? Both see the lasting truth beneath the surface of mere outward appearance. Both try to help nature successfully accomplish its plan. The one may strive to visualize the perfect form and to realize it in his work; the other to grasp the perfect deformity, and *thus* reveal the very essence of a personality. A good caricature, like every other work of art, is more true to life than reality itself.

Annibale Carracci, sixteenth century

Introduction

The obituaries called him a national institution, which was true even if it was a cliché. They described him as a cartoonist, and indeed he was one of the wittiest and most prolific there have ever been. But he was more than that. *Who's Who* described him as 'artist and writer', which is nearer the mark. It is no disparagement of his work as a cartoonist to say that his activities in other fields, though perhaps less celebrated, were even more considerable.

He was one of the most stylish writers of his generation, both in prose and verse; he was a superlative illustrator and a much underrated painter; he was one of this century's most perceptive historians of architecture, and one of its most prophetic critics. As a diplomat he played an important role in Greece at the end of the Second World War, a crucial time in that country's history. He was a great dandy, a brilliant public speaker, a bon viveur, raconteur and wit. He was one of the finest stage designers this country has produced. And so on. Not just a cartoonist.

Versatility is suspect in this age of specialization. Renaissance man could get away with it, but nowadays one is expected to stick to one last. Those who do otherwise are put down as jacks of all trades and masters of none, dabblers, amateurs, dilettanti, and not to be taken seriously.

If versatility is suspect, facility is even more so. When Osbert was writing, he did not toil over endless drafts in order to produce that highly polished prose. On the contrary, his manuscripts (usually written in pencil on lined paper) show that he hardly revised anything; his work emerged fully formed like Venus from the sea. Likewise, his drawings and paintings were almost always done straight off, without roughs, sketches or discarded versions.

The dandy is obliged to make whatever he does look easy. Many hours in front of the mirror were required in order to produce the precise casual elegance of Beau Brummell's cravat. A favourite story

11

of Osbert Lancaster's concerned Nikolaus Pevsner and Kenneth Clark. Pevsner once turned up at the National Gallery for a meeting with Clark a few minutes early. Pevsner never wasted a second, and when Clark emerged to greet him, he found Pevsner reading a book and taking notes. '*Immer fleissig, Herr Doktor,*' said Clark, '*Immer fleissig.*' ('Always busy, Herr Doktor, always busy.') It is hard to imagine the dandyish Clark or Lancaster being caught in this way, actually working, but there can be no doubt that the work was done, and that the learning was there, however lightly worn.

As architectural historians and critics, Pevsner and Osbert Lancaster were as different as they could be, in taste as well as style. Pevsner was an ardent advocate of *Modernismus*, Lancaster was not. Pevsner impressed the reader with his high seriousness and prodigious industry. Osbert Lancaster's works instruct through entertainment. They are easy to read, they do not have massive bibliographies (or, indeed, bibliographies at all), nor do they carry a baggage-train of critical apparatus and footnotes. His books are fun. Indeed, they are funny. In one of his letters Byron mentions a Methodist preacher who 'on perceiving a profane grin on the faces of part of his congregation exclaimed, "No *hopes* for *them* as *laughs*" '. For more than half a century Osbert Lancaster delighted and gave hope to them as laughs.

At this point I must, for reasons that will soon become apparent, introduce a personal note.

As a schoolboy my first attempts to understand something about architecture relied on the works of Nikolaus Pevsner and Banister Fletcher. I can now see that theirs are admirable tomes but perhaps they are not really for beginners. At any rate my architectural studies made very little headway until I came across Osbert Lancaster's *Pillar to Post* and *Homes Sweet Homes*, described by Professor Sir Ernst Gombrich as 'the best textbook of architecture ever published'. These little books changed everything. So *that*'s what architecture was all about. It was all around you. The parish church was architecture. The school chapel was architecture. The High Street was full of architecture. The cowshed was architecture. The stuff was everywhere. Like the character in Molière who was astonished to learn that he had been speaking prose all his life, I was amazed to discover that the buildings I saw every day were architecture, and that in order to appreciate and enjoy it you didn't need the massive erudition of a Banister Fletcher or a Nikolaus Pevsner, but just a pair of open eyes. In so far as my eyes have been opened to architecture I can say, with enormous gratitude, that it was Osbert Lancaster who did it.

Some years later, in the 1960s, I saw the man himself. He was standing in Fleet Street, opposite the *Express* building, hailing a taxi. A short figure, stocky but erect, nattily dressed in a pinstriped suit with a carnation in the buttonhole and neatly folded handkerchief in the breast-pocket, umbrella tightly rolled and hat perched slightly back on top of a head which seemed much too big for the body that carried it, like an Edwardian caricature by Spy. He looked furious. The moustache bristled, the eyes bulged. I murmured to myself 'Good grief,' and passed on.

As did the years. In 1973 the *Guardian* asked me to review *The Littlehampton Bequest*. I was captivated by it. As far as I remember, my review expressed total admiration for the wit and erudition both of the paintings and the written commentary. I said it was as good as *Pillar to Post* and *Homes Sweet Homes*. I said it was better than Max Beerbohm.

A few weeks later I happened to be house-hunting. My requirements were simple, but hard to meet. I wanted to rent somewhere in the country, not too far from London; preferably a cottage with a garden. Innumerable phone calls to estate agents were eventually rewarded. The agent in Goring-on-Thames drove me up to Aldworth, a Berkshire village, where he showed me an enchanting thatched cottage with garden. The house was so small that there was not a single doorway I could walk through without ducking, and the rent was equally low. On the spot I said that I would take it. The owners apparently lived next door, and the lights showed that they were in.

We were welcomed by a very tall, very elegant lady who invited us in for tea. While she went to put the kettle on, the agent and I were left with her husband, the subject of this book. His wife, I suddenly realized, was Anne Scott-James. He looked much less choleric than when I had seen him in Fleet Street. Indeed he was relaxed, affable and not at all the terrifying figure I had come to imagine. In the course of small talk it emerged that I had been the reviewer of *The Littlehampton Bequest* in the *Guardian*. Anne Lancaster came in bearing a tea-tray. 'Darling,' he said, 'our new *neighbour* is the man who said those *nice* things about me in the *Manchester Guardian.'*

I stayed in the cottage as the Lancasters' tenant for about five years, and then bought a house of my own in another part of the village. For some dozen years hardly a week passed in which we did not visit one another for meals, drinks or a chat.

This preamble has two purposes. One is to establish that my admiration for Osbert Lancaster predated my acquaintance and friendship with him. The other is to explain why in this book I have had the presumption to refer to him throughout as Osbert, and to his wife as Anne. Normally it is a bad thing for a biographer to be on first-name terms with the subject: it would be hard to put much trust in a book on Cromwell that always called him Oliver, or one on Wellington that called him Arthur. On the other hand it would be taking literary propriety too far to be on surname terms with someone with whom you have more than once shared Christmas dinner – someone you have seen, indeed, pulling crackers and wearing a paper hat.

Besides which, just as Max Beerbohm was Max, Osbert Lancaster was Osbert. When in London, wearing his impeccably cut suit with the carnation in the buttonhole, he may have been Mr Lancaster, and later Sir Osbert, but I rarely saw him like that. The man I knew was the country-weekend figure in baggy corduroys, venerable pullover and carpet slippers, a powerful martini in one hand and in the other a cigarette of which the ash could reach an astonishing length before being dropped into the ashtray, or more likely falling on to his pullover, or his trousers, or the carpet. To call that smiling, genial, witty, hospitable and (in every sense) entertaining figure 'Lancaster' or 'Mr Lancaster' or 'Sir Osbert' would be completely artificial. He was Osbert.

There have been problems in writing this book. Someone who led such a busy life, socially and professionally, someone whose experiences ranged from the Foreign Office to Glyndebourne, from Fleet Street to clubland, someone with such an avid appetite for gossip, with such acute observation of the foibles, fashions and follies of mankind and the ability to record them so wittily both in words and drawings; such a person was in a position to be a uniquely entertaining and informative diarist. Osbert did write two splendid volumes of autobiography, and when travelling abroad he kept journals which alternated detailed drawings with written day-by-day accounts. Otherwise, regrettably (though characteristically), he kept no diary.

There is a further problem. Had he been merely a cartoonist, or merely a painter, writer or stage designer, his career could be traced chronologically. But he pursued his various activities not consecutively but simultaneously. Furthermore his style in art and life were fully developed early on, and did not change greatly thereafter. It has therefore often proved convenient when discussing an early period of his career to mention activities of many years later. Sometimes I have unavoidably had to get ahead of the story and then backtrack. I hope that this approach is not too confusing. If it is, I can only excuse myself by pointing to Osbert's own autobiographical writings, which weave together time past and time present as intricately as the first lines of T. S. Eliot's 'Burnt Norton'.

I

THE IMPORTANCE OF
BEING OSBERT

ONE of the less celebrated of the many and varied achievements of Queen Victoria's Prince Consort was to have done
more for the name Bert than anyone before or since.
According to the *Guinness Book of Names*, analysis of the first names
of boys called Smith recorded in England and Wales shows that
Albert was the twentieth most popular name in 1850, eleventh in
1875, ninth in 1900, tenth in 1925, and made no appearance at all in
the top fifty names before or after this period. The turning-point
came when the Prince of Wales defied Queen Victoria's expressed
wish that he should become King Albert and chose to become
Edward VII instead.

At its peak the popularity of Albert surpassed even the perennial
Robert, and dragged Herbert in its wake. Berts abounded
everywhere, from Burlington Bertie to Bertie Wooster. There were
even Ethelberts, Huberts, Egberts and Cuthberts. There were
Bertrams and Bertrands. And there were a few, a very few, Osberts.
In fact it was so rare a name that Osbert Sitwell took a decidedly
proprietorial attitude to it and bitterly resented the existence of a
literary gentleman called Osbert Burdett, author of books on such
subjects as Carlyle, the Brownings, the art of living, and cheese.
Osbert Sitwell was further put out when the name of Osbert
Lancaster began to be mentioned in the circles in which he moved.
However, Sitwell eventually came round to the view that at least the
youngest of the three extant Osberts was not entirely unworthy of
the name. This emerged when Osbert Burdett died, on which
occasion Osbert Lancaster received from Osbert Sitwell (whom he
had never met) an invitation to lunch in order to celebrate the fact
that there were now only two of them. The surviving Osberts
remained on friendly terms thereafter.

Osbert Lancaster too was jealous of the name. Indeed, it was a
subject on which he could become a little tetchy. I once, rather

mischievously, asked him when he had first become aware of the existence of an American film-actor called Burt Lancaster. The reply was mumbled, but clear enough to indicate that he did not think the subject worth pursuing.

Unusually for someone of his background, he had only one forename. This was as a result of a policy laid down for the whole family by the paternal grandfather, Sir William Lancaster: during his very long and busy career Sir William had found the signing of documents to be a time-consuming chore, and thought that for his descendants to have only one forename would economize on time, effort and ink all round.

Osbert Lancaster was born on 4 August 1908, the only child of Robert Lancaster and Clare Bracebridge Lancaster (née Manger). He was thus born six years to the very day before the declaration of the war which, as everyone always says, changed everything; he came to consciousness in that pre-war period. He was born an Edwardian, and in many respects an Edwardian he always remained.

In his autobiography Osbert referred to the 'perpetual sunlight of the days before 1914', but he also commented that vast social changes were in the air. To recognize the truth of this, one has only to look at a few of the events that occurred in the year of his birth. In 1908 Northcliffe bought *The Times*. The song 'It's a long way to Tipperary' was first heard. E. M. Forster published *A Room with a View*. At the Paris Salon some paintings were exhibited which a critic said consisted of 'little cubes': Cubism was born. It was the year when Belgium annexed the Congo, when the Young Turks had their revolution, when Asquith became Prime Minister. Austria annexed Bosnia and Herzegovina, and Taft was elected President of the United States. The Hughes Tool Company and the General Motor Company were founded, and Henry Ford introduced the Model T Ford or 'flivver', a motorcar with a wooden body on a steel frame which made it 'stronger than a horse and easier to maintain' and which came in any colour you wanted as long as it was black.

Perhaps it was the last of these events that proved in the long term to be the most important. At $850.50 the Model T cost more than most Americans earned in a whole year, yet it heralded the age of popular motoring. During Osbert's lifetime this was to change everything, from the structure of society to the appearance (or disappearance) of ancient landscapes and cities. That this did not go without notice at the time is shown by Kenneth Grahame's *The Wind in the Willows*, first published just two months before Osbert was born. It is a work of nostalgia, but at the same time it is every bit as

prophetic as H. G. Wells's *The War in the Air*, also published that year. Grahame saw clearly what would be the impact of the motorcar:

> 'Glorious, glorious sight!' murmured Toad, never offering to move. 'The poetry of motion! The *real* way to travel! The only way to travel! Here to-day – in next week to-morrow! Villages skipped, towns and

cities jumped – always somebody else's horizon! O bliss! O poop-poop! O my! *O my!*'

Of course Toad was more than a little cracked, but almost everyone else was too. It turned out that the new century did not belong to sensible chaps like Rat and Mole and Badger with their rowing boats and horse-drawn vehicles but to the brash vulgarian Toad and his infernal internal combustion engine.

The stoats, weasels and other horrid little lumpenproletariat animals of the Wild Wood fail in their insurrection against the solidly bourgeois heroes, but it is a damned close-run thing. The social system of power and privilege based on inherited wealth is not brought down, but it is badly shaken. Grahame's nostalgia for the past is accompanied by an uncomfortable awareness that the future belongs to the Common Man (or stoat). Osbert, whose life coincided with the Age of the Car, made the same connection between social change and the motorcar in his autobiography, in such books as *Drayneflete Revealed*, in the drawings he executed for the Victoria and Albert Museum's exhibition 'The Destruction of the Country House' (reproduced in *Scene Changes*, 1978) and in the large mural he produced for the Shell Centre in 1963.

His own preferred method of transport was, he always said, a pram. His memories from this vantage-point were vivid and much cherished, but in the interest of accuracy one must point out that they sometimes benefited from hindsight. For example, his autobiography records 'a purple-lettered poster, seen from my pram, in the Upper Richmond Road, announcing the death of Kitchener'. Kitchener was drowned in 1916, by which time the eight-year-old Osbert would surely have grown out of his pram. Even if he was thinking of the Kitchener recruiting poster with the pointing finger and the message that his country needed HIM, he would have been aged six.

Be that as it may, he achieved consciousness in time to experience the old order, both in the streets of London and in his own home:

> ... due largely to the patriarchal organisation of my family I was the fortunate victim of a time-lag ... From the death of the old Queen until the outbreak of war this small society upheld the standards of Victorianism with the same unruffled tenacity with which the Sephardic community at Salonika persisted in speaking fifteenth-century Spanish; fully aware of Bernard Shaw, Diaghilev and Alexander's Ragtime Band, their outlook remained as resolutely unmodi-

fied by these phenomena as that of the Adobe Indians by the airplane and the radio.[1]

The patriarchal organizer was Osbert's formidable grandfather, Sir William Lancaster, who established the family fortunes as a founding father of the Prudential Assurance Company. Harold Speed's rather good portrait of Sir William shows a classically impressive Victorian paterfamilias with a massive forehead and an aquiline nose (Osbert's own very differently shaped nose came from his mother's side of the family). The white beard is of impressive length, though not quite as long as his grandson used to claim. Even so it was very big, as was his head which, Osbert wrote, was

> enormous, square and completely, shinily bald; but, for the austerity conditions prevailing above the line of the ears he had been richly, perhaps over-compensated on a lower level. Beneath immensely thick brows, jutting out like cornices, were just visible a pair of extremely bright hazel eyes, a determined nose, romanesque rather than Roman, and two round and polished cheeks, thrusting up like twin tumuli from a hawthorn thicket. And that was all. From immediately below the nostrils right down to the navel there cascaded a snow-white beard of that particular strength and thickness only achieved by those who have never in their life employed a razor.

Though Osbert found the general effect benevolent, he was conscious that 'Father Christmas could, if necessary, double the part of Jove'. Sir William was very much the head of the family, and was held in awe by his numerous relations.

The Lancasters were descended on one side from large Norfolk landowners, and on the other from 'gloomy farmers and manic-depressive yeomen'. Though he had a multitude of sisters, William Lancaster was an only son. His mother was a widow, and he was largely dependent for his education on the charity of friends. While still in his teens he took the stagecoach from his native King's Lynn to Cambridge, which at that time was as far as the railway network extended. Thence he proceeded by train to London, with the determination of a Dickensian hero to restore the family fortunes. He fulfilled this ambition amply.

The Prudential Assurance Company was started in 1848. Its staff of three had the names of John Shillinglaw, Goodman Jenkyn and

[1] Unless otherwise indicated, quotations that appear in the first three chapters of this book are taken from *With an Eye to the Future* (Century Hutchinson, 1986), the joint edition of Osbert Lancaster's autobiographies.

Mrs Jobbins, the housekeeper. In 1858 these three were joined by Frederick Fishe and William J. Lancaster. The official history of the Prudential Company comments of this tiny staff that 'the smallness of their numbers promoted a degree of intimacy unknown to-day but, more important, these young men were in at the beginning of things and each had a part in the creation of what thirty years later was to be described as "The Mighty Prudential" '.

Under the direction of Shillinglaw, Jenkyn, Fishe, Lancaster and Mrs Jobbins, the Prudential flourished. The staff worked not only extremely hard but also with a degree of accuracy of a kind hard to grasp in this age of computer foul-ups. In 1862 the Company Secretary was able to report that in the previous year not a single posting error had occurred: Frederick Fishe had made 30,000 flawless entries. In the same year another clerk, Alexander Monro, spent many hours searching for a penny that had been lost in the company's accounts. Failing to find it, he opened an 'error' account for that sum in order to regularize the figures.

Presumably William Lancaster conducted his business in an equally meticulous fashion. At any rate he became Assistant Secretary of the company in 1873, by which time the staff had grown to nearly eight hundred (this was also the year in which the Prudential bought its first typewriter). In 1874 William Lancaster became Secretary of the company, one of only eleven in a period of a hundred years. He kept this position until 1900, more than a quarter of a century. In 1906 he received a knighthood in recognition of the philanthropic benevolence he bestowed on King's Lynn: he was extraordinarily generous to anyone who could claim the remotest relationship with those who had helped pay for his education. He financed the re-building and re-equipping of the grammar school, and founded prizes and scholarships. He endowed hospital beds and charities, and gave large sums of money for the restoration of numerous ecclesiastical buildings in East Anglia (not always with the happiest results, according to his grandson). Sir William was Deputy Chairman of the Pru from 1910 to 1917; when he gave up his directorship (being replaced by his son John) in 1920 he had served the company for no fewer than sixty-two years.

He combined financial acumen with an interest in the arts that was keen if not always successful. Late in life he attempted but failed to master the violin. He wrote poems, a slim volume of which was actually published (albeit at his own cost). And while the results of his interest in architecture may not always have been fortunate as far as the churches of East Anglia were concerned, it was, to his credit, almost certainly Sir William who was responsible for spotting Alfred Waterhouse at an early stage in his career and appointing him as the Prudential's architect. The late Sir John Betjeman may have exaggerated in saying that Waterhouse's achievement is rivalled among English architects only by Wren, but even so his was an enormous output and one that remains with us. He built everything from museums and colleges to churches, town halls, hospitals and country houses. His work is conspicuous in the universities of Manchester, Liverpool, Oxford and Cambridge, and in London is to be seen in the form of the wonderful Natural History Museum, the scarcely less impressive National Liberal Club, University College Hospital and the Prudential's colossal headquarters in Holborn, the crazy exuberance of which rivals even that of St Pancras station. This was the first and greatest of no fewer than twenty-two Prudential buildings to be erected in central sites of the major towns of Britain, all built in the distinctive style that makes them one of the first examples of what is now called 'corporate identity'. Waterhouse's taste for red brick and terracotta earned him the nickname 'Slaughterhouse'. Opinion of his work is sharply divided; Osbert was certainly less enthusiastic about it than his friend Betjeman.

Sir William's interest in the arts extended beyond architecture and poetry to music, and infected the rest of the family. While he himself struggled with the violin, Aunt May played the clarinet 'competently', Uncle Harry was a 'powerful' baritone, Aunt Hetty was an 'infinitely painstaking' performer of early Beethoven piano pieces, Cousin Barbara played the cello, Cousin Peggy the violin, Cousin Ruth sang contralto and little Osbert was assigned to 'that beautiful but temperamental instrument, the flute'.

Sir William's London house, called South Lynn, was a large, four-square, yellow-brick Victorian mansion on Putney Hill, which Osbert visited on Sundays. The smell of Havana cigars and Knight's Castile soap left an abiding memory, as did the never-varying greeting:

> ... after prolonged chuckling, as though my appearance recalled some side-splitting joke temporarily forgotten, my grandfather always made the same announcement which dated, I fancy, from my first visit in some early sailor-suit, ' 'Pon my word, ain't he a howlin' swell.'

Having smirked embarrassedly at this familiar sally, I dived into the undergrowth and planted a kiss in what I hoped was the general direction of his cheek, after which I respectfully saluted whatever aunts happened to be present in the same manner.

Osbert's aunts were impressive both in quantity and quality even by the standards of that great age of aunts (and aunts of great age) as chronicled by Saki and P. G. Wodehouse. Although Sir William was the only son of an only son, he had plenty of sisters, and before his blissful marriage ended with his wife's early death the couple had produced seven children. Since five of these in turn had families of their own, Osbert (an only child) was provided with aunts, uncles and cousins in abundance. They included an Uncle John, said to have been the last man to drive a coach-and-four in Wimbledon, an Uncle Hugh who fought in the Boer War, and a barrister Uncle Harry. There was Aunt Minnie, Aunt May, Aunt Bessie, Aunt Hetty, and Aunt Alice among others. All these aunts and uncles were backed up by a large extended family of poor relations known as the Grateful Hearts, as well as multitudinous and entirely unrelated beneficiaries of Sir William's generosity.

Most impressive of all was Great-Aunt Martha, who had been born early in the reign of George IV. Visiting her brother in London she would arrive in a victoria drawn by greys. Osbert remembered vividly her jet-black eyebrows, 'thick as doormats', her black bonnet enriched with violets, her black-trimmed shoulder-cape and tight black kid gloves. She spoke with a strong Norfolk accent and (according to Osbert) bore a close resemblance to Sir Robert Walpole. Alone among the Lancasters she was keenly interested in food: her dumplings were reputed to be the best between King's Lynn and Norwich. 'In addition she was never at pains to conceal an early relish for scandal which, linked to a prodigious memory, made her a far more entertaining, and quite possibly more accurate, authority on the genealogies of most Norfolk families than Burke.'

Osbert's father, Robert Lancaster, was educated at Charterhouse and at Leipzig University before going to work in the City. He was a Freemason and a churchwarden, a cheerful, good-natured man and an affectionate father. Like all Lancasters up to Osbert's generation he was an enthusiast for vigorous physical exercise and used to ride in Richmond Park before breakfast. He liked the music hall, was an ardent Wagnerian, and his favourite artist was Phil May.

Osbert saw little of his father except at weekends, but clearly

25

delighted in his company. His early memories include going with him to visit Sir William on Sundays; his churchwarden father carrying out small financial transactions in the vestry after the service; his father taking him to the White City exhibition; his father back from the City in the evening, sitting by the fire and reading one of the pastel-coloured newspapers of the day.

When war broke out in 1914 Robert Lancaster immediately enlisted in the Army. On the very day he was due back on leave the news arrived that he had been killed in action in the battle of the Somme. By then he had been away so long that the memory of him had already begun to fade for his young son. 'Although he had always remained a cherished and deeply missed figure, his image was fast becoming legendary.' Thus it was that for the eight-year-old boy the realization that his father was never to return came as a 'shattering disappointment rather than overwhelming grief'.

*   *   *

Osbert's birthplace was 79 Elgin Crescent, an area near Notting Hill which was already beginning to go down, achieving full seediness by the beginning of the Second World War, and subsequently becoming distinctly smart again. 79 Elgin Crescent (which still stands) was a semi-detached stucco house, consisting of three floors and a basement with a pillared porch flanked by geraniums in urns, a front door gleaming with brass, and at the back a small private garden leading to a large garden held in common by the houses south of Elgin Crescent and north of Lansdowne Road. The house had previously belonged to Madame Blavatsky, and neighbours included foreign diplomats and various people connected in one way or another with the stage, such as the celebrated conjuror Mr Maskelyne.

Next door to Number 79 lived an old lady called Mrs Ullathorne with whom Osbert would take tea at regular intervals. He found her an 'imposing and always slightly mysterious *grande dame*' who seemed to belong to a more sophisticated world than Edwardian Notting Hill. She was reputed to have been a great success at the court of Napoleon III and her drawing-room was liberally adorned with photographs of dashing military figures 'sporting waxed moustaches and elegant lip-beards'. Instead of giving the normal handshake, Osbert had to bow smartly from the waist and kiss her outstretched hand, alarmingly criss-crossed as it was by what he remembered as 'the purple hawsers of her veins standing out in as high relief as the yellowish diamonds in her many rings'. One day this exotic old lady gave him a large leather-bound volume which had been her childhood scrapbook. For Osbert, opening it was like passing through the doorway into a magic garden. Old Mrs Ullathorne, as a child long, long ago, had pasted into the book page after page of hand-coloured and highly coloured vignettes of shakoed infantrymen, steel-engraved lakes, knights in armour with enormous plumes, gendarmes in tricornes, and little girls practising archery in pork-pie hats and striped stockings.

Further contributions to Osbert's store of visual imagery were to be found in the nursery library, which was well stocked with the illustrated fairy tales of his mother's childhood, full of the wood-engravings which were executed with such virtuosity in that period. Then there were H. C. Andersen, Charles Kingsley's *The Water-Babies*, the Tenniel *Alice*, and (best of all) the bound volumes of *Picture Magazine* which had come down from his father's Victorian

27

schooldays. Combining instruction with entertainment, this periodical contained startling images such as a daring criminal escaping from prison by parachute, a cock mesmerized into following a chalk line with its beak, or bewhiskered tourists being hauled up in nets to the monasteries of the Meteora in Greece. Further riches came in the form of the strip cartoons of Caran d'Ache, and four-page supplements of distinguished soldiers, politicians, divines, scientists, artists and rulers of sovereign states. The sovereigns fascinated him especially:

> Those long rows of royal torsos adorned with every variety of epaulette, plastron and aiguillette, the necks compressed into collars of unbelievable height and tightness, the manly, if padded chests hung with row upon row of improbable crosses and stars crisscrossed by watered silk ribbons and tangles of gold cords, surmounted by so many extraordinary countenances adorned with immense moustaches, upstanding in the style of Potsdam or downsweeping in the style of Vienna, some fish-eyed, some monocled, some vacant, some indignant but all self-conscious. . . . Less colourful but more familiar were the pages devoted to the more prominent contemporary divines. No flourishing moustachios nor jewelled orders here, but every variety of whisker from the restrained mutton-chop to the full Newgate fringe, and billowing acres of episcopal lawn.

Osbert not only pored over these fascinating images (to his inestimable profit in later working life) but also read everything he could lay his hands on, from the popular papers of the Harmsworth Press that were read Downstairs to his mother's occult literature Upstairs, from the Book of Common Prayer to the leaders in *The Times*. In an age before television, transistor radios and tape-recorders there were few distractions from reading for a child who was both solitary and bright, apart from taking tea with Mrs Ullathorne, or doing his bit on his mother's 'At Home' days. Clad in 'a *soigné* little blue silk number, with Brussels lace collar', his job was to pass round the cucumber sandwiches, *petit-fours* and chocolate cake while making diverting comments or asking questions which, while sometimes mildly embarrassing, fell short of being offensively personal. This usually went down well, except with such Lancaster relations as Aunt Hetty who frowned at what she considered a deplorable tendency to 'play to the gallery'.

*   *   *

When Osbert was born his parents' joint income was £600 a year. This was sufficient for them to keep up a comfortable house in Notting Hill with a staff of cook, housemaid, nurse and boot-boy. Even so, and allowing for the huge change in monetary values, it was not as much as might have been expected, considering that Robert Lancaster had a job in the City and that there was very solid wealth on both sides of the family – for Osbert's maternal grandfather could match Sir William in cash terms. He had made a pile at an early age in Hong Kong. However, for different reasons, neither grandfather believed in showering money on his descendants. Sir William preferred to direct his largess towards more public recipients. Alfred Manger, on the other hand, took the view that the best person to spend his money on was himself. Having retired in his mid-thirties he never did a stroke of work again (in contrast to grandfather Lancaster, who worked tirelessly until he was nearly eighty). Alfred Manger did not share the fervent Lancaster belief in work. The 'great Lancaster ethos', Osbert said, was that 'provided you were out of the house by nine or nine-thirty it didn't matter what you did. "A regular job" was the great phrase.'

The two sides of Osbert's family differed in other ways. While the Lancasters robustly despised ill health as a sign of moral feebleness, the Mangers went in for valetudinarianism. While the Lancasters would cheerfully eat a cow-pat if it was put in front of them, the precarious health of the Mangers necessitated a more discriminating attitude to food: the simple country fare available at their Dorset house was always reinforced by regular supplies sent down from Jackson's of Piccadilly.

Alfred Manger's first wife (Osbert's grandmother) died young. He soon married again, returned to China and left Clare, Osbert's mother, with her grandmother, a formidable lady of Low Church persuasion. The finishing-school that Clare went to in Brussels came as a release from a stifling atmosphere. She studied art first in a studio in Brussels, and then with G. F. Watts, of whom she was the last surviving pupil. Osbert used to put it about that she was the model for Watts's painting of *Hope*, but would readily concede that this information was not strictly accurate. She was a painter of by no means negligible ability, and always fostered Osbert's own talents in this direction.

Osbert described his mother as 'very short, robust, with great width of jaw and very beautiful pale blue eyes', an account which fitted himself closely enough to make it clear that physically he took after his mother rather than after the Lancasters. Some found her bossy, others (more politely) 'very capable' – not such a bad thing for a widow with a house and young son to look after on her own. Clearly she was tough, physically and temperamentally, but she also had an excellent sense of humour, and by the standards of the time was enlightened and liberal. She was a New Woman, a Shavian and a supporter of Votes for Women. She liked painting, theatre, ballet and travel. She was also keenly interested in such subjects as the Hidden Wisdom, spiritualism, faith-healing, Rosicrucianism, the Perfect Oneness, the Prophet Ezekiel, Rudolf Steiner, the Great Pyramid, St John of Patmos, the Lost Ten Scribes, the Second Coming, the Astral Plane and Armageddon (which she firmly declared was *not* the First World War).

Some idea of her originality may be gathered from the way in which she taught Osbert to read. This was by means of a chocolate alphabet. Twice a week the edible letters were spread out on the dining-room table and he was allowed to eat the letters he could recognize. Once he had full command of the alphabet he was allowed to eat those which he could make into a word. By the time he could spell 'suffragette' he was deemed to have mastered literacy by means of a system of teaching which seemed designed to develop equally a taste for chocolates and long words.

He soon became an omnivorous reader (though no longer literally), and eagerly perused the various journals to which his mother subscribed, such as the *Occult Review*, *Rosy Cross* and *Theosophists' Monthly*. Not that this was his mother's only reading matter. Sometimes she would retire for the night conspicuously bearing a copy of the *Bhagavad Gita* or *The Cloud of Unknowing*; when Osbert later went in to say goodnight he might well find her engrossed in the latest fiction of Ethel M. Dell. 'Always on such occasions her response, uttered in a very reproachful tone, to any expression of surprise was the same. "You know quite well, dear, that the bent bow must be unstrung." '

However dotty the subjects of her enthusiasms and interests, she did not take them without a dash of salt, always retaining 'a curious ability to achieve, suddenly and without warning, an almost cynical detachment when the spectacle of others' credulity would provoke her to hoots of happy laughter'. She may sometimes have appeared intimidating, but Clare Lancaster was evidently intelligent, humorous, lively and warm. Her granddaughter Cara remembers her as 'splendid, very down-to-earth. You knew where you were with her. She was exactly what a grandmother ought to be.'

Osbert was devoted to his mother. His portrait of her (in words and drawings) in *With an Eye to the Future* is comic but very affectionate. She died in 1955 at the age of seventy-nine.

About his much-loved pram Osbert wrote, 'The motion is agreeable, the range of vision extensive and one has always before one's eyes the rewarding spectacle of a grown-up maintaining prolonged physical exercise.' Only the gondola, he said, can compare with the pram for pleasure, and then only if someone else takes care of the 'nerve-racking financial dispute which will inevitably mark the journey's end'.

Amateur psychoanalysts may make what they will of the absence of a strong masculine presence in Osbert's childhood. Perhaps grandfather Lancaster's dominating personality in the background was powerful enough to compensate for the missing father. However much his formative years were dominated by women, Osbert could never be described as in any way effeminate. On the other hand, throughout his life he retained the assumption of a privileged Edwardian male child that it was somehow pre-ordained that a capable and devoted woman would always be on hand to see to his every need.

In addition to his mother and the aunts, there were female servants. He said that though the ideal of a servantless civilization was doubtless noble, and he admired those who felt degraded by the idea of being waited on by their fellow human beings, he personally could tolerate without discomfort being waited on hand and foot. He added that for a child, 'A mother's love is all very well, but it is only a poor substitute for good relations with the cook.' Good relations also with the housemaid, named Kate, who introduced him to reading matter very different from the occult literature upstairs. Kate avidly followed the popular press, and derived from it the catch-phrases and political slogans of the day which peppered her conversation. 'Hands off the people's food,' she would say on catching him foraging in the larder. If he enquired what was for dinner she would reply in Asquith's words, 'Wait and see.'

Kate loved the music hall. Through her, Osbert gained an early (albeit second-hand) knowledge of the songs and ballads of the top performers of the day which she rendered while going about her domestic duties. While Clare Lancaster's musical tastes lay in the direction of *Traumerei*, Kate's were closer to those of Robert Lancaster (though he rated Harry Lauder more highly than she did).

Though 79 Elgin Crescent was a world sharply stratified into Upstairs and Downstairs, there was much that the two levels had in common. The child of the moneyed class was not brought up in ignorance of the less privileged. The streets through which the pram was propelled were peopled not only by fine ladies and gentlemen but also by a varied cast of characters such as errand-boys, the Italian organ-grinder with the monkey, the old lady selling balloons, the crossing-sweeper, the lamplighter, the toy-vendors, and the man in checked coat and bowler hat who sold tiny thumb-nail Bibles to the cry of 'Li'l 'Oly Boible! Orl the Good Book for tuppence!'

Nurse would cautiously navigate the pram along a route that skirted round such districts as Notting Dale, which were considered highly dangerous. Yet the pram afforded distant views of exciting places like the Portobello Road, of which it was said that a well-dressed man could not walk its length and emerge at the other end intact. Later, pramless now, the visit with his father to the White City Exhibition revealed to Osbert 'the seething Saturday night crowds, the women all in tight sealskin jackets and vast plumed hats, the men in pearl-buttoned waistcoats and flared trousers, jostling round the street market in the theatrical light of the gas-jets'. Such childhood memories of characters and costumes, of buildings and pavements and streets, provided a rich source of material for the future cartoonist, illustrator and designer of stage sets and costumes. Osbert was born and blessed not only with exceptional powers of observation but also with a remarkably retentive memory. He was doubly lucky in retaining these qualities into adult life.

Holidays provided perspectives on the world outside London. The Sussex resort of Littlehampton was a place and name to play a key role in the world of Osbert's imagination. The rows of bow-fronted Regency villas, the promenade and the sands provided a setting for a cast as rich as the streets of London, with pierrots and minstrels, donkey rides, Evangelical missionaries on Sundays, and the German brass-bandsmen in braided hussar uniforms who were to disappear so abruptly during the August holiday of 1914.

Other holidays were at grandfather Lancaster's Norfolk home at East Winch, a small village between King's Lynn and Swaffham, with one shop and four pubs (only two of which were licensed: the local potentate, Sir William, had decreed that as far as pubs were concerned two was a number sufficient for the needs of the small population), the vicarage, and a fourteenth-century church drastically over-restored by Gilbert Scott. East Winch Hall, Sir William's country seat, was approached through imposing entrance gates giving on to a croquet lawn fringed with copper beeches. The house itself was a four-square late-Georgian residence built by a tea-trade nabob: its appearance supported the story that its design had been deliberately modelled on a tea-caddy.

At East Winch Osbert's reading was further enlarged by sharing, surreptitiously, his cousins' *Comic Cuts*, *The Perils of Pauline*, *Buffalo Bill* and the works of W. W. Jacobs (concealed in the covers of the more acceptable G. A. Henty). On Sundays these were replaced by such dull Sabbath matter as bound volumes of *The Quiver*, mercifully enlivened by wood-engravings of whiskered curates. Then there were volumes of pious fables which he came to find abominably deceitful:

> The hero, some gallant knight, would don his armour, leap on his trusty steed and go galloping off in pursuit of dragons in the most approved style, and then, just as my interest was getting aroused, it was revealed that the armour, on the exact style and manufacture of which I had been speculating, was the armour of Righteousness, the steed one learnt answered to the name of Perseverance, and the dragons against which the hero was set off to do battle were called Self-Love, Indolence and Bad Temper.

For six days of the week Osbert's cousins would trounce him at tennis. On Sundays, through some mysterious logic of the Victorian mind, the one permitted game was croquet. It was also the only game at which Osbert was ever to achieve prowess (though he was an enthusiastic skier).

Very different were the Dorset holidays at the Manger family home near Gillingham, a small town that smelt of beer. Grandfather Lancaster may have had a town house and a country house, a title and even more money than Grandfather Manger, but the Dorset house was approached by a much longer drive, with a Gothic lodge at the beginning and a butler at the end. There were grand gardens with terraced lawns and geometrical flower beds, summerhouses, wooden footbridges, waterfalls and even a ha-ha. Instead of the Lancasters' drab Renault there was a splendid crimson Talbot-Darracq, and indoors there were vast quantities of intricately decorated post-Ming *chinoiserie*. The food was excellent, there was freedom to read what you liked, and there was a further collection of maiden aunts.

As at East Winch there were family prayers, when his grandfather Manger would read from the Bible, usually the Epistle to the Ephesians. 'Wives, submit yourselves unto your own husbands,' he would say, with a look at Mrs Manger; 'Children, obey your parents' (his monocle was directed at Osbert's mother, aunts and uncles); 'Servants, be obedient to them that are your masters,' the domestic staff were told. Osbert did not remember ever hearing on these occasions the verses concerning the obligations of the head of the household.

In spite of a world war and the loss of his father, Osbert's childhood was a happy one both at the time and in retrospect. The distinction is an important one in his case because he was one of those people for whom the act of looking back, the remembrance of things past, is if anything even more intense than the original experience. Proust and Joyce evidently felt likewise, and it was from recollections of childhood that Wordsworth gathered his intimations of immortality. Such importance given to the act of memory is connected (I would conjecture) with loneliness, for which it provides compensation, solace and reward. Proust was a sickly and solitary child who became a recluse. Osbert too was an only child. Like Dr Johnson, who was terrified by solitude, he was to stave off loneliness by being almost compulsively sociable and by working exceptionally hard. It was as though, one way or another, every minute had to be filled so that the terrors of emptiness (of boredom perhaps?) were kept at bay. Work is one way of keeping the yawning gulf temporarily filled. Company is another, and the pleasures of memory are a third. Osbert emphasized the point in his choice of epigraph to *With an Eye to the Future*. It comes from Delacroix, another artist whose experience was intensified through the inner eye of memory.

> *Je crois que le plus grand attrait des choses est dans le souvenir qu'elles réveillent dans le cœur ou dans l'esprit, mais surtout dans le cœur. . . . Le regret du temps écoulé, le charme des jeunes années, la fraîcheur des premières impressions agissent plus sur moi que le spectacle même.*

> (I think that what lends things their greatest charm is the remembrance they awaken in the heart or in the mind, but particularly in the heart . . . The nostalgia of time gone by, the magic of early years, the freshness of first impressions move me more deeply than the sight itself.)

The past is not just another country; it is a better one.

When Osbert was eleven he went to the Diaghilev production of *The Sleeping Beauty*. Many years later he wrote that all he remembered of it was Lopokova as the Lilac Fairy, the dazzling beauty of the Bakst sets and 'the intensity of my own response'. Like Delacroix, he gives as much weight to his reaction to the experience

35

as to the experience itself, but then it was an event which shaped his life:

> Nothing I had ever seen had in any way prepared me for the magnificence that was disclosed on the rise of the curtain of The Alhambra, and for weeks afterwards my drawing books were packed with hopeful but pathetic attempts to recapture something of the glory of that matinée, and there and then I formed an ambition that was not destined to be fulfilled for more than thirty years.

There was only one other such remembered moment of what can only be called ecstasy to rank with this. It occurred on a childhood visit to Venice with his mother:

> Waking very early next morning I went out into the brilliant sunshine on a solitary exploration before breakfast, and after negotiating several narrow alleys found myself in a long arcade hung with canvas awnings through which the sun filtered in a golden glow and one of which after a moment's hesitation I firmly pulled aside. For what was then revealed – the whole Piazza backed by the west front of Saint Mark's, all the golden balls and crosses gleaming and shimmering in the rays of a sun that was only just above the Doge's Palace – I could not have been less prepared. Slowly, in a state of exalted trance, I crossed the great Square, at that time empty of all but the pigeons, and then, having arrived opposite the glittering façade, I glanced right and saw for the first time that most staggering of all views, S. Giorgio Maggiore floating above a dancing sea framed between the twin columns of the Piazzetta.

The accounts of these two intense childhood experiences have much in common. They are both vivid demonstrations of the powerful effect that the visual could have on Osbert; they are evidence of the detailed retentiveness of his memory; and they show the extent to which it is true in his case to say that the child was father of the man.

II

UNWILLINGLY TO SCHOOL

I N the last year of the war Osbert was sent to St Ronan's preparatory school in Worthing, a seaside resort with considerably less charm than Littlehampton. It was winter, and the bleak sea-front was sparsely populated. A few old ladies bravely shivered in the shelters. The occasional Bath chair struggled against the bitter east wind. There were convalescent soldiers, wounded or shell-shocked, in bright blue suits, and Sunday afternoons provided the spectacle of a crocodile of small boys from St Ronan's, with a pipe-puffing tweed-capped master striding out at the front and Lancaster a straggler at the back. On one occasion they heard, far away across the sea to the south-east, the guns of the artillery barrage that launched the last German offensive of the war.

After the protected feminine world of mother and aunts and cooks and housemaids, the all-male environment of a boarding school must have come as even more of a shock to Osbert than to most new boys. For his first few terms he suffered the constant misery that is so common among the small victims of the British fee-paying educational system. As an only child with virtually no playmates of his own age or sex, he had never before encountered the bullying and teasing which are brought to such acute refinement in private schools. Furthermore, he neither enjoyed nor excelled at games. As one term followed another he proved that he was equally hopeless at soccer, rugby and cricket. Failure on the playing fields is a dreadful misdemeanour at any prep school, but at St Ronan's it was especially terrible since the headmaster, Stanley Harris, was an all-round sportsman of tremendous prowess. At soccer he had captained for Westminster School, Pembroke College, Cambridge University, the Corinthians and England, and he had performed almost as spectacularly at rugger and cricket. Such a superlative exemplar of sport must have been an uncomfortable one for an unathletic boy, but Osbert managed to cope with the situation, and to do so with precocious and characteristic urbanity. A contemporary at a near-by school remembered not only playing an away rugger match against St Ronan's but also Osbert's distinctive contribution to the game. The visitor had broken from the scrum, taken the ball, tucked it under his arm and, leaving all behind him, was heading for a touchdown and glory. Nobody stood between him and a certain three points for a try – nobody except Osbert. As the visitor charged towards him, Osbert stood his ground, and spoke. 'Do you wish', he asked politely, 'to pass me on the left or on the right?'

Though this was not an approach to games that was likely to endear anyone to the muscular Stanley Harris, the headmaster treated him well, and by his final year Osbert actually reached the dizzy height of being a prefect. He remembered with pleasure Harris's Sunday-night readings of the hair-raising ghost stories of M. R. James and A. C. Benson; and though Harris was no great intellectual and clearly saw athletic distinction as the highest possible achievement, learning was not neglected. In fact Osbert said that he doubted whether his subsequent studies at Charterhouse and Oxford added anything of importance to the solid foundation of conventional learning that he acquired at St Ronan's. His best subjects were Scripture, Latin and English. He showed no aptitude whatsoever for mathematics.

The staff consisted of the usual comic types with which Messrs Gabbittas and Thring so unfailingly provided the prep schools of England. There was, for example, the terrifying spinster Miss Eakin who may have had the body of a frail woman but could quell scenes of rowdiness and indiscipline which would have been intractable to mere male physical force. There was Mr Hoffman, who was epileptic and rumoured to be a German spy. And there was the sadistic school sergeant who has the distinction of being one of the few people Osbert ever really detested. Osbert was not given to personal hatreds, but in the case of the sergeant he was ready to make an exception. This tyrant not only drilled the boys in the quadrangle and made them box in the gymnasium but was also in charge of administering punishments. For offences more serious than those which could be punished by the setting of lines, the boys were handed over for half an hour to the sergeant, who would make them stand with arms outstretched holding iron dumb-bells for anything up to ten minutes. Signs of weakness and tiring were corrected by a sharp crack on the back of the knee with the drill-stick.

When one was finally released one was, as like as not, subjected to a sinister demonstration of bonhomie which involved being clasped tight to his bemedalled breast while, in an overpowering cloud of whisky-laden breath, he rubbed his close-shaven but still abrasive chin up and down one's cheek, behaviour which seems to me in retrospect to have required rather closer investigation than, so far as I know, it ever in fact got. Revenge was long in coming but none the less sweet. Some ten or fifteen years later on answering the telephone one winter's evening I heard again that once dreaded voice. 'Is that Mr Lancaster, sir? It's your old sergeant 'ere – you remember old sarge at St Ronan's, sir! 'Ow are you keeping, sir? I'm still fit and well but just at the moment, sir, I'm in a bit of temporary embarrassment and I was wondering, sir, whether for old time's sake . . .' I am sorry to say that it was with keen if unworthy pleasure that I pleaded total ignorance, and no cock crowed.

Fellow-pupils at St Ronan's included an Irish peer, a baronet, Roger Fulford and (a year or two Osbert's senior) Patrick Gordon-Walker, remembered as a keen rather than outstanding footballer 'enthusiastically charging up and down the touch-line like a conscientious chimpanzee'.

On Osbert's bookshelves I came across a small volume called *The Master and His Boys* by Stanley S. Harris, published in 1924 (not long after Osbert had left St Ronan's). It is inscribed 'To Osbert from his mother in remembrance of his schooldays with the author, S. S. Harris, 1946'. It was a curious present to give to a man of nearly forty. The author's note at the beginning of the book expresses gratitude to two of the leading church figures of the day, Canon C. E. Raven and the Rev. H. R. L. Sheppard. Dick Sheppard, who was to found the Peace Pledge Union, asks of Harris in his preface to the book, 'Was there ever a finer footballer?' and says of the book itself that 'There would be much hope for the future if the youth of to-day would be willing to mould life on the principles here set out and to make an effort to acquire that simple, sincere and sane religion that is behind all that the Author writes.'

The book has chapters on Religion, School-boy Honour, Character, Public Schools, Swearing, Parents, Creative Spirit, Games, Points of General Interest, The Master and His Boys. The schoolmaster with vision 'sees in himself the means of fitting hundreds of God's young creatures to play the game of life as the Lord Himself would have had them to do it'. Pluck and grit are, as one would expect, held up for admiration. Parents and boys are warned that although at the average public school there is 'comparatively little gross immorality', there are, on the other hand, some who talk in 'a gross and bestial manner'. Furthermore there are 'a number of men who actually consider it natural and justifiable, before they are married, to have sexual relations with a woman'. Such matters should be treated in a 'frank, natural, open manner', says Harris, while being somewhat vague about what it is that he is being frank, natural and open about other than that it involves 'the big questions of life'.

The Master and His Boys is in its way a minor masterpiece of unconscious humour, and its comic aspects would not have been lost on Osbert. Indeed, there are parts of his children's story *The Saracen's Head: or The Reluctant Crusader*, which read like a straight parody of Harris. *The Saracen's Head*, the first of the Littlehampton trilogy, was published in 1948. When Osbert was writing it, and reading it as a bedtime story to his children Cara and William, the words of Harris's book, recently given to him, would have been fresh in his mind. Since *The Saracen's Head* clearly draws on Osbert's own childhood it seems best to consider it here rather than in a later chapter.

> Once upon a time, in the reign of King Richard Cœur-de-Lion to be precise, there lived in Sussex a certain landowner known as William de Littlehampton. He was exceedingly rich, the lord of five manors with the rights of soccage, corkage and drainage between Chanctonbury Ring and Bognor-supra-Mare and in addition he enjoyed the rare privilege of fishing for sturgeon in the river Arun. (In fact there are no sturgeon in the river Arun but this was nevertheless regarded as a very rare distinction.) His principal residence was the castle of Courantsdair . . .

In spite of the 'Once upon a time' opening, the jokes about socage and corkage assume a high level of sophistication on the part of the story's first listeners, Cara and William, to whom the book is dedicated. Their French, too, must have been pretty good if they got the point of the name of the family castle, Courantsdair, an exceptionally draughty pile. Doubtless some of the jokes were above their heads, but like most of the best children's stories, *The Saracen's Head* entertains on two levels, both that of the child listeners and that of the adult bedtime reader. There are, of course, plenty of drawings to look at, full not only of architectural and armorial detail but also exciting episodes of derring-do and farcical violence, such as when

41

the terrifying wolfhound Charlemagne has his tail snapped off by a Numidian lion. There's plenty of gore, too, with blood more than once cascading from the headless trunks of decapitated warriors. And plenty of good food, such as a dish of roast flamingo stuffed with a whole turkey, stuffed with a whole goose, stuffed with a whole duck, stuffed with a whole chicken, stuffed with a whole partridge, stuffed with a whole quail, stuffed with a whole snipe, stuffed with a whole lark, stuffed with a whole nightingale, stuffed with a locust. 'None of the Crusaders had ever eaten such a meal before; but for William whose mother had never approved of fancy, "frenchified" dishes and had always insisted at Courantsdair on what she called "good plain English cooking", it was a revelation.'

William's mother, the Dame de Littlehampton, resembles Osbert's own mother not only in her style of *cuisine*. She is 'a remarkably tough old lady of sixty-eight of whom, I am sorry to say, [William] was very much afraid'. It's probably going too far to say that Osbert was very much afraid of his own mother, but she was undoubtedly tough, and he undoubtedly treated her with considerable respect. There are other ways in which, without need of Freudian analysis, William's and Osbert's circumstances can be seen to be similar. Both are surrounded by womenfolk, Osbert by innumerable aunts, William by eleven older sisters (a further six having died of the colds, croup and bronchitis endemic in freezing Courantsdair). Like Mrs Lancaster, the Dame is a widow: her awesome husband, Sir Dagobert, a mighty man-at-arms, had been killed (albeit in a ludicrous manner) in battle, as was Robert Lancaster. The Dame devotes herself to bringing up the fatherless boy 'with the fond intent that he should grow to resemble his beloved father as closely as possible and in every way'. William is, of course,

as inept as Osbert at sports and such manly pursuits as killing boars (at the age of ten he is still terrified of the domestic cat), wrestling, boxing and archery, thereby incurring the mockery of his beefy contemporaries. Whether or not William is an aesthete, he is certainly not a hearty.

He is especially hopeless at tilting, at which he is quite unable to keep a Straight Lance (a significantly Harris-like phrase). This turns out to be his salvation, as emerges in the chapter 'Incompetence Justified'. William's lance is so far from straight that – his eyes glued shut with fear – he accidentally topples the terrifying killer of Christians, El Babooni, who 'When . . . he saw approaching a horseman whose lance, so far from being inflexibly straight, wavered from side to side, describing circles with its point, he was completely dumbfounded and his carefully acquired technique became of no avail.'

All in all *The Saracen's Head* is a most satisfying tale for any reader who is unable to identify with the Captain of the First Eleven or other *Boy's Own Paper* heroes. Still better, it is completely free of moral uplift.

The Times Literary Supplement hailed *The Saracen's Head* and C. Day-Lewis's *The Otterbury Incident* as the first outstanding children's books to have appeared since T. H. White's *The Sword in the Stone*. 'Astringent, snappish, odd and incalculable, Mr. Lancaster is also the most practical of men; his appeal lies in his daunting descent to brass tacks, his genius expresses itself in his manner of pricking the balloon.'

If, as I would suggest, the balloon in question was that little-known work *The Master and His Boys*, it need not mean that Osbert remembered Stanley S. Harris other than with affection and respect. However little Osbert shared Harris's prowess at games and the importance he attached to them, and however droll Osbert must have found the Speech Day rhetoric about the game of life and keeping a straight bat, he would have felt the moral standards behind the platitudes far from despicable. Harris, the muscular Christian, may not have imparted to Osbert much muscularity, but Osbert always remained a devout member of the Church of England, and a regular communicant.

A special cruelty of the English private boarding-school system is that the horrors must be endured not once but twice. The child leaves the security of home at the age of about eight and finds himself to be not only in the lowest form of the preparatory school but also to be the lowest form of humanity – if indeed he can properly be considered to belong to humanity at all rather than to the realms of entomology, a point made explicit in those prep schools and public schools (including Charterhouse) where he is not even a 'new boy' but a 'new bug'. At prep school, through long and weary terms and years, he rises to the lofty height (in status and in stature) of prefect. Then he goes to public school and the whole process has to be repeated all over again.

The prep school he leaves at thirteen may have prepared him for the Common Entrance examination, but no amount of avuncular admonitions from the likes of Stanley Harris can prepare him for the public school's brutality. This is not only that of the prep school writ large but with the addition of repressed (and not-so-repressed) all-male sexuality. An extensive literature from *Tom Brown's Schooldays* to *Vice Versa*, *Stalky & Co.*, *Tell England* and a sizeable library of other first-hand reports have left no one with an excuse for pleading ignorance of the physical and psychological violence of these expensive and privileged establishments.

For many public school boys the singing of 'Lord dismiss us with thy blessing' at the last chapel service of their last term at school is one of the happiest moments of their lives. They shake the dust of the detested place from their feet, and vow never to go near it again. In *Summoned by Bells* Osbert's friend John Betjeman says of his five years at Marlborough, 'Thank God I'll never have to go through them again.' Another contemporary, Evelyn Waugh, commented that prison holds no terrors for anyone who has been to a public school.

The strange thing is that almost invariably the victims of the system send their own sons back to the very same school, or to one almost exactly like it. Somehow each generation convinces itself that Greyfriars is very different now from what it was in *their* day. Thus, as Osbert was about to set off for Charterhouse, his uncles reassured him that 'there was nothing to worry about, that the beatings and bullyings of their youth were things of the past, now as obsolete, they understood, as the thumbscrew and the rack, and that school was a totally different place from what it had been thirty years ago'.

It was not. Osbert soon found that conditions at Charterhouse had changed not at all from those of the 1890s, when his father and uncles were there. The idiotic slang and customs were the same. The lavatories were the same – earth-closets. In the 1890s the school doctor had landed Osbert's father with rheumatic fever: the same man still held the post in Osbert's time.

In *Goodbye to All That*, Robert Graves wrote of his time at the school, a few years earlier than Osbert's: 'From my first moment at Charterhouse I suffered an oppression of the spirit that I hesitate to recall in its full intensity.' Osbert also hated the place. On arriving he at first found himself deeply shocked by the foul language and behaviour but, as is the way of such things, was soon himself admiring the prowess of a contemporary who could fart 'Abide with me' in tune. He escaped sexual harassment but not bullying or corporal punishment: beatings were carried out with a whipping-rod, a chalk line being first marked on the victim's trouser-seat to make sure that all six strokes fell in the same place.

He suffered but survived, contriving to cope by means that resembled his rugger-playing at St Ronan's. He simply didn't play the game the way others did. When it came to fagging (the public school's form of institutionalized slavery) he showed such total and consistent incompetence at shoe-shining, running baths, making toast, carrying messages and otherwise performing the menial tasks imposed by the big boys on the small ones that the cry for 'Any fag but Lancaster' soon became familiar. Even so, and despite sporting and athletic performances that more than confirmed his lack of promise, he in his turn rose to the rank of monitor.

The late Philip Hope-Wallace used to say that he had been Osbert's fag at Charterhouse and that Osbert had been 'beastly' to him. Osbert denied this, saying that he had never been head of house, that only heads of houses could beat fags, and that he was in a different house anyway. Certainly Philip was never one to let tiny details of fact mar his stories, but they usually contained a kernel of truth, and Osbert himself admitted that his promotion to the rank of monitor demonstrated the validity of Lord Acton's dictum about the corrupting effect of power.

Another Carthusian contemporary, Richard Usborne, remembers that Osbert looked grown-up at sixteen. Evidently his personality, style and appearance were almost fully developed by the time he went to Oxford. This appearance was unusual. By conventional standards the adult Osbert was never good-looking. His eyes were wonderful, brilliantly blue and greatly expressive, but they did protrude. He was short of stature, and his body seemed too small to carry his great head. His nose, always snub, became bulbous, and the child's clear complexion was to be pitted by the cruel scars of acne. For someone of his sensitivity the psychological scars from this must surely have been as deep as the physical ones.

The Headmaster's final report on Osbert pronounced him to be 'irretrievably gauche' and 'a sad disappointment'. The feeling was mutual. For his part Osbert found Charterhouse 'intolerably irksome' at the time, and the education lamentable in retrospect. Yet, in spite of his sharp comments, he clearly got a lot out of Charterhouse. For one thing there was the acquaintance of the precociously gifted Ronald Cartland, who was a year or two his senior. Cartland was dreadfully snobbish, but his charm enabled him to get away with rebelliousness against a school which he considered to be distressingly middle-class. He derided the school's traditions and customs, and refused to comply with them. He openly announced that the first thing he would do on leaving Charterhouse would be to buy an Old Etonian tie. He edited the irreverent and gossipy magazine *Green Chartreuse*, set up in opposition to the school's official, pedestrian *The Carthusian*.[1]

For Osbert, Cartland's sophistication opened up a glittering sartorial and social world (his sister was Barbara Cartland, later to

---

[1] In *With an Eye to the Future* Osbert says that Cartland started *Green Chartreuse*: he may have re-animated it after the war, but in fact it was started in 1913 by, among others, George Mallory (of Everest fame) and Robert Graves.

make her name as a prolific romantic novelist). At the same time he brought Osbert's reading up to date, introducing him to the works of Galsworthy, H. G. Wells and Aldous Huxley, causing him to set aside *The Yellow Book* in favour of Lytton Strachey, and drawing his attention to such luminaries of the day as the Sitwells and Noël Coward.

Graves had noted in his time at Charterhouse the clash between sixth-form intellectuals and the 'bloods', more usually known as the aesthetes and the hearties. In this respect Charterhouse was actually healthier than most public schools. At least intellectuals and aesthetes like Graves and Cartland existed, and in sufficient numbers to provide some opposition to the bloods and hearties. This was in part thanks to some distinguished Old Carthusians – the hearty Baden-Powell, for example, was offset by Ralph Vaughan Williams and Robert Graves, while talented Carthusian artists had included Thackeray, Leech, Lovat Fraser and Max Beerbohm.

The artistic opportunities at Charterhouse provided some mitigation of Osbert's dislike of the school: the foundations in drawing and painting that had been laid by his mother were built upon in the studio, to which he would slip off when other boys were playing games. The art school was presided over by a genial old-fashioned water-colourist called 'Purple' Johnson, his nickname being derived from his extensive use of that colour when painting shadows. His artistic credentials were proclaimed by his wearing thick tweeds and a spotted bow-tie. He sturdily maintained that drawing and painting were not for self-expression: technique was the thing. 'Quite right too,' Osbert used to say. Even so, once a certain level of proficiency had been achieved, 'Purple' Johnson became more permissive. In autumn the representational was replaced by the decorative, with all the pupils painting and varnishing little boxes and book-ends to give to relatives for Christmas.

Johnson also tolerated Osbert's composing large historical and oriental scenes in a style that he hoped combined the best of Lovat Fraser with the best of Bakst. And then in summer they would get on their bicycles and ride through the Surrey lanes on sketching trips, returning after drawing and painting a lych-gate or a water-mill

> through a still rustic landscape, doomed all too soon to become a commuter's paradise, with the low sun sparkling through the elms, gilding the clouds of midges hanging above the hedgerows and

turning the thatch on the old-world cottages from burnt umber to raw sienna beneath a crimson lake sky noisy with rooks.

Such a description could not have come from a boy who found his time at Charterhouse wholly irksome; in fact, thanks to Ronald Cartland, 'Purple' Johnson and the connection with Max Beerbohm, it was valuably formative. However, his attitude to the school may be deduced from the fact that when the time came for him to send his son William to school he broke with family tradition and sent him to Eton. (The tradition was restored in the present generation: Osbert's granddaughter Louisa was sent to Charterhouse.) Even so, his attitude remained ambivalent. Near the end of his life Sir John Betjeman said, 'Osbert's very fond of Charterhouse. In a time [when they were at Oxford together] when it was unfashionable to refer to one's school he was very proud of it. He liked it mentioned. I remember he amazed me by not decrying his public school.'

Osbert's feelings were probably close to those of Max Beerbohm, who wrote that 'My delight in having been at Charterhouse was far greater than had been my delight in being there.' It seems to be a common experience to loathe the place at the time and then become nostalgic about it. Even Robert Graves (in his 1957 epilogue to *Goodbye to All That*) says that 'Charterhouse certainly has a good name nowadays'. Graves tells how when he met Vaughan Williams in Palma they talked of Max Beerbohm (who had been in the same form as Vaughan Williams) and then found themselves singing 'Carmen Carthusianum' in unison, to the surprise of a crowded restaurant. Ben Travers, who was born in 1886 and would have been a contemporary of Osbert's father, was another who hated the place and yet throughout his extremely long life remained a loyal 'old boy'. Osbert said that with Max the conversation always came round to Charterhouse. 'He was a tremendously loyal *old boy*. I *always* wore the old school tie when I went to see him.' In his will Osbert left his Beerbohm cartoons to the school.

Why, I once asked him, do Old Carthusians keep harking back to the place they detested so much? 'I expect', Osbert replied, 'that you would find much the same with former inhabitants of Dartmoor.'

III

WHILE OXFORD SLEEPS

HAVING PASSED the School Certificate examination and gained his entrance to Oxford, Osbert left Charterhouse at the age of seventeen – '*Not* under a cloud,' he would always emphasize. The first thing he did was to grow a moustache. He used to quote 'some old boy' who had said that a moustache was no good unless you could see it from behind. His own moustache never achieved quite such dimensions, which one would have thought were exclusively the property of Second World War Squadron Leaders, if not Wing Commanders. Even so, Osbert's was a very fine moustache and it served him well for some sixty years.

He had a few months to fill in before going to Oxford. This he did by attending life classes at the Byam Shaw School of Art. The General Strike was on at the time and, like most people of his background, he volunteered for strike-breaking. The offer of his services as a bus driver was turned down politely but firmly: even at a time of national crisis the interests of road safety could not be ignored completely. Instead he worked in Princess Marie Louise's canteen, and in recognition of his services received an illuminated testimonial signed by HRH.

In 1926, Osbert arrived at Lincoln College, Oxford.[1] It was a small college, and not particularly distinguished apart from having some very fine seventeenth-century glass.

Lincoln's lack of both athletic and intellectual distinction made it something of a no-man's-land in the war between the aesthetes and the hearties, which was contested at Oxford even more fiercely than at Charterhouse. But even at Lincoln the choice had to be made. For an artistic dandy who had firmly established his incompetence at games, there could not have been a moment's hesitation as to where

---

[1] In recent years there have been many descriptions of the Oxford of the 1920s, in the autobiographies, biographies and memoirs of such people as Cyril Connolly, Evelyn Waugh, John Betjeman and C. Day-Lewis, and in Martin Green's *Children of the Sun*. Osbert's account, in *With an Eye to the Future*, was not only one of the first of these but also the funniest.

his allegiance lay. Or so one would have thought. One would have been wrong. Amazingly, Osbert started off in the direction of heartiness.

Lincoln had close connections with Charterhouse – too close for comfort, in Osbert's view. The Rector, Dean and several Fellows of the college were Old Carthusians, and the undergraduates included many of Osbert's former schoolmates. The hateful 'house spirit' of school was duplicated by a similar pressure to 'do something for the college'. Of all improbable things, Osbert took up rowing.

> The incurable optimism which had at St Ronan's sustained my belief that there must be one sport at which Lancaster was destined to shine was not, even yet, finally quenched by bitter experience and when the President of the Boat Club came round on a recruiting drive I proved a sucker. After a few days on the river it became abundantly clear to me why rowing had in more rational societies been confined to the criminal classes and prisoners of war, and not all the efforts of Sefton Delmer [later a colleague at the *Express*] – then a willowy, curly-haired heart-throb, the toast of St Hilda's – to whom my instruction in the rudiments of what it would be ridiculous to call either an art or a science had been entrusted, could arouse, let alone maintain, my enthusiasm, so that after a grim two weeks I cast in my lot with the aesthetes, laid down my oar and joined the O.U.D.S. [Oxford University Dramatic Society].

The Oxford aesthete tradition went back to Walter Pater, Oscar Wilde and Max Beerbohm's *Zuleika Dobson*. In the period before the First World War the aesthetes came to be countered by the hearties. The opposition was not just one of contrasting lifestyles but also of actual physical conflict.

Maurice Bowra described the 'boisterous years' of pre-1914 Oxford when 'the privileged young relieved their ebullience in outbursts of violence'. Young aristocrats chased Philip Sassoon out of Balliol with whips, and at New College 'It was a common amusement on summer evenings to take the furniture from a man's room and burn it. The victim need not necessarily be unpopular or have come from the wrong school; what counted was the thrill of incendiarism.' In Compton Mackenzie's Oxford novel *Sinister Street*, published in 1913, the young gentlemen wreck the room of one man simply because his name is Smithers and he has a cockney accent.

The war had a sobering effect on the universities. When Captain Robert Graves returned from the trenches in 1919 he found Oxford 'remarkably quiet':

The returned soldiers did not feel inspired to rag about, break windows, get drunk, or have tussles with the police and races with the Proctors' 'bulldogs' as in the old days. The boys straight from the public schools kept quiet too, having had war preached at them continually for four years, with orders to carry on loyally at home while their brothers served in the trenches, and make themselves worthy of such sacrifices.

Goodbye to All That

For a while the war brought peace to the university. Those who had survived the Somme and Passchendaele had had more than enough of violence. But undergraduate generations are brief and soon the last of the 'beribboned brigadiers masquerading as undergraduates' (in Osbert's phrase) had gone down, to be replaced by a new intake which quickly reverted to the irresponsibility of pre-war Oxford. They divided themselves into two rival groups, as distinct and as hostile to one another as Montagues and Capulets, mods and rockers, skinheads and punks.

Evelyn Waugh in *Decline and Fall* memorably describes a reversion to pre-war behaviour with the hearties of the Bollinger Club 'baying for broken glass', assaulting the aesthetes and destroying their possessions:

They broke up Mr. Austen's grand piano, and stamped Lord Reading's cigars into his carpet, and smashed his china, and tore up Mr. Partridge's (black) sheets, and threw the Matisse into his water-jug; Mr. Sanders (who had been to dinner with Ramsay MacDonald) had nothing to break except his windows, but they found the manuscript at which he had been working for the Newdigate Prize Poem, and had great fun with that.

Waugh's Bollinger Club was the fictionalized version of the Bullingdon, whose members on one occasion smashed 256 panes of glass. Osbert described them as wearing 'well-cut tweeds or old Etonian ties, or jodhpurs, yellow polo-sweaters and hacking jackets, slit to the shoulder-blades'. This attire distinguished them from the less aristocratic hearties, who dressed in grey flannel trousers or elaborate plus-fours, with 'extravagantly long striped scarves indicative of athletic prowess'.

The aesthetes by contrast favoured high-necked pullovers, or shantung ties in pastel shades. For the aesthetes clothes, in Cyril Connolly's account, were an intoxication. The war had provided only a brief interruption to the tradition of sartorial flamboyance and elegance of Wilde and Beerbohm. The epicene Beverley Nichols, president of the Union in 1920, and in the same year author of the Oxford novel *Patchwork*, is said to have been the first man to wear suede shoes in Oxford. Harold Acton wore outrageously broad trousers, twenty-six inches at the knee and twenty-four at the ankle, so that they covered his shoes and gave his legs the appearance of an elephant's. This set the fashion which was to be called 'Oxford bags'.

Alan Pryce-Jones (an exact contemporary of Osbert's at Oxford) wrote that the aesthetes saw themselves as a heroic minority like the Albigenses. The hearties were stronger in numbers and in brawn, and continued their room-wrecking activities. In a letter to Brian Howard, Harold Acton described how his rooms were attacked by thirty men: 'I, tucked up in bed and contemplating the reflection of Luna on my walls, was immersed under showers of myriad particles of glass, my head powdered with glass dust, and my possessions vitrified.'

Evelyn Waugh remembers Hertford College as being agreeably free of schoolboyish 'college spirit' and the hooliganism against eccentrics that was prevalent in the larger colleges. Even so his room was once invaded by a belligerent 'tipsy white colonial' who demanded to know what Waugh 'did for the college'. He replied that he drank for it.

Not that the aesthetes confined themselves to verbal retaliation. When a hearty sneered at the bottle-green suit and raspberry-coloured crêpe de Chine shirt of Harold Acton's brother William, he simply knocked the man down. Osbert recalled 'one heroic evening' when beefy invading rowing hearties 'fell like ninepins before a barrage of champagne bottles flung by Robert Byron from a strategic position at the head of the stairs with a force and precision that radically changed the pattern of Oxford rowing for the rest of the term'.

Another non-hearty who was equally capable of looking after himself was Randolph Churchill. Whatever he may have looked like in his later years, Randolph Churchill was at that time, according to Osbert, 'without exception the best-looking young man I've ever seen. He had a self-assurance which most of us at that age lacked, which in his case amounted to down-right arrogance, and great moral courage.' He and Osbert once, slightly tipsy, took a motor-boat out on the river. They behaved thoroughly badly and nearly removed the oars from the university boat. On disembarking they were met by a dozen hefty rowing blues obviously, and probably rightly, intent on throwing the miscreants into the river.

Osbert recalled the subsequent events in a radio tribute to Randolph Churchill after his death in 1968:

> Before they could get a *word* in edgeways Randolph, aged seventeen, instantly attacked them, saying 'Extraordinary behaviour, going up and down in that boat as if you own the river just because you've got all those OARS.' This went on for about half an hour, at the end of which the great rowing hearties slunk away and we went quietly home.

Louis MacNeice said that in the Oxford of that time 'homosexuality and "intelligence", heterosexuality and brawn, were almost inexorably paired. This left me out in the cold, and I took to drink.' Certainly heterosexual intellectuals such as MacNeice, Day-Lewis and Rex Warner did not shine in a milieu that was almost entirely male, and often actively homosexual. Harold Acton, Tom Driberg, W. H. Auden, Maurice Bowra and many other influential figures of the time were homosexual. Even Evelyn Waugh and Cyril Connolly, who in later life were heterosexual, at that time directed their attentions towards other men.

Osbert did not, but in other respects he was now the very model of a 1920s Oxford aesthete. In a book review for *The Isis* he savaged Renée Haynes's *Neapolitan Ice*, the first novel to describe life in a women's college at Oxford. The rival Oxford magazine, *The Cherwell* (both took the definite article in those days), commented (12 May 1928): 'That chap Lancaster doesn't care for this book; so one gathers from his powerful indictment of it in the *Isis*. But Lancaster is such an aesthete.'

Most undergraduates were still in their teens, having come straight from their public schools, and there were very few women undergraduates. University was thus simply a continuation of the all-male education of preparatory and public schools, and many undergraduates suffered from what Cyril Connolly diagnosed as arrested adolescence. Arrested childhood, too. Beverley Nichols had a toy rabbit called Cuthbert, Sebastian Flyte a toy bear called Aloysius, and Betjeman kept his teddy bear Archibald to the end of his life. The aesthetes and dandies also preserved a taste for children's literature to an advanced age. Evelyn Waugh used to read *Wind in the Willows* to Lady Diana Cooper when she was resting on tour with *The Miracle*, and W. H. Auden said that Lewis Carroll's Alice was 'What, after many years and countless follies and errors, one would like, in the end, to become.' Apart from his yearning to return to the luxury of being pushed in a pram, Osbert avoided the Peter Pan element in the aesthetes, as he did their effeminacy and what was later called 'camp' behaviour, such as Harold Acton crying, in Betjeman's *Summoned by Bells*:

> My dears, I want to rush into the fields
> And slap raw meat with lilies.

On the contrary, Osbert was remarkably grown up by the standards of his contemporaries. Alan Pryce-Jones remembers him as 'above all, debonair'. Reviewing the second volume of autobiography, *With an Eye to the Future* (*New York Times Book Review*, 29 October 1967), Pryce-Jones writes:

> As his exact contemporary, I can see him very clearly in those days. To my eyes, indeed, he has not changed over 40 years. He might, then as now, have been an Edwardian dandy, moustached and pinstriped; perhaps a trifle trimmer at twenty than today, but already with the communicative air – since he has remained passionately interested in the doings and the foibles of countless friends – of a bigger and rounder Max Beerbohm.

John Betjeman remembered Osbert as being different from the other aesthetes:

> They wore tweed and hand-woven ties, and identified themselves with outdoor life and hay-carts and wains. They differed, too, from polished Etonians and Harrovians. The rest of us wore grey flannel trousers, tweed jackets and club ties. Osbert, with that round head, those round observing eyes and huge moustache, unique in a clean-shaven age, looked like Max Beerbohm.

He wore checks, and for a while sported a monocle.

Osbert's social circle at Oxford centred on the hospitality of three dons – G. A. Kolkhorst, F. F. Urquhart and C. M. Bowra, who rivalled one another as hosts for the brighter undergraduates. Kolkhorst, university lecturer in Spanish, was known as the Colonel because, according to Betjeman, he was so little like a colonel. Maurice Bowra at times affected to believe that Kolkhorst had actually been invented by Betjeman, though he recognized his reality sufficiently to put it about that Kolkhorst had 'a touch of the tarbrush'. Kolkhorst, who was wholly white, retaliated by always referring to Bowra as Mr Borer, and by becoming visibly irritated by any mention of his rival that struck him as over-appreciative.

Osbert, who described Kolkhorst as 'highly ridiculous, but dearly loved', would, like all the other smarter aesthetes, regularly attend the Colonel's salon at half-past twelve every Sunday in term-time. Sherry and marsala were served: the choice was made by the Colonel and depended on how far the recipient stood in his favour. Sherry went to those in good odour, marsala to anyone who had caused offence through such crimes as insufficient laughter at the Colonel's jokes, or excessive laughter at one of Bowra's.

Osbert conceded the childishness of these occasions. People would write four-letter words under the mantelpiece in the hope that they would shock female students seated on the low sofa by the fire for their tutorials. Another jape was, at a given signal, for everyone to sway from side to side chanting, 'The Colonel's drunk! The Colonel's drunk! The room's going round,' or for everyone to sing words by Betjeman to the tune of John Peel:

> D'ye ken Kolkhorst in his art-full parlour
> Handing out the drinks at his Sunday morning gala?
> Some get sherry and some marsala
> With his arts and his crafts in the corner.

It all sounds very convivial and, if rather silly, must at least have provided a break from the relentless sophistication that the aesthetes had to keep up for the rest of the time. Betjeman describes Kolkhorst's Sunday-morning 'rout' in *Summoned by Bells*:

> The over-crowded room was lit by gas
> And smelt of mice and chicken soup and dogs.
> Among the knick-knacks stood a photograph
> Of that most precious Oxford essayist,
> Upon whose margin Osbert Lancaster
> Wrote 'Alma Pater' in his sloping hand.

Francis Fortescue Urquhart, the history tutor and Dean of Balliol, had a more direct connection with Walter Pater, having been the model for the chief character in the latter's *Emerald Uthwart*. He was known as 'Sligger', a name said to be derived from 'the sleek one'. He is commonly reputed to have been the model for the character of Sillery in the *Music of Time* novels, but Anthony Powell has denied it.

By far the most influential of the three hospitable dons was

Maurice Bowra. With the best will in the world, it is not easy for those of us who never met Bowra to understand quite why and how he was able to cast such a spell on those around him. His many friends and admirers claim that his brilliance went into his conversation and that, because of the fugitive nature of the spoken word, those who did not experience it at first hand cannot know how dazzling it was. There is little hint of it in his writings, as even his admirers point out.

Bowra acolytes never tire of repeating his verbal sallies, but few who were not members of the charmed circle are likely to be won over to the Bowra Admiration Society by his feeble puns, class snobbery, and plain rudeness. Yet Bowra did have positive qualities. In an otherwise largely hostile essay (the *new Review*, January 1975) John Carey, an Oxford don of a later generation, pays tribute to Bowra's breadth of learning which, he says, offers a challenge and a reproach to modern dons with their increasingly narrow specializations. Bowra read Russian, French, German, Italian, Spanish, Greek and Chinese:

> World literature to him was not a set of linguistic cupboards, mostly closed, but a warm and welcoming ocean in which he splashed about freely. He spanned time as well as space. From Homer, Pindar and Sophocles his love and knowledge extended to Yeats, Valéry, Rilke, George, Blok, Cavafy, Apollinaire, Mayakovsky and Lorca. Pasternak, Quasimodo, Neruda and Seferis were his personal friends. Set against these riches, the burrowings of the typical modern researcher shrivel into absurdity.

Osbert's precocious degree of sophistication was undoubtedly reinforced by the influence of Maurice Bowra. He was one of those who spoke of the excitement generated by Bowra's mere presence, and of the 'unquenchable and astringent enthusiasm with which he proffered both sympathy and encouragement during their formative years' to people as various as himself, John Betjeman, Hugh Gaitskell, John Sparrow and Isaiah Berlin. Bowra's circle of favoured undergraduates also included Cyril Connolly, Evelyn Waugh, Rex Warner, Cecil Day-Lewis, A. J. Ayer, Norman Brook, Henry Green, Kenneth Clark, Harold Acton, Brian Howard, Anthony Powell ... the list could easily go on.

Bowra did an immense amount to widen the cultural horizons of those who met him, to free them from English provincialism and the dead hand of Victorian social and moral values. No less a man than

Sir Isaiah Berlin called Bowra a major liberating influence, and Professor Hugh Lloyd-Jones wrote that:

> In Bowra's early years in Oxford the constricting stuffiness of Victorian convention still lay heavily on much of English social life. Much of intellectual life was correspondingly inhibited; till well into the thirties most senior academics and schoolmasters reacted with sheer horror to any movement in literature that seemed to break away from the Victorian tradition. Against this tradition Bowra was an open rebel.

It is normal for the younger generation to react against the values of the previous one. Osbert was later to write, rather self-critically, of the shame of adolescents at the 'supposed inadequacy, intellectual or political, of their families', and of his own 'uncritical rejection of all the artistic values which my parents still upheld, and a ridiculous exaltation of contemporary masters at the expense of those they reviled'.

Whether or not he was in retrospect being a bit hard on himself, Osbert had certainly followed up Ronald Cartland's lead with enthusiasm. He subscribed to Wyndham Lewis's *Blast*, he listened to Brecht and Weill's *Die Dreigroschenoper*, to Cole Porter and Noël Coward. To improve his French he went during vacations to the Riviera, staying with family friends at Roquebrune, where he encountered the work of Valéry, Matisse and Stravinsky.

Even Bowra's explosive form of speech infected his group. Betjeman detected an echo of Bowra's voice in those of both Isaiah Berlin and Osbert. This is slightly surprising, since Bowra's speech was noted for its rapid, explosive delivery (like that of Sir Isaiah and of Lord David Cecil) and booming volume. Osbert, by contrast, spoke fairly quietly, slowly and with great deliberation, the chief characteristics being to put enormous emphasis on certain syllables while at the same time widening his eyes even more than usual, raising his eyebrows, bristling his moustache, and announcing the end of the sentence with something between a chuckle and a laugh which sounded like a small bark. But Betjeman was not the only one to have remarked on the resemblance between Bowra's way of speaking and Osbert's. According to Rex Warner, when Bowra visited Athens at the end of the war (when both Warner and Osbert were working there) someone ventured to comment to Bowra that he spoke like Osbert. This remark made Bowra extremely huffy: he thought the man should have said that Osbert spoke like him.

Although the General Strike had stirred many of the undergraduates of Osbert's generation into political action, interest in issues outside the university had for the most part proved temporary. Political awareness, of a highly traditional kind, was discernible only in the Union, a place visited by the aesthetes hardly at all except to use the commodious lavatories. The only occasion of political excitement Osbert remembered, other than at the Union, was during an election, when he noticed a large crowd outside the Conservative Committee Rooms being addressed with characteristic ebullience by Quintin Hogg (later Lord Hailsham). At first he thought the listeners were held spellbound by the power of Hogg's oratory. It was not until he noticed wisps of smoke snaking up the façade that he realized that they were in fact rooted to the spot by an understandable curiosity as to how soon the speaker would be consumed by the fire which, unknown to Hogg, had broken out in the piano-showroom on the ground floor. As for the politics of the Left, these were virtually the sole preserve of Tom Driberg, but his poetry, 'of which he gave a memorable recital to the accompaniment of typewriters and flushing lavatories in the Music Rooms, owed, as I recall, rather more to Dada than to the Communist Manifesto'.

Oxford at that time was, indeed, more interested in poetry than in politics. It was the Oxford of MacSpaunday (the composite name later given to Louis MacNeice, Stephen Spender, W. H. Auden and C. Day-Lewis). Auden kept himself in hermit-like seclusion, and was not a frequenter of the dons' salons. Nor were Day-Lewis, Rex Warner or Louis MacNeice, though MacNeice at least looked like a poet. Indeed his appearance at that time struck Osbert as 'uncompromisingly and defiantly poetic; the curly black hair, the carelessly draped scarf above the brown velvet jacket, the walking stick, all combined with an habitual air of bored and slightly arrogant detachment to arouse intense astonishment without immediately inspiring sympathy'. Stephen Spender, who arrived in Oxford in Osbert's second year, was 'type-cast for the young Apollo golden-haired, a role to which he brought all the touching grace of a performing bear'. Other poets included Norman Cameron, and two of Louis MacNeice's contemporaries from Marlborough, Bernard Spencer and John Betjeman (or Betjemann, as his name was then spelt).

A Marlburian friend of Betjeman's at Lincoln was Graham Shepard, the son of E. H. Shepard who illustrated A. A. Milne's Pooh books, and it was through him that Osbert and Betjeman met.

Betjeman was to be of crucial importance in directing the way Osbert's career was to go, both at Oxford and afterwards. Osbert remembered Betjeman's appearance at that time: '... Betjeman, idiosyncratic as ever, made a sustained and successful effort to present a convincing impersonation of a rather down-at-heel Trac-

tarian hymn-writer recently unfrocked' – this in spite of wearing Sulka shirts and Charvet ties.

Betjeman was a year ahead of Osbert, and it is the way of second-year students to despise freshmen. This seems at first to have been the case with Betjeman. Asked (in 1983) for his first memory of Osbert he said, 'I think we had a difference of opinion. I was faintly jealous of him because he was so prominent so young. I was envious of him. I thought of him as an upstart. The Charterhouse connection made him so prominent socially.'

Betjeman was in the habit of giving people nicknames, sometimes quite cruel (he himself had the luck to get away with nothing worse than JB or Betch). In the conversation of Betjeman and Osbert, Lord (Kenneth) Clark was always K. Clark, and John Piper invariably Mr Piper. When Betjeman first met Osbert Lancaster he shifted him to another county and called him Sidney Derbyshire. 'To his face?' I asked. 'I think so,' said Sir John. Fortunately Derbyshire was soon forgotten. Osbert was Osbert.

Osbert liked Betjeman straight away: 'We liked the same jokes, we liked the same people. It started off with hoots of laughter about – I can't remember – some joke figure.' Had there not been a difference of opinion to start with? 'Yes, I think there was a small row but mercifully that period passed.' Betjeman said that Osbert was his greatest friend in the mid-Oxford period 'and ever since', a sentiment which Osbert undoubtedly reciprocated. The two had so much in common, from their sense of humour to their love of tradition and their distrust (often dislike) of the new, their passionate interest in architecture, and their lifelong commitment to the Church of England. Unlike so many of their contemporaries they did not *find* their faith: they never lost it.

It was the hoots of laughter that brought them together. 'We liked unimportant people,' Betjeman remembered. 'Hackforth Jones, who lived in Barnet.' (This recollection caused the Poet Laureate to laugh so immoderately that he was unable to explain who Hackforth Jones was.) Osbert confirmed this interest.

> Betch would go miles by bus to the other end of Oxford to see someone of no interest. His enthusiasm for the dimmest person he could find was very salutary, a sort of inverted snobbery. There was another trick of J.B.'s. He'd take up a crashing bore of no interest whatsoever and land him on all his friends and never be seen again. That was a well-known manoeuvre.

Betjeman was responsible for Osbert's first appearance on the Oxford stage. The OUDS at that time had a high reputation. Max Reinhardt had put on an enormously successful production of *A Midsummer Night's Dream* in 1925, and in Osbert's first year Theodor Komisarjevsky, one of the greatest producers of his day, did *King Lear*. Betjeman, who was cast as the Fool, was at the time editing *The Cherwell*. He published a photograph of OUDS rehearsing, under which there was a ribald caption. Denys Buckley, the president of OUDS, and Harman Grisewood, who was playing Lear, became extremely pompous and insisted on Betjeman's expulsion from the Society. This necessitated a hasty shuffling of the cast less than a fortnight before the opening. John Fernald was promoted to Fool, the part left vacant by Betjeman. The role of the Duke of Cornwall was taken over by Peter Fleming, previously the Duke of Cornwall's servant. Osbert, who had hitherto had a non-speaking part as one of Goneril's drunken knights, became the Duke of Cornwall's servant.

It is not a large part, but it is an important and active one, for it is the servant who tries to prevent the putting out of Gloucester's eyes. For his pains he is set upon by the Duke who promptly kills him in a swordfight. The university sabre champion gave the Duke (Peter Fleming) and servant (Osbert) special training for this scene, which was one that Komisarjevsky gave full treatment, ending with the slain Osbert falling from a great height. Osbert survived the combat rather better than the Duke, who one night received a nasty crack on the skull from Osbert's four-foot steel blade. Another night Peter Fleming forgot his mail gauntlet, and received from Osbert a wound which lent unexpected realism to his exit-line, 'I bleed apace!'

> Nor was he the only victim, for one night as I swung Excalibur over my left shoulder a loud groan signalled that I had dealt an effective backhander to one of those old men whom Shakespeare so frequently leaves hanging about the stage, invariably in one of the pools of darkness without a superfluity of which no continental producer can possibly make do. The very next evening my trusty weapon finally failed, snapping off smartly at the hilt, flying across the stage, tearing through a flat and, after narrowly missing Miss Martita Hunt who was playing Goneril, buried itself in the prompt-side wall.

John Fernald was also editor of *The Isis*, for which Osbert worked for a year, doing caricatures of such contemporaries as Fernald himself, Peter Fleming, Harman Grisewood and many others. He then moved to *The Cherwell* where he started by contributing a series of 'Little Known Gems of Victorian Art'.

The Cherwell was, in contrast to *The Isis*, irreverent and frivolous. Recent editors had included Evelyn Waugh (whose lino-cut captioned 'Europe listens while Oxford sleeps' continued to adorn reports of the Union debates for many years), Robert Byron, Edward James, Christopher Sykes and John Betjeman. Other contributors included Brian Howard, Tom Driberg, Mark Ogilvie-Grant and

Edward Hulton. In due course Osbert was to share the direction of the magazine with Maurice Green, later editor of the *Telegraph*.

In some ways *The Cherwell* foreshadowed *Parson's Pleasure*, the scurrilous Oxford magazine of the late 1950s which itself was the forerunner of *Private Eye*. *The Cherwell* contrived to get itself into quantities of hot water, and Osbert and Maurice Green had many awkward interviews with the Proctor. They were fined £10 each for publishing an indecent joke about Godfrey Winn, and they were threatened with legal action by Quintin Hogg or, to give him his full name (as *The Cherwell* liked to), Quintin McGarel Hogg.

Not that *The Cherwell* was a scandal sheet. In the issues of 1928 and 1929 one finds, for example, reports on Union speeches by such as G. Boyd-Carpenter, E. M. Lustgarten, Quintin Hogg and Randolph Churchill ('. . . hesitating and youthful, while his diction remains somewhat pompous . . . His remarks about Moslems and Hindoos provoked much indignation among the Indian members.'). One finds a report on M. Maurice Ravel receiving the honorary degree of D.Mus., and a note congratulating the former editor Edward James on his marriage to Miss Tilly Losch. Betjeman wrote about novels and poetry of the day that included Evelyn Waugh's *Decline and Fall*, Aldous Huxley's *Point Counter Point*, Virginia Woolf's *Orlando* and the 'Ariel' poems of T. S. Eliot (or Thomas Eliot, as *The Cherwell* called him).

Osbert's name, writings and drawings crop up frequently. The Sayings of the Week quote such remarks of Mr O. Lancaster's as 'I cannot say that I concur in the general high opinion of Abraham Lincoln.' His drawing of 'Colonel' Kolkhorst's salon is captioned 'The Colonels and the Queens depart' – a comment on the sexual proclivities of the Kolkhorst set that must have seemed distinctly risqué at the time. There is a report of a debate at the Poetry Society in which Mr Osbert Lancaster propounded the thesis that all Forms must have a Purpose, in fact 'a moral conclusion, preferably at the end'. Exactly what this means is a trifle obscure, but according to *The Cherwell* Mr Lancaster defended his view 'with such torrential rhetoric that Mr Green was very soon convinced, and threw himself into the combat on Mr Lancaster's side; shortly even Mr (Stephen) Spender was driven into compliance'.

In May 1930 *The Cherwell* carried a report of an exhibition of caricatures by Mr Angus Malcolm and Mr Osbert Lancaster, and in the same term there was a review by O.L. which is of interest not

only for showing how early his prose style was fully developed, but also for presenting him in the unpredictable act of defending D. H. Lawrence and his views on pornography and obscenity: 'Mr Lawrence's pamphlet is a book that needed writing and the fact that he is shouting at the top of his voice throughout does not rob what he says of its proper value.'

While leading an active social life, acting with OUDS and drawing and writing for *The Isis* and *The Cherwell*, Osbert had to find at least some time for the academic studies which purport to be the reason for an undergraduate's presence at university. At Oxford the honourable choice of degree was between an effortless First on the one hand, and on the other a Fourth, the lowest degree of all, reputedly reserved for those who combined brilliance with indolence. Anything between a First and a Fourth suggested that the recipient was an industrious but not particularly bright plodder. Osbert used to say, 'If you don't take a First it doesn't matter what the hell you take.'

Clearly such contemporaries as Kenneth Clark and John Sparrow must have worked, and worked hard, to acquire their erudition. Rex Warner in fact overdid it and had a nervous breakdown which necessitated his taking an extra year. So what did Osbert read? When asked this question on *Desert Island Discs* many years later, he replied, 'What did I read? I hardly read anything. I read English Literature, like a fool. The stupidest school I could have taken.' In fact, as we have seen, he read a great deal. In the space of a few pages of *With an Eye to the Future* he mentions Aldous Huxley, Virginia Woolf, Saki, Ronald Firbank, Richard Aldington, Stefan Zweig, T. S. Eliot's *The Waste Land*, Sacheverell Sitwell's *Southern Baroque Art*, Robert Graves's *Goodbye to All That*, Wyndham Lewis's *Time and Western Man* as well as Stendhal, Julien Benda, Proust, and a good many other French authors read during vacations in France. Unfortunately these were not part of the Oxford English Literature syllabus.

Robert Graves memorably recalled the rebuke he received at the college board at the end of his first term: 'I understand, Mr Graves, that the essays which you write for your English tutor are, shall I say, a trifle temperamental. It appears, indeed, that you prefer some authors to others.' Some ten years later Osbert found himself equally discouraged from exercising his critical faculty. 'Personal judgements were not called for; what was required was the largest possible collection of *idées reçues*.' He found himself forced to spend as much time on 'an affected bore such as Spenser' as on Chaucer. Worst of all (as countless Oxford generations reading Eng.Lit. have bemoaned) was the compulsory Anglo-Saxon. Osbert made no attempt to conceal his lack of interest in this language. One can see how little he learnt about it from the fact that when he writes about Anglo-Saxon literature in *With an Eye to the Future* he lumps together *Beowulf* and *Sir Gawain and the Green Knight*: not only are these works separated by six centuries, but *Gawain* is not even written in Anglo-Saxon.

Half-way through Osbert's third year it became apparent that his neglect of the boring bits of the syllabus had been too dedicated for him to sit his finals with much hope of success. He managed to be allowed a fourth year, the idea being that he would abandon his social, dramatic, journalistic and artistic activities, and apply himself single-mindedly to Grimm's Law, *Piers Plowman* and other of the less cherry-like parts of the Oxford Eng. Lit. cake. Accordingly he handed over *The Cherwell* to Angus Malcolm, made his farewell to the OUDS stage and moved out to the less socially tempting regions of lodgings off the Iffley Road, where he shared rooms with his old friend Graham Shepard.

Since most of Osbert's friends had gone down at the end of his third year, and Betjeman before even that, this plan stood some chance of working. A new distraction appeared, though, in the form of the Ruskin School of Drawing which had suddenly been rejuvenated by Albert Rutherston and a talented team that included Gilbert Spencer (the brother of Stanley), Eric Ravilious and Barnett Freedman. Osbert's original intention was to spend only one morning a week at the Ruskin, but those who have once felt the lure of the life class can never resist it when the opportunity presents itself. That one morning soon invaded large areas of the rest of the week. Come the summer term, the inevitable panic set in as Osbert realized that he knew no more about Grimm's Law now than he had a year earlier, that he had small Middle English and less Anglo-Saxon, that he had not finished *Paradise Lost* or started *Paradise Regained*, and that a reasonable knowledge of Chaucer and the Metaphysicals was not enough. The worst part of the exams was the Viva, which left him

> scarred for life . . . The moment when a particularly aggressive female
> don thrust at me a piece of Anglo-Saxon unseen, of which the only

intelligible words were 'Jesus Christ' which I promptly and brightly translated, leaving her with the unfortunate impression, as they were followed by unbroken silence, that I had employed them expletively, still occasionally haunts my dreams.

To his surprise and delight he was awarded what he always referred to as 'by the skin of my teeth, an honest Fourth'.

IV

ENTR'ACTE

MANY of the aesthetes who left Oxford in the 1920s found that their long and expensive education had not equipped them well for earning a living in a congenial manner. Anthony Powell went into publishing, Henry Green into his family business. These were exceptions. Most of them showed a fastidious disdain for anything that smacked of trade or commerce. Betjeman, for example, resolutely resisted parental pressure to join the family firm manufacturing household gadgets in the Pentonville Road. How, he asked in *Summoned by Bells*, could he go by tram in a Savile Row suit and Charvet tie?

> How could I, after Canterbury Quad,
> My peers and country houses and my jokes,
> Talk about samples, invoices and stock?

One way of earning a living that was considered not too *infra dig.* was to take the route (via Gabbitas and Thring) back to the detested prep schools. Such was the course taken by John Betjeman, Evelyn Waugh, Graham Greene, W. H. Auden, Cecil Day-Lewis and Rex Warner. Most of them brushed the chalk from their clothes as soon as possible and usually went abroad, following in the footsteps of wealthier contemporaries such as Harold Acton who had never been forced by financial necessity to stand in front of a blackboard or to take games.

There were any number of reasons why abroad was so attractive. They varied from sex (as in the case of Auden and Isherwood) to architectural exploration (as in the case of Robert Byron) to sheer wanderlust (as in the case of Peter Fleming). There was, of course, a long tradition of literary travel from Sterne and Smollett to Byron and Kinglake.

In the first decades of the century it was almost mandatory for artists and writers to make their homes anywhere other than where they were born. Henry James, T. S. Eliot, Ernest Hemingway, Scott

Fitzgerald from the United States; Shaw, Joyce and Beckett from Ireland; E. M. Forster, D. H. Lawrence and Aldous Huxley from England; Picasso from Spain; Stravinsky from Russia – these and many others chose exile. Had it been left to those who stayed at home there would have been no Modern Movement.

Between the wars this emigration became a flood. Paul Fussell's *Abroad* describes what he calls the British literary diaspora of the twenties and thirties. In a brief space he mentions Gerald Brenan in Spain, Graves in Majorca, Norman Douglas in Capri, Naples and Florence, Lawrence Durrell on Corfu, Aldous Huxley in California, Isherwood in Berlin, Bertrand Russell in China and Russia, Somerset Maugham on the Riviera, Stephen Spender in Vienna, V. S. Pritchett everywhere from Tenerife to Afghanistan, Edmund Blunden in Tokyo, Peter Fleming in Brazil, Harold Acton in Peking, William Empson in Tokyo and Peking, and Evelyn Waugh, Graham Greene and Robert Byron all over the place. It is easy to see why Lawrence Durrell should have written home from Corfu in capital letters, 'IS THERE NO ONE WRITING AT ALL IN ENGLAND NOW?'

Osbert's family, on both sides, was well enough off for him not to have to contemplate going back to the classroom, and at first it looked as though his choice too would be to go abroad. He had already travelled a good deal. He had first crossed the Channel at about the age of twelve with his mother. A dutiful trip to his father's grave in one of the vast cemeteries of the Somme was followed by the pleasure of three days in Paris, where he saw Notre-Dame and the Louvre, and then a motor-trip to Chartres and round the châteaux of the Loire. It was immediately apparent that abroad would vastly expand the cast of comic characters that the streets of Notting Hill and Littlehampton had provided. 'The bloused porters who rushed on board in a cloud of garlic and ferocious high spirits, the waxed-moustached gendarmes, the formidable alpaca-bosomed ladies rummaging in the *douane*, had none of them any counterparts in my experience . . .'

Thereafter there were annual holidays abroad, to Venice and Florence and to Roquebrune in the South of France where he stayed at the home of the Van den Eckhoudts, Belgian friends who had sought asylum during the war at his grandfather's house. Monsieur 'Van den' was a painter in the modern style, which rather shocked the Lancaster aunts, and he more than shocked grandfather Lancaster by speaking approvingly of Oscar Wilde: the old patriarch informed him firmly that had he not been a foreigner he would have known that this was not a name that could be mentioned in a gentleman's house.

Roquebrune introduced Osbert to all that was new in painting, literature and music.[1] The novels were not Dickens but Proust, the music not Sir Arthur Sullivan but Poulenc and Satie. At the opera house in nearby Monte Carlo there were the ballets of Diaghilev. Roger Fry was a frequent visitor. A near-neighbour was Paul Valéry. Osbert records a tea-party at which a chameleon was being shown off and after close study of the creature Valéry proclaimed the words:

> *Vert parmi les vergers,*
> *Rose parmi les fraises,*
> *Dans les apartements,*
> *Il grimpe sur les chaises.*

During his first long vacation from Oxford Osbert had set off with £50 in traveller's cheques in the company of Graham Shepard. After a week on the Loire, he met up with John Fernald in Paris and went via Munich and Vienna to Budapest. Subsequent holidays (twice with Angus Malcolm) took him to Germany and Austria, following the boundless enthusiasm for the Baroque that had been aroused in him by the Sitwells. He found that an unexpected pleasure in travelling in German-speaking countries was that his name on documents and luggage-labels was frequently misread by customs officials, railway porters and hotel staff, who would address him deferentially as 'Herr Oberst' (Colonel).

He visited Salzburg but didn't enjoy it much. Nor did he warm personally to the Bavarians and Austrians sufficiently to share 'one of the most widespread and dangerous illusions then current – namely, that the Bavarians and Austrians were kindly, sensitive people, the predestined and unwilling dupes of the brutal and callous Prussians to whom all the more disagreeable phenomena of German history were exclusively attributable'.

Otherwise, Osbert's response to abroad was almost invariably favourable. Left to himself he might, like so many of his friends and contemporaries, have gone (as Evelyn Waugh titled one of his travel books) while the going was good. Perhaps, but I doubt it. Unlike Browning's Waring he loved pacing up and down the streets of

---

[1] One exponent of the new to whom Osbert never warmed was the architect Le Corbusier. It was at Roquebrune that Le Corbusier met his death by drowning many years later.

London town. He had a very deep love of England and, like his friends John Piper and John Betjeman, he realized early on that its architecture was every bit as well worth exploring as that of abroad. Hitherto it had gone largely unexplored, from its stately homes to its parish churches, its street architecture and vernacular buildings from railway stations to public houses.

Furthermore there was family pressure to stay at home and put his honest Fourth to proper use. The Lancaster family fortunes had been built on a sturdy belief in the work ethic. In an interview with Michael Bateman (in *A Funny Way to Earn a Living*, 1966) Osbert replied to the question as to whether he was rich:

> Well, I have had to think about money. My mama, though rich, had the impression that she was as poor as a church mouse. Psychologically there was a tremendous pressure from the family that unearned income was a disgrace. It was an almost pathological thing to get the earned money ahead of the unearned income.

What then should he do, now that Oxford was behind him? His mother turned for advice to the head of the family, Uncle Jack. When Osbert tentatively suggested art as something he would like to do, Uncle Jack quickly made it clear that art was not work. 'It's all very well drawing pictures, but it don't get you anywhere,' he said. 'Why, I remember an awfully clever chap in my form at Charterhouse who did wonderful caricatures of all the masters. We all thought he had a great future but I've never heard of him since. Can't remember his name but he was a half-brother of that actor fellow Tree.' (Osbert never found quite the right moment to tell Max Beerbohm this story.)

The Bar. That was the decision arrived at by the councils of the Lancaster elders. This choice met with the enthusiastic approval of Osbert's mother, who (he discovered many years later, when going through her papers after her death) had cast his horoscope when he was born and discovered that what the stars foretold for him was a brilliant legal career. Accordingly he went off to a crammer's in Chancery Lane and ate his dinners in the Middle Temple. Predictably law studies turned out to be every bit as uncongenial as Anglo-Saxon, and in swift succession Osbert failed Roman Law once and Common Law twice. After one look at the paper on Real Property he went out to watch the latest Marx Brothers film.

Clearly the law was a misdirected target for his talents, and his studies would doubtless not have continued for long anyway. What terminated them abruptly was a violent fit of coughing in which he brought up blood. The haemorrhages did not recur but he had lost weight and X-rays showed dark areas of the lung which the various specialists interpreted as either old pleurisy scars or, possibly, tubercular patches. Accordingly, accompanied by a large supply of books, he set off for a sanatorium in Switzerland.

This was not a propitious start to a career, and it meant turning his back on an enjoyable and stimulating social life in London. More to the point, tuberculosis was then (and for some years after) a killer. No amount of humorous identification with Keats and Chopin can have lightened Osbert's spirits as he made his solitary journey to the upper Rhône valley. When he got off the train at Sion it was in a state of gloom more profound than any he had previously experienced. 'As the funicular to Montana crawled up into the blanket of cloud my heart sank to hitherto unplumbed depths.'

But he was resilient physically and in character. As the fog lifted and the beauty and grandeur of the Bernese Alps were revealed, his spirits soared and the depths of depression were replaced by a euphoric sense of liberation. Not for the first or last time his acute visual awareness proved a solace:

> The sky was of an intense dazzling blue and though no more snow was at the moment being added to the fresh fall which covered all the distant peaks and adjacent slopes, the air appeared to be full of minute specks of glittering mica mysteriously suspended. When to this visual surprise was joined the novel sensation of a sleigh-ride I managed to arrive at my destination in a far more balanced state of mind than an hour before I should have thought conceivable.[1]

It was rare for Osbert to be so open about his inner life, and the fact that on this occasion he recorded the ups and downs of his state of mind indicates that they were more than commonly extreme.

His friend Graham Shepard had given him a copy of Thomas Mann's *The Magic Mountain* but (half-deliberately) Osbert left it on the train. Had he read it, he could not have failed to recognize the similarities between Doctor Roche's sanatorium at Montana and the one in Mann's great novel. The food was just as copious and just as excellent, for Dr Roche's son-in-law was the chairman of the Savoy and used to send out members of his kitchen staff for healthy working-holidays. Drink (one glass of stout with meals) flowed

[1] *With an Eye to the Future.*

rather less freely than in *The Magic Mountain*, but there was the same routine of sputum tests and thermometer-watching, the short walks, the long rests in bed, and the endless games of bridge. Like Mann's Hans Castorp, Osbert found that the great world 'down there' lost its reality: what mattered was the minutiae of the daily goings-on of the sanatorium and the precise medical state of the patients.

> Very soon the outside world grew shadowy and remote, the fall of governments and the movements of Wall Street paled into insignificance alongside questions of such burning interest as whether or not Mrs Padstow-Trench was going to have a pneumo-thorax or how far the authorities were aware of Colonel Golightly's regular morning visits to that chic little bar in the village.

In its very different way the sanatorium was every bit as far removed from the realities of ordinary life as Oxford. Dr Roche's establishment was entirely English and maintained a high moral tone. There was not only less alcohol than in the German-speaking sanatoria, but also less sex. 'The other sanatoria', Osbert said, 'were run by Swiss who were of the opinion that sex was necessary three times a week – it was like cleaning your teeth, something to be done regularly. Even in the English sanatoria no one ever slept in their own beds, a fact which to my regret I only discovered very late in my stay.' Sir Malcolm Sargent, who was a patient at Dr Roche's shortly after Osbert, made the discovery early on.

After a few months Osbert was declared fit and ready to return to the real world. He decided to join friends in Venice for Easter. The night he arrived there he was seized by a panic of depression as severe as the one he experienced on arriving in Switzerland. He attributed this to the effect of going from the pure air at five thousand feet straight down to sea level and a very different quality of air. Whatever the physiological effect of this change of altitude, one cannot but suspect a psychological origin for this depression. Returning to the harsh realities of the everyday world from the cocoon of the sanatorium must have been every bit as much a shock as leaving them had been.

Nor had the months on the magic mountain done anything to resolve the question – what was he to do? A week in Venice soon restored his spirits, and he returned to London primed with well thought out arguments against returning to the law. Though he was now in the pink of health, it would surely be tempting providence to expose his vulnerable lungs to the dusty, musty atmosphere of a barrister's chambers. He would be coughing blood again in no time. The smell of turpentine, on the other hand, presented no such dangers. Accordingly he started studying at the Slade School, as he should have done in the first place.

He arrived at the Slade shortly after the terrifying Henry Tonks had been replaced as Head by Randolph Schwabe, and after the distinguished generations of students that had included Augustus John, Stanley Spencer, William Coldstream and Rex Whistler. Osbert spent long and absorbing hours in the life class and dutifully produced from time to time Slade-ish paintings ('some sombre still-life or discreet understatement of landscape which duly appeared in the annual exhibition of the New English Art Club').

What he enjoyed most, though, was studying stage design under Vladimir Polunin, who had for many years been Diaghilev's principle scene-painter and had worked with Picasso on *The Three-Cornered Hat*. The techniques and practical skills of scenery-painting that he learnt from Polunin were to prove invaluable when, some years later, Osbert was to work at Covent Garden, Sadler's Wells and Glyndebourne, and to execute his enormous wall-painting in the Shell building. It was Polunin too who introduced him to Karen Harris, a fellow-student five years younger than himself, with whom he fell in love. He married her in 1933 after two years' 'long and frustrating courtship'.

Osbert was twenty-two and Karen barely seventeen when they met. Her parents objected to an early marriage. Their daughter was of tender years. Also they had reservations about whether Osbert was a suitable match. These doubts were overcome after his probation-ary visit to the Harris home at Bembridge on the Isle of Wight in the company of John Betjeman, then in hot pursuit of Karen's cousin Camilla Russell (later Mrs Christopher Sykes). Camilla Russell's father was Sir Thomas Wentworth Russell, known as Russell Pasha. He served under no fewer than 29 Ministers of the Interior after Egyptian independence in 1922, and when he finally retired in 1946 he was the last British officer in the Egyptian service. He was a dandy, and an equestrian who made history by jumping his camels over fences.

Russell Pasha was not the only unusual member of Karen's extended family, and her nuclear family was by any standards odd.

Her father, Sir Austin Harris (1870–1958) was vice-chairman of Lloyds bank and an art collector. He was close to the seats of power, or so he thought. He claimed that the decision to go off the gold standard had been taken in his drawing-room where he was entertaining Sir John Simon and Sir Montagu Norman at the time. His reactions to financial affairs were highly emotional. The Wall Street Crash had him in almost continuous tears for months. He was liable to sob helplessly at the sight of the household accounts, and tried to economize on electricity by going round the house in the evening switching off lights regardless of whether or not there was anyone in the room.

Whether or not the gold-standard decision really was made in his drawing-room must be a matter for doubt, because Sir Austin's grasp on reality was not strong, and became increasingly weaker. He deceived himself rather than others, telling stories worthy of Baron von Münchhausen. He once told a dinner guest that when Blériot made the first air crossing of the Channel he was not alone, as is generally thought, but in the company of Sir Austin himself; he then proceeded to give a detailed eyewitness account of the whole perilous and historic journey.

Then there was Lady Harris, who was even odder. Just how odd is hard to say, because she was always being confused with one of the many other Lady Harrises who were around at the time, and some of the stories told about her may properly belong to another Lady Harris. There was Lady Harris who was the wife of the famous cricketer Lord Harris. There was the wife of Lord Harris of Seringapatam and Mysore. There were also the wives of a knight in Canada, another knight in Berkshire and one who was a Brazilian boundary arbitrator, as well as the spouses of a veteran of the Griqua campaign, an ex-chairman of the London County Council and an anti-slavery expert.

This information comes from an unidentified newspaper cutting in the scrap-book of the late Miss Honey Harris, elder sister of Karen. The journalist (probably Tom Driberg) was prompted to line up this identification parade of Lady Harrises because a few days previously he had made a bit of a blunder.

In addition to all the Lady Harrises listed above there was the wife of Sir Percy Harris, MP and Liberal chief whip from 1935 to 1945.

Lady (Percy) Harris was an artist, who under the name of Jesus Chutney painted pictures which were meant to be shocking and had titles like *The Blue Christ*. Lady (Austin) Harris also painted, and she too used a pseudonym, which was Rognon de la Flèche (Kidney of the Arrow). John Piper remembers Rognon's paintings as 'little roses, very delicate chi-chi things. I must say they were terrible.'

At any rate, Lady (Percy) Harris threw herself under a tube train at Bond Street with fatal consequences. The newspaper report was accompanied by a photograph of Lady Harris. The wrong Lady Harris. Not the wife of the MP but the wife of Blériot's co-pilot.

Karen's mother was also said to have healing hands, and massaged Lady Violet Powell for fibrositis with the help of a rosary and a 'poop-poop motor-horn which was part of her campaign for bullying servants'. The treatment, however unconventional, was (Lady Violet says) quite effective.

Lady Harris was a keen enthusiast of the psychic, mediums, Ouija boards, table-turning and other spiritualist and paranormal matters. She was anti-alcohol and obsessed with health to such a point that she would keep her bathroom and lavatory locked in case someone should in some way misuse them. She was terrified by the idea that her maid might have been using her hairbrushes. When travelling abroad she took not only her own bed linen but also her own bidet, which she had decorated with hand-painted violets and lilies of the valley. On one occasion this was mislaid on the quayside at Calais, as a consequence of which Osbert found himself in the embarrassing situation of having to carry the conspicuous object the entire length of the Blue Train. Karen explained to him that 'You must realize, darling, that my poor dear mother suffers from a bidet-fixe.'

Before being Lady Harris and Rognon de la Flèche she had been Cara Veronica Batten, the only daughter of an Edwardian beauty who was painted by Poynter and was said to have been the lover not only of Edward VII (when Prince of Wales) but also of Radclyffe Hall, the lesbian author of *The Well of Loneliness*.

Lady Harris had an orange-and-blue macaw which had the disconcerting habit of saying 'Fuck off, you silly bitch' at the least appropriate moment. She also made amateur films at her home in the Isle of Wight, with the often reluctant co-operation of relatives, friends and neighbours who were roped in willy-nilly.

These films seem to have been much influenced by the Marx Brothers. In *Treason's Bargain*, a silent film in 5 acts and 106 scenes, the part of the King was played by the composer Lord Berners, Mrs Tarchtree (a Margaret Dumont role) by Lady Harris, and the villainous Captain Desmond Sneyke by Osbert. The credits thanked Lady (Sybil) Colefax for providing an elephant (there was no elephant in the film), and the Girl Guides were supplied by the London Mediums' Psychic College.

The next year, 1937, there was another film with an equally wild plot: *The Sun Never Sets: An Epic of Endurance*. Though this too was filmed in the Isle of Wight, it was set in the African jungle. The cast included Mrs Peter Quennell, Lady Harris, Osbert (as Professor Schweppes), Angus Malcolm (Commander Bughouse), Honey Harris, Karen Lancaster and the artist Adrian Daintrey. The lion was played by the family cat, shot in close-up. Shot for real by the big-game hunter (Professor Schweppes), its demise is recorded by a picture of Osbert, shot-gun in hand, pith helmet on head, standing over a tiger-skin rug.

In yet another film (for which Karen was cameraman) Osbert played the part of a sinister Black Hussar who, disguised as a parlour-maid, perpetrates dastardly deeds which shake half the chancelleries of Europe. At least one of these films was shown for charity, and greeted with acclaim and hilarity.

Opinions of Lady Harris vary from that of Lady Violet Powell who found her 'great fun', to those of Penelope Betjeman ('a formidable person'), Tom Driberg ('one of the greatest senses of humour it has

been my fortune to meet'), John Piper ('frightfully affected') and her granddaughter Cara ('a very tiresome woman'). Osbert himself found her a woman of 'enormous charm and strong personality [and] of quite remarkable although unfashionable beauty'.

After Osbert's initial probationary period, they all got on very well together. So did Karen with Osbert's mother, who had little in common with Karen's other than an interest in the occult. Shortly before the wedding Mrs Lancaster took Karen aside for a little word of advice about the physical side of marriage. 'Now, dear, I want you to promise me that you won't let Osbert be tiresome. I know what those Lancasters are like when given half a chance and I was always very firm with his dear father.' This was probably the nearest Osbert's mother ever got to an explicit mention of sex.

As by far the youngest child of Sir Austin and Lady Harris, Karen had been very much the pet of the family. She was never sent to school apart from a nearby dame school, hardly ever left the house, and went to bed at seven o'clock until quite a late age. Her over-protected upbringing was partly due to Lady Harris's obsessive valetudinarianism but, unfortunately, only partly. Karen was diabetic from the age of eleven and one of the first people to be regularly on insulin, the long-term effects of which were as yet unknown. Her health cannot have been improved by smoking some sixty Turkish cigarettes a day. She was in very poor health in her later years, and was only fifty when she died. She was clever, and very amusing. She did not share Osbert's appetite for party-going, but did not try to check it. She was always supportive of him, both emotionally and in practical matters, domestic and professional, from proof-reading to helping with models and costumes when he came to work for the theatre.

Osbert's friends all very much took to Karen. John Piper says she was 'a marvellous woman, very sensitive and intelligent and really creative, terribly kind, frightfully funny. She was clearly in love with him when they married – they both were in love.' She would keep Betjeman in hoots of laughter for hours. With his usual habit of tinkering with people's names he called her not Karen with the stress on the first syllable but Kar-*een*: he thought it sounded like a car lubricant. The only time in their long friendship that Betjeman ever saw Osbert in tears was when Karen died. As for the genuine-ness of Betjeman's affection for her, this can be seen in 'Autumn 1964', the poem he wrote on her death.

77

She was quite strict with Osbert. Piper remembers her saying 'Oh, *Osbert*, don't do that.' Betjeman too remembered her cry of 'Osbert! *Osbert!* OSBERT!!!' Osbert's friends of that time are not in full agreement as to whether his failure to hear was because he was concentrating on something else and wasn't listening, or because he was even then slightly deaf. What they are agreed on is that Karen and Osbert were very fond of one another, and very kind to one another, and found one another extremely funny.

She is described as beautiful and quite tall; at least compared with Osbert. Photographs of the two of them together usually show Osbert with one foot on a step higher than Karen's. With the notable exception of Osbert's mother, most of the women in his life were taller than him.

Karen was also a good carpenter and could master an electric circuit. As far as domestic matters were concerned Osbert hardly lifted a finger in his life. What is surprising to someone of a later generation is that neither his mother nor Karen nor his second wife Anne seems to have objected to Osbert's laziness about the house. Both he and Betjeman assiduously fostered a little-boy-lost persona where practical matters were concerned, and were more than happy to be seen as hopeless and helpless if it meant that an efficient woman could and would cope with the tedious details of everyday life. In actual fact, until his last years Osbert was perfectly capable of looking after himself when necessary, as was evidenced by his mostly grass-widow time in Greece and by the highly organized professional efficiency and self-discipline without which he could not have produced such a large and varied quantity of work.

John Piper, himself immensely capable at everything he turns his hand to, confirms that Osbert never did any washing up. 'We all slaved at the sink and did all the cooking while Osbert amused us. One has to remember that he wasn't brought up to do any tedious chores. Gentlemen of Osbert's generation and class were expected to lead lives of permanently being waited on. He took to it absolutely naturally. It was like a bird flying – Osbert doing nothing.'

Karen and Osbert were married on a scorchingly hot day in June 1933 in the High Anglican church of St Peter's, Eaton Square. They honeymooned in Venice, and then moved into a flat with a studio in West Kensington.

Osbert was now aged twenty-six. Four years at Oxford, the false start at the Bar, the sanatorium in Switzerland, and studying at the Slade had provided a varied but prolonged preparation for his working life. Any lost time, however, was soon made up for. The large body of work he produced in the years up to the beginning of the war ranged from book reviews to anything from Christmas cards for laundries to posters for church bazaars, and the occasional exhibited painting. He held an exhibition at the Whitechapel, and executed some large murals at the Crown Hotel, Blandford Forum, Dorset (22 feet by $7\frac{1}{2}$, and $7\frac{1}{2}$ feet by 4), showing uniformed men on horses and other military figures in a setting of classical architecture. (Regrettably these have been damaged, and the brewery, Hall & Woodhouse, has covered them up.) He did illustrations for a number of books, including John Betjeman's *An Oxford University Chest*, worked on the *Architectural Review*, was art critic for the short-lived *Night and Day*, published four books (*Progress at Pelvis Bay, Our Sovereigns, Pillar to Post* and *Homes Sweet Homes*) and started the *Daily Express* pocket cartoons which were to continue with only brief interruptions for more than forty years.

The owner of the *Architectural Review*, Percy Hastings, was (Osbert said in an interview for *Desert Island Discs*) 'an old chum of my mother's, so it was graft'. It must also have been a help that the assistant editor was John Betjeman. The magazine, edited first by Christian Barman and then by Hubert de Cronin Hastings (son of Percy Hastings) was a lavish affair. Even today the issues produced in the 1930s seem adventurous in typography and layout.

Osbert's work at the *Architectural Review* varied from the humble chore of caption-writing to producing book reviews, art criticism, full-length feature articles and a monthly column of architectural chit-chat, sometimes illustrated by his own drawings. In the last Osbert's style is already recognizable, though not fully developed. The written contributions, however, show once again that his prose style was already fully formed. The cadences are classically balanced, the tone is one of dandyish superiority that fully exploits the comic potential of taking a reductive Gulliver's-eye view of the absurdly minuscule activities and aspirations of the Lilliputians. Thus he writes of the Royal Academy's 1932 summer exhibition:

> On going round Burlington House one experiences that feeling of relief and surprise that assails one on revisiting the Zoo; relief that some of the old favourites are still there, surprise that they should be

playing exactly the same games as before. This year, however forti-
fied one may be by previous experience, a gasp of admiration and
astonishment is with difficulty suppressed, so true to form do the old
favourites run. Never, surely, have Mr. Farquharson's Highland
sheep had to fight their way through so fierce, so snowy, a blizzard as
they do in No. 89, Gallery 1. On many a wall Mr. Olsson's sun sinks in
treacly glory beneath the wine-dark sea of the Cornish Riviera, just as
it used to do thirty summers ago . . . One of the pleasantest spots in
the whole Academy is always the Architectural Room; it has more
seats than the others, is light, airy, and seldom overcrowded.

Mocking the Royal Academy is easy: the summer exhibition has
been derided annually for as long as anyone can remember. What
showed more originality in his criticism was his choice of what to
praise. A 1934 book review, for example, extolled contemporary
British posters. 'No other country possesses a poster artist of the
calibre of Mr. McKnight Kauffer,' he wrote, 'nor can boast of
employers so enlightened as the Underground and Shell.' He could
have added the *Radio Times* to the list of enlightened patrons, and
(without in any way wishing to detract from the brilliant work of
McKnight Kauffer) surely Cassandre in France was at least of his
calibre. He might also have mentioned his old Ruskin teacher
Barnett Freedman, and John Hassall ('Skegness is *so* bracing') whom
Osbert described in his obituary notice in 1948 as supreme. Incidentally, Osbert had himself worked for both Christian Barman of
London Passenger Transport (as it was then called) and Jack Beddington at Shell. But he was right (and at the time unusual) in
making high claims for what was then contemptuously called
'commercial art' and in recognizing that most of the best visual art in
Britain at that time was to be found in posters, illustrations and
advertisements rather than in the easel paintings of the Academy
and the galleries.

As one would expect, some of his *Architectural Review* contributions are jokes, such as the rather prophetic account (with his own
illustrations) of the liner SS *Pelvishernia*: 'Next month we hope to
show you the seventy-thousand-pound first-class swimming pool
which is fitted with a unique gyroscopic device that ensures, no
matter how rough it may be outside, a perfectly calm surface for the
first-class luxury bathers.' Other contributions are less tongue-in-
cheek. In 1936 he wrote a long article (with drawings by Hugh
Casson) on 'The Culture of the Hadhramant', reviewed Freya

Stark's book on Arabia and Sacheverell Sitwell's *Narrative Pictures*, and wrote appreciatively of Victorian water-colours.

Neither architecture outside Europe nor the art of the Victorians was then a fashionable subject to enthuse about, and might seem out of place in a journal committed to the Modern Movement and what Osbert called 'that Bauhaus balls'. In the *Architectural Review*'s offices in Queen's Gate he found 'a stirring, almost hot-gospelling, determination to spread the doctrine of fitness for purpose and to proclaim from the roof-tops that there was no style but the international style and Le Corbusier was its prophet'.[1] This doctrine was reinforced when Betjeman left the *Architectural Review* and was replaced by J. M. (now Sir James) Richards. Around the same time there arrived in Britain such refugees from Hitler as Nikolaus Pevsner, Walter Gropius and Erich Mendelsohn. An earlier arrival had been that of Berthold Lubetkin who came from France in 1931: he designed the London Zoo's Penguin Pool and was one of the first men to fasten his trousers with a zip fastener rather than fly-buttons.

In 1933 the MARS (Modern Architectural Research) Group was set up with members who included Wells Coates, the *Architectural Review* writer P. Morton Shand, Maxwell Fry and Ernö Goldfinger. Osbert saw Betjeman as 'a built-in counterweight to too much *Modernismus*' on the *Architectural Review*, but it would be wrong to take the view that Betjeman and Osbert were a beleaguered pair defending the architecture of other ages and other continents against the grim-faced advocates of the twentieth-century architecture of Teutonic countries. For one thing Betjeman was briefly a member of the MARS group himself; he also wrote in the 1939 pamphlet *Antiquarian Prejudice* that architects should emulate those of Soviet Russia and produce 'an honest, plain structure of steel, glass and/or reinforced concrete'. For another, contributors to the *Architectural Review* included not only Betjeman and Osbert but such un-MARS-ish people as D. H. Lawrence, Brian Howard, Vanessa Bell, Raymond Mortimer, Robert Byron, Evelyn Waugh, Penelope Chetwode, Cyril Connolly, John Piper, Osbert Sitwell, Clive Bell and Wyndham Lewis.

The year 1936 saw the beginning of the Spanish Civil War, the hunger marches and the founding of the Left Book Club. There was a general feeling that the old order was disintegrating, combined

[1] *With an Eye to the Future.*

with desperate attempts to find something to cling to. For some it was Communism, for some Fascism, for others Roman Catholicism. Osbert remained detached from the great political upheavals of the day. If he heard the siren voices he did not listen to them. He was not seduced by Rome, as were Evelyn Waugh and Graham Greene, or by the Kremlin as were Anthony Blunt, Guy Burgess and Kim Philby, or by the far Right as were such as Harold Nicolson, Sacheverell and Osbert Sitwell, Cecil Beaton and John Strachey, who all joined, however briefly, Oswald Mosley's New Party, the precursor of the British Union of Fascists.

There were others who were seduced in the more usual sense of the word and joined the boys. Looking back on the twenties and thirties one cannot help being struck by the extraordinarily high incidence of homosexuality in the arts – Auden and Benjamin Britten are but two of the distinguished names that leap to mind. And not only in the arts but also in politics (Tom Driberg, Guy Burgess) or (in the case of Anthony Blunt) art and politics. In their various ways all these groups, or gangs – Roman Catholics, Communists, Fascists, homosexuals – were rejecting the values of their parents' generation. Osbert was unusual in steadfastly and resolutely remaining where he always was, a Church of England conservative heterosexual. He remained the small boy on the rugger field politely inquiring of the burly forward thundering down on him, 'Do you wish to pass me on the left or the right?'

He took the same attitude to architecture. Thus in *Homes Sweet Homes* he satirized both Nazi and Stalinist architecture by showing two virtually identical, brutal public buildings; the only differences are that the 'Third Empire' building is topped by an eagle and a swastika and the statues are giving Heil Hitler salutes, whereas 'Marxist non-Aryan' has a star and hammer-and-sickle, and the statues are giving clenched-fist salutes; another difference, Osbert comments, is that the Soviet architect has eschewed the use of capitals on the columns on ideological grounds.

Osbert never lost his head, never fell for the latest creed currently being hawked about, but remained his own detached, quizzical self, 'a little quietly facetious upon every thing' (in Byron's phrase about *Don Juan*).

The editorial team of the *Architectural Review* would seem to have been something of a house divided against itself. On the one side were the Modernists such as P. Morton Shand, J. M. Richards and

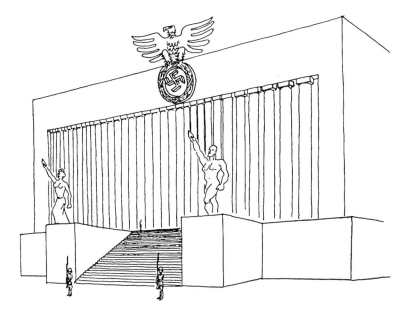

Nikolaus Pevsner, on the other conservatives and what we would now call conservationists such as Osbert and (fundamentally) Betjeman. The central figure, somehow holding the whole thing together, was the proprietor and editor Hubert de Cronin Hastings. His achievement was all the more remarkable since he would absent himself for long periods without anyone having the slightest idea where he was or who had been delegated to do what. Hubert de Cronin Hastings was a deeply eccentric man, who struck wonder into his staff with the information that certain members of his family had webbed feet. It was never clear whether this was a matter of concern or pride to him, or whether or not his own toes were joined together. If they were, it would have been far from the oddest thing about him. In general he refused to appear in public if at all possible, and made every effort to avoid meeting people. In the 1950s he was prevailed upon to read a paper to a meeting of architects. He did so, but insisted on sitting with his back to the audience. Betjeman called him 'Obscurity Hastings'.

Osbert liked Jim Richards, and was likewise impressed by the scholarship of Nikolaus Pevsner. He was not impressed, however, by Pevsner's Teutonic humourlessness and 'total lack of imagin-

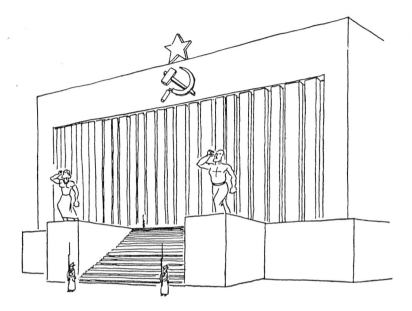

ation'. Indeed the two of them were so utterly different in manner and outlook that in a way they complemented one another: this is why Osbert's *Here, of All Places* and Pevsner's *Outline of European Architecture* together provide such a sound and balanced introduction to the subject.

Another influential member of the *Architectural Review* team was P. Morton Shand, a product of Eton and King's, a writer on wine and food as well as architecture (and, incidentally, father-in-law of both the architect James Sterling and Sir Geoffrey Howe). Having extolled everything Swedish in the twenties, in the thirties he proselytized for Dutch, Swiss and German architecture, and above all the Bauhaus. Later, as will be seen shortly, Morton Shand recanted.

Osbert lived to see his views on architecture and town planning vindicated. The tower blocks with flat roofs and glass walls proved uniquely impractical and especially unsuitable for the English climate and way of life. Far from being, in Le Corbusier's phrase, *machines à habiter* they have been rejected by those awkward creatures who, architects decided, ought to like living in them, and in some cases have proved so far from habitable that they have had to be demolished with dynamite. (Walter Goetz remembers accompanying Osbert to the house of Wells Coates, a founder member of the MARS group who had a certain reputation for his fondness for the opposite sex. As was the fashion of the day, the rooms had few chairs, but plenty of cushions for tumbling on. 'Ah,' said Osbert as he took in the scene, 'a *machine à co-habiter*.')

Defenders of Modernism argue that what was wrong was not the original ideas but the mis-application of them by insensitive or wicked people after the war. Even so, an authoritarian streak is detectable from the beginning in the teachings and preachings of Le Corbusier and the Bauhaus. Modernist architects knew that it would be better for the inhabitants if the street were turned on end and they were made to live in soaring vertical rectangles instead of little houses with sloping roofs and small gardens. To think otherwise was, according to Pevsner, blasphemy.

Morton Shand, shortly before his death in 1960, wrote in a letter to Betjeman that he was 'haunted by a growing sense of guilt in having, in however a minor and obscure degree, helped to bring about, anyhow encouraged and praised, the embryo searchings that have now materialized into a monster neither of us could have foreseen'. Well, they could have foreseen it, because Osbert evidently did.

These disputes lay some years ahead, and it would be wrong to suggest that the *Architectural Review* in the 1930s suffered from a split personality. In fact the disparate crew co-operated and collaborated. Surprisingly it was Frederick Etchells who translated Le Corbusier's *Vers une architecture* (as early as 1927). J. M. Richards worked with Betjeman on the *Shell Guides*, and Betjeman's *Ghastly Good Taste* shows that his own tastes extended from Voysey to Modernism, while Pevsner's *Pioneers of Modern Architecture* likewise goes from William Morris to Gropius.

Whatever their view on the architecture of the future, the Modernists do seem to have been insouciant about the destruction of that of the past that was already taking place on a widespread scale in the thirties. Osbert chronicled this in *Progress at Pelvis Bay* (1936) as did Robert Byron in his short but blistering polemic, *How We Celebrate the Coronation: A Word to London's Visitors*. The way we celebrate the Coronation, Byron said, is by pulling down our most beautiful buildings. He gave details of the damage (Chesterfield House, Pembroke House, Whitehall, Waterloo Bridge, Wren's All

Hallows Church, Lombard Street), listed the individuals and institutions responsible (including the Archbishop of Canterbury) and even gave their telephone numbers, while urging visitors to London to 'deluge your contempt upon the only nation in Europe that destroys its birthright for the sake of a dividend'.

Osbert never knew Byron so well as he did Bowra or Betjeman, but Byron's influence was at least as important. Robert Byron (1905–41) was of the undergraduate generation previous to Osbert's, but returned to Oxford fairly frequently after going down. He was certainly eccentric, perhaps a little mad. Not the least of his achievements was winning the Rosebery history prize at Eton with an essay which contained only one full stop.

In photographs he looks a bit like the young Evelyn Waugh – a comparison both would have hated since they quarrelled bitterly. This was partly for the simple reason that they were both so quarrelsome, partly because of Byron's strong dislike of Roman Catholicism. He himself thought he resembled Queen Victoria, and often went to parties dressed up as her. When he filled in his passport application form he wrote in the space asking about 'any special peculiarities' the words 'Of melancholy appearance'. In the square left for a photograph of the bearer's wife he drew a cartoon, resulting (according to Anthony Powell) in the document's being withdrawn.

Some considered that he was asexual, others that he was actively homosexual. What all who knew him were agreed on was that he was extremely funny. When in 1965 Nancy Mitford was remembering her friends who had died she noted that 'except relations I miss Robert the most . . . It's the jokes.'

Byron was a vigorous defender and champion of English architecture, not only the grand buildings whose vandalizing he castigated in *How We Celebrate the Coronation* but also the vernacular architecture which few at that time thought worth their notice. Paddington, he said, was the symbol of all that Bloomsbury was not (he meant that part of London, not the Bloomsbury Group). In place of Bloomsbury's 'refined peace' there were public houses, fun-fairs, buses, tubes, and vulgar posters, also 'small brick houses, Gothic mews, and great tapering tenements in which to live'.

Byron travelled widely abroad in search of architecture, and not to the MARS group's Germany, Sweden and Holland but to Greece, Persia, Afghanistan and India. His discovery of architectural

87

masterpieces was discovery both in aesthetic terms and also quite literally: many of the great buildings he found and wrote about had never previously been photographed.

His best-known book nowadays is *The Road to Oxiana: An Inquiry into the Origins of Islamic Art*. This, published in 1937, was the last of his nine books. He had impressed his Oxford friends long before, having published *Europe in the Looking Glass* in 1926, when he was only twenty-one, an account of a journey through Germany, Italy and Greece. Thereafter he produced a book almost every year, notably *The Byzantine Achievement*, *The Birth of Western Painting*, *An Essay on India*, *The Appreciation of Architecture*, *First Russia then Tibet* and the *Shell Guide to Wiltshire*. The titles alone show how different were his interests from those of the MARS group, as do the illustrations of buildings discussed in *The Appreciation of Architecture* (a book of which he was quite wrongly ashamed) – the Villa Rotonda at Vicenza, the Black Pagoda at Kanarak, Shad Sindah at Samarkand, Beauvais cathedral, Gunbed-i-Qabus tower in northern Persia, Angkor Vat, Hardwicke Hall and so on: not one building from Sweden, Switzerland, Holland or Germany. (When Byron did write about German architecture it was not always with great respect: at Nuremberg, for example, 'The buildings convey the same impression of affectation as the baronial rafters of the Queen's Hotel, Margate'.)

Byron not only opened up vistas in many directions other than the Bauhaus. His prose style was also an influence on Osbert. The crack about Nuremberg could easily have come from *Pillar to Post*, but it is not only in the more jokey remarks that the resemblance can be seen. Here is Byron on the Tower of Qabus:

> A tapering cylinder of café-au-lait brick springs from a round plinth to a pointed grey-green roof, which swallows it up like a candle-extinguisher ... Up the cylinder, between plinth and roof, rush ten triangular buttresses, which cut across two narrow garters of Kufic text, one at the top underneath the cornice, one at the bottom over the slender black entrance.

Byron and Osbert shared an enthusiasm for colour in architecture. They had the same sharpness of eye and ability to translate what they saw into words, judiciously mixing technical terms like 'plinth' and 'cornice' with vivid images like the café-au-lait, the garters and the candle extinguisher.

*   *   *

The proprietors of Eno's Fruit Salts celebrated the Silver Jubilee of George V by producing a Monarchy Chart which consisted of colour reproductions of portraits of Kings of England from Alfred onwards. John Murray acquired the plates of these portraits and had the idea of making them into a book to come out in time for the coronation of Edward VIII. The text was originally to have been written by Philip Guedalla, but he backed out at a late stage and John Murray asked Osbert to take it on. Osbert said he wasn't sure how well a Fourth in English qualified him, but he gamely buckled to and made a very good job of it. *Our Sovereigns* was duly published in November 1936 and sold quite well. On 10 December the king abdicated, so a new edition was required with necessary revisions concerning Edward VIII, and a new section on his successor George VI.

The contemporary portraits of the fifty-four English sovereigns from Alfred to George VI start with coins depicting the pre-Conquest Alfreds, Edwards, Edmunds, Edgars, Ethelreds, Edwyns, Canutes, Hardicanutes and Harolds, then go on to the Bayeux Tapestry for Harold II and William I, and thence through such celebrated portraits as Holbein's Henry VIII, Van Dyck's Charles I, and Kneller's James II to a *Times* photograph of Edward VIII and a studio photograph of a tremendously bemedalled George VI by Speaight Ltd of London. In view of Osbert's later books one regrets that he did not illustrate *Our Sovereigns* himself, but this would hardly have been possible since the whole idea of the project was to use the plates of the Eno's Fruit Salts collection. Nor should the value of these plates be underestimated. By the standards of the time the quality of the colour reproductions was high. Furthermore one must remember that colour reproductions were far less common at that time than today, as a result of which many people had only the haziest notion of what our kings and queens actually looked like, based usually on stage and screen interpretations (as Osbert pointed out in his introduction). Consequently, he said, Henry VIII, for example, had developed a family likeness to Rembrandt and Captain Bligh in the public imagination, since Charles Laughton had so impressively played these three parts. Not only did these portraits of English monarchs from 871 to 1937 show what they looked like, but the collection also constituted an instructive and entertaining little history of portrait-painting and fashion over more than a thousand years. The plates were accompanied by Osbert's word-portraits, which themselves made up an entertaining potted history of England. *Our Sovereigns* contained the germ of the idea that came to such splendid fruition nearly forty years later in *The Littlehampton Bequest*.

Osbert's witty and concise text is still to be recommended to anyone wanting a painless refresher course on English history as seen through the lives of our kings and queens. The failings of individual sovereigns are gleefully pointed out but the general drift is one of staunch admiration for the institution of monarchy as opposed to republican or dictatorial alternatives. Quite rightly Osbert likes some kings better than others, though quite wrongly he (like Shakespeare) libels the excellent Richard III. As might be expected he favours the more dandyish kings. Richard II was 'unfortunate, intelligent and artistic . . . a strangely sympathetic and individual figure'. Charles II was 'a notable wit' and 'one of the cleverest of our kings'. George IV is praised for his interest in architecture, his encouragement of Nash and his discovery of Brighton. 'In addition, he possessed all the social graces and was universally admitted to be a charming companion; his conversation was witty and entertaining and his imitations justly renowned.' This praise is immediately qualified by the magisterial statement that 'In his personal relationships he exhibited a truly royal inconstancy, and though affable and full of charm his insincerity was never called in question.'

Edward VII is praised, like the equally amorous Charles II, for his love of peace, and the sensitive subject of Edward VIII is dealt with tactfully but frankly (mentioning, for example, the fact that Mrs Simpson had divorced not one but two husbands). Edward was a Prince

> in whom the charm and affability of the Hanoverians were rather more conspicuous than the judgment and discretion of the Coburgs. No one questioned the fact that the private life of the sovereign was his own affair provided that it remained private . . . owing either to a mistaken estimate of the popular feeling or to a highly creditable but unfortunate longing for the pleasures of domesticity [he] was induced to place his personal problem on a plane where it automatically became of national importance.

The word-portraits are never more than two or three pages long. Such brief accounts of what are often complex and bizarre goings-on invite a *1066 and All That* approach. Admirable though that work undoubtedly is, it was not the kind of book Osbert had been asked to produce and he wisely resisted the temptation. Given the nature of Osbert's talents it is not surprising (or indeed to be regretted) that it contains a strong comic element, but the general tone is one of levity rather than facetiousness. The prose has an eighteenth-century balance, and the wit is very much that of Gibbon's footnotes. Thus the account of the 'unfortunate accident' which concluded the reign of William Rufus ends: 'Whether some peasant had taken revenge for the enclosure of his lands, or some friend turned traitor or whether Henry's well-known patience had at length been exhausted will never be known. The lack of curiosity which his contemporaries displayed on the death of the Red King was only equalled by the restraint with which they mourned him.'

King John receives equally scathing treatment: 'Of all our kings John has probably the least to recommend him. As cruel as Richard III, as lecherous as Henry VIII, as untrustworthy as Charles I, and as ineffectual as Stephen, his sole redeeming feature seems to have been that, like so many criminals, he was invariably kind to his mother.'

As for Edward II, 'to presume, as some have done, that his moral code was high, on the evidence of his reported remark that after seeing his wife he found himself unable to like another woman, is to overlook a certain ambiguity inherent in that rather improbable utterance'.

Our Sovereigns was bound in primrose yellow, as almost all the hardback editions of Osbert's subsequent books were to be. I had always assumed that this was a deliberate act of homage to the dandy-aesthete *Yellow Book* of Beerbohm and Beardsley fame, but Osbert denied this, saying that he simply liked the colour.

In a book review of James Thurber's *Fables for Our Time* (*Spectator*, 31 January 1941) Osbert wrote:

> From time to time there appears upon the literary scene that rare figure, the writer who is also an artist. Frequently one of his two talents is out of all proportion to the other; even more frequently he is a bad writer and a worse draughtsman. But on the very rare occasions when he is a man whose gifts are equally well developed and complementary, what an extraordinary effect he is able to produce.

Osbert was himself such a man. Whereas in *Our Sovereigns* he wrote about other people's pictures, in all his subsequent books he

91

1790

produced both the text and the illustrations (except *The Pleasure Garden* on which he collaborated with Anne Scott-James). *Progress at Pelvis Bay*, which appeared the same year as *Our Sovereigns*, is a

1890

1840

tongue-in-cheek account of the 'splendid metamorphosis' from 'poverty-stricken fishing village to the present-day magnificent marine metropolis covering many acres of what had hitherto been

1930

virgin downland'. The attack on the horrors being perpetrated on England's towns and countryside (or in this case, seaside) takes the form of a deadpan defence, outright praise indeed – for among other things *Progress at Pelvis Bay* is a parody of the kind of municipal guide that can be found on the railway-station bookstall of any sizeable town or city. The characteristic of these publications which Osbert pounces on is that while every prospect pleases, nothing at all that the visitor's attention is directed to, however vile, is subject to even the slightest of criticism. All is for the best in the best of all possible towns. Thus the Panglossian authorities of Pelvis Bay 'have never had any sympathy with town-planning or any such Socialist nonsense, preferring rather to leave things to the natural good taste of the individual. Their policy, it will, I fancy, be conceded by all unbiased observers, has been abundantly justified. In the following illustrations the uniformly high standard of building, some particularly in the modern examples, is very noticeable.' The Regency terraces, built in 'a uniformly monotonous style' have 'happily' been pulled down in recent years and replaced by fake Tudor shops. 'In these circumstances, to regret the passing of the dingy old row of houses, is to lay oneself open to the charge of odious sentimentality.' The recent domestic buildings are modern labour-saving villas which are charming, quaint and cosy. Their chaotic variety of style is defended as an avoidance of monotony. Praise is also given to the cinema, the railway station, the Cottage Hospital, the Country Club (the work of the distinguished Continental architect, Hans Krautenbaum 'whom the political events in his own country had forced to eat the bread of exile in a foreign land'), the Lead Gnomes Ltd factory, the Municipal Waterworks and Ye Olde Toffee Shoppe. The account of the progress in building, amenities and transport concludes with a rhetorical flourish that anticipates by many years the late Peter Sellers's travelogue paean to 'Bal-ham, gateway to the South':

> Here then we take leave of our reader, after first leading him up to the top of the massive tower overlooking the swimming pool, whence we can see far away in the distance the glittering sea, and take a farewell glimpse of lovely Pelvis Bay, the Queen of Watering Places.

Progress at Pelvis Bay was not the first polemic of its kind. As early as 1928 Clough Williams-Ellis's *England and the Octopus* had denounced the ribbon development, bungaloid growth, petrol-stations and advertisement hoardings which were increasingly disfiguring the landscape. Osbert's original contributions were his wit and satire, and the precision with which he pinned down the beast, identified its nature and detailed its various manifestations.

Progress at Pelvis Bay was enthusiastically received on publication, though there was one review which deserves to rank with the (probably apocryphal) one of *Lady Chatterley's Lover* in a field sports magazine which complained that the novel was not an accurate account of modern game-keeping practice. The *Town Planning Review* wrote of *Pelvis Bay* that 'If there is one criticism to be made against the book it is that lay readers may find it very difficult to differentiate between serious comment and sarcasm or humour.'

The illustrations are deadly accurate satires of contemporary styles, but by the standards of his later books the drawing in *Pelvis Bay* is a little hesitant, and the irony repetitive; we are told too often, for example, that Regency architecture is monotonous. Nor is the ironical device consistent. For the most part the book adopts the Swiftian method whereby the reader, unless impenetrably dense, can assume that what is praised is bad and what is blamed is good. But when town planners and 'such Socialist nonsense' are attacked, is the author defending them, or is he having it both ways?

If to a reader half a century later the satire of *Pelvis Bay* looks too easy, too much like scoring a bull's eye on a target at point-blank range, then the fact that we now see it as an easy target is in large part thanks to this book. Certainly at the time its wit and irreverence were greeted with delight, and doubtless it would be rated more highly now had it not been overshadowed by his later and better books in a similar vein.

These followed very soon: *Pillar to Post* in 1938 and *Homes Sweet Homes* in 1939.[1] Like all his other books they were published by John Murray, to whom Osbert was introduced by Betjeman with the suggestion that a book might be made out of the *Architectural Review* articles about Pelvis Bay.

[1] In 1959 these were published together, with the addition of some entries on the buildings of the United States, under the title *Here, of All Places: The Pocket Lamp of Architecture*. The 1976 edition, now titled *A Cartoon History of Architecture*, brought the story up to date with entries on Pop Nouveau and finally High Rise, in which a tower block is depicted at the very moment that a balcony is falling off, casting its contents of mother and pram to the concrete far below. The concluding words of the book comment on High Rise: 'Nor was the prevalence of vertigo-induced angst among the older generation in any way lessened by occasional mishaps due to an imperfect understanding, on the part of the builders, of the exciting new structural methods and materials made available by modern technology.'

Jock Murray says that Osbert was the most stimulating author any publisher could have: 'He added to the excitement of life.' He was a frequent visitor to Murray's offices in Albemarle Street, the same address as that of the first John Murray who was the publisher of Lord Byron. His arrival always caused a buzz of excitement in the office, and he cheered up everyone with his jokes and apparently unlimited supply of gossip. He was always very willing to do a drawing at the shortest notice for any occasion such as a staff dinner or an anniversary.

Jock Murray noted in Osbert both a streak of laziness and a capacity to work extremely hard and with incredible swiftness. When he was working on *Pillar to Post* and *Homes Sweet Homes* he would, Murray recollects, come in with two more spreads almost every day. 'If he agreed to do a book it would come at a rate of knots. If he lost impetus, wild horses, money, entreaties, nothing would get it out of him.'

A disclaimer at the beginning of *Here, of All Places* states that 'All the architecture in this book is completely imaginary, and no reference is intended to any actual building living or dead.' It consists simply of Osbert's drawings of imaginary exteriors and interiors each faced by a page of witty and observant information and comment, not of particular buildings but invented exemplars of styles and periods. In his introduction to the 1959 edition Osbert says that he had a twofold object:

> First, to do for buildings what so many popular writers have done for birds, to render them a source of informed interest and lively excitement for the passer-by so that his quiet satisfaction at having identified a nice bit of Bankers' Georgian might equal that of the keen bird-watcher on having spotted a red-breasted fly-catcher; second, and with no very sanguine hopes of achievement, that such an interest, once stimulated, might become so widespread as to cause inconvenience to speculative builders, borough surveyors, government departments and other notorious predators.

He was supremely successful both in his educational objective and in his polemical one. If anything he was too modest in his educational claim. The mere process of identification, which bird-watchers call 'twitching', is even more rewarding if it leads to the more complex business of making observations about the behaviour of individual examples of a species. In the same way, Osbert provides the architecture-spotter with a solid foundation on which

Wimbledon Transitional

to base aesthetic judgements of particular buildings.

Osbert was the first to identify and name some of these species: Pont Street Dutch, for example, and Wimbledon Transitional, Aldwych Farcical, Stockbroker's Tudor, By-Pass Variegated, Le Style Rothschild, Greenery Yallery, and so on. He modestly insisted that some of these terms were already in circulation, but Pseudish and Stockbroker's Tudor were certainly coined by him, and Pont Street Dutch probably was. Even if he did not himself invent all of the terms, he was the first to give them general currency.

The drawings in *Here, of All Places*, far more confident than those in *Pelvis Bay*, are notable not only for the accuracy with which the architecture of a style or period is presented but also for the comic details of the daily life around it – the dog cocking its leg in the Gothic hall, for example, or the bald, bespectacled, bearded Fabian hiking in knickerbockers past the whimsy Art Nouveau cottage.

Very Early English is represented by a Stonehenge-type structure in front of which are tourists taking snaps, and a wooden hut for the sale of teas and ices. The prehistoric megaliths show that 'even then British architects were actuated by a profound faith, which has never subsequently wavered, in the doctrine that the best architecture is that which involves most trouble'. This point is confirmed a few pages later by Norman, which shows at a glance 'that its construction has cost a great many people a great deal of hard work'. Norman also has the advantage for the amateur of being very easy to recognize on account of its round arches, otherwise only to be found in railway tunnels. Perpendicular fan-vaulting 'arouses enormous enthusiasm on account of the difficulties it has all too obviously involved'. In Queen Elizabeth's time the well-dressed man wore padded breeches: when these went out of fashion in the Jacobean period 'he was in a position to appreciate the painful disadvantages of the plain wooden chair he sat on, and upholstered furniture was introduced for the first time to a grateful public'.

In spite of its Olympian prose, *Here, of All Places* does not avoid controversy. Dissent from Modernism recurs especially frequently. The very first page, 'Earliest, Earlier, Early', calmly but effectively confronts the functionalist doctrines of Modernism. Osbert traces the development in Greece from the crude hole in the ground with low stone walls and tent-like roof of branches, to the flat lintel and thatched roof supported by wooden pillars, a form that was later translated into brick and stone in the form familiar to us as the classic Greek temple. The sting in the tail comes where it is noted that in the change of material from wood to stone

> various traces of the technique involved in wooden construction, such as the projecting beam-ends with their securing-pegs, were retained as decorative adjuncts carried out in stone for as long as the Doric style continued to flourish. Thus early, heedless of what Messrs. Corbusier and Gropius were going to say, did the first, though perhaps not the least accomplished, of European architects light-heartedly compromise with the strict principles of structural truth.

As one would expect, Greek is preferred to Roman. Victorian is mocked, though quite gently, while such enthusiasm as there is for the Arts and Crafts movement is reserved for William Morris's wallpapers. Osbert praises the vernacular of Public House Classic, and lambasts the Olde Worlde half-timbered pubs of By-Pass Elizabethan and Brewers' Georgian. He reveals his strong dislike for

99

terracotta, and Art Nouveau is suggested as a rich field for the researches of Herr Freud. He denounces the destruction of Edwardian Baroque plaster-work at Harrods to make way for some tasteful modernistic improvements. Twentieth-century Functional is seen as inappropriate to the English climate and as evidence of barrenness of spirit.

Unlike most architectural illustrations, Osbert's always have people in them. After all, buildings do have people living in them, and their behaviour, their clothes, dogs, ornaments and plants are every bit as much part of the place as are the furniture, wallpaper, pictures on the wall and carpets. For example, the interior of Scottish Baronial, with its huge fireplace flanked by a suit of armour on one side and a stuffed bear on the other, with family portraits and stuffed heads of horned animals on the walls, and fish, birds and other taxidermist's items in glass cases, also contains a monocled and kilted laird with a shooting-stick in conversation with a gentleman in a deer-stalker and thick tweed, with a shot-gun in one hand and a glass of what can only be whisky-and-soda in the other. This is not simply a cartoonist's comic detail: it shows that this is an indoors for people who live outdoors; for people, indeed, who make indoors as like outdoors as possible, who wear thick clothing even while downing their drinks, and who are standing in front of the crackling but thermally negligible fire not just for effect but because it is the only place in the house that is above freezing-point.

The text on the facing page describes Scottish Baronial as 'vast, castellated barracks faithfully mimicking all the least attractive features of the English home at the most uncomfortable period of its development'.

One of the many extraordinary things about the proponents of the Modern style was the gulf between what they preached and what they practised. They declared that houses should be machines to live in but not a single one of the illustrations in Pevsner's *Introduction to European Architecture* contains a human being. The Modernists were considered to be on the Left, Osbert on the Right. Yet it was the Modernists who were the élitists, seeking fastidiously to confine architecture to grand buildings; people like Osbert took a far more democratic view which embraced the vernacular, the domestic and the humble. The first words of Pevsner's book are: 'A bicycle shed is a building; Lincoln Cathedral is a piece of architecture.' By contrast Osbert's introduction to *Here, of All Places* declares that:

> Architecture, it cannot be said too often, is not confined to temples, palaces, state capitols, churches and public libraries; the term extends, and with equal force [he is writing here to an American audience] to drugstores, tram-depots, comfort stations and saloons.

Osbert's ties with the *Architectural Review* began to loosen not so much because of disagreements about policy as of the steady increase in his other work. He published four books in the four years 1936 to 1939 as well as numerous drawings and a variety of journalism, especially as art critic of *Night and Day*. The idea for this brilliant but short-lived magazine was that of Ian Parsons, a director of Chatto & Windus. The company started with a capital of £20,000, and the chairman was Victor Cazalet (the Tory MP who was killed in a plane crash in the war). The first issue, costing sixpence, appeared with a cover by Feliks Topolski in July 1937. It openly set out to emulate the *New Yorker*. The contributors made up a galaxy of talent: theatre critic, Elizabeth Bowen; chief book reviewer, Evelyn Waugh (who in the first issue lauded David Jones's *In Parenthesis*); art critic, Osbert Lancaster; architecture, John Summerson and Hugh Casson; films, Graham Greene; broadcasting, John Hayward; music, Constant Lambert; restaurants, A. J. A. Symons; football, Walter Allen. Occasional contributors included Anthony Powell, Herbert Read, Malcolm Muggeridge, Louis MacNeice (on the Dog Show), Peter Fleming, Antonia White, Rose Macaulay, Christopher Isherwood, Pamela Hansford Johnson, T. F. Powys, V. S. Pritchett, Nigel Balchin and James Thurber. There were poems by, among others, Walter de la Mare, Stevie Smith, William Plomer, Herbert Read and William Empson.

The first issue sold 40,000 copies, and then settled down to a circulation of about 20,000 which was almost the break-even point. However, like most brilliant magazines, *Night and Day* did not flourish financially. What finally did for it was a review by Graham Greene of John Ford's film *Wee Willie Winkie*. Greene's suggestion that the then pre-pubescent Shirley Temple had 'a certain adroit coquetry which appealed to middle-aged men', prompted Twentieth-Century Fox to claim that Greene had accused them of procuring Miss Temple for immoral purposes. The court awarded Miss Temple £2,000 and the film company £1,500, and with costs that was the end of *Night and Day*.

Osbert did one joyful full-colour cover for *Night and Day*, showing two exuberant kilted figures leaping in the air in a wild Highland fling. Most of his contributions, though, were as art critic and, as Christopher Hawtree says in his book on the magazine, 'There has surely never been more enjoyable art criticism than the pieces contributed by Osbert Lancaster.'

He visited the Paris Exhibition in 1937 and was scathing about the pavilions both of the Nazi Germans and of Soviet Russia. He gave rather low marks to Picasso's *Guernica* which (at least in that setting)

he saw as a propaganda poster. He says that while an artist may comment (as Daumier and Lautrec did) he must never preach (which Courbet and David are reprimanded for having done). Poussin, on the other hand, scored well, as did (less predictably) Hubert Robert. Géricault he found 'enigmatic and slightly sinister'. He was enthusiastic about Sisley (whom he preferred to Monet), Corot and Degas, luke-warm about Matisse, Manet, David and Courbet, and didn't like Diego Rivera or Gauguin. He wrote of the 'towering genius of Degas', but described Manet as 'an artist who somewhere, somehow, missed the bus'. Without at all detracting from Degas's genius, more people now than fifty years ago would probably agree with Degas's words on Manet's death: 'He was greater than we thought.' When I reminded Osbert of this piece, he stuck by his opinion of *Guernica* but said his comments on Manet were presumptuous.

Osbert's best *Night and Day* contributions as art critic were when he operated as a cartoonist in words. Thus, on the recently unveiled statue of the First World War military donkey Earl Haig:

> From the aesthetic standpoint the statue is completely negligible; and not even the persuasive tones of Sir Herbert Baker (speaking in the kindly, indulgent accents of Mr. Herbert Read explaining the beauty of one of Miss Hepworth's obscurer achievements), who tells us that the statue must not, of course, be regarded as a piece of representational art but rather a three-dimensional embodiment of the sculptor's conception of military triumph, can persuade us to the contrary. From the purely equine point of view the statue is equally unsatisfactory. Is this curious charger of doubtful breeding, walking forward, standing still or preparing to indulge in a capriole or one of the other decorative feats which have earned the Lipizaner horses in Vienna such deserved commendation? Is the fact that its hind quarters appear to be stationary while its forelegs advance a subtle indication of the dual nature of the late Field-Marshal's command, or an unkind sculptural suggestion that his strategy suffered from divided counsels? These are questions which each man must decide for himself, but personally we can never feel that an equestrian statue is really equestrian if the steed is not rearing up in a dramatic manner with its stomach supported by a small iron rod and its rider's hand waving a baton.

In July 1937 he wrote about the Tate's Duveen sculpture gallery, which was designed by Russell Pope, whose previous major work had been a railway station in New York. Osbert did not fail to spot the similarities.

> ... In this instance it must be admitted that the ample scale so suitable in backgrounds for locomotives is perhaps a trifle overwhelming; few pieces of sculpture are calculated to appear to the best advantage in the surroundings of the Pennsylvania Railroad Station.[1]

This is merely the prelude to a deadly demolition job. In spite of subsequent changes to the Duveen gallery, visitors to the Tate can still easily see the truth of Osbert's comments. Not for the first or last time, what he objects to is the arrogance of architects and patrons who think they are more important than the work they do. He points out that in order not to ruin the architectural vista ('which would, of course, be an unthinkable outrage') the sculpture has to

[1] One wonders what Osbert would have thought of the Musée d'Orsay in Paris.

be arranged in rows against the walls, which is far from being the ideal way of displaying three-dimensional objects. Nor is that all. The colour of the stone is such that any material other than bronze merges gracefully into the background. Posterity when confronted with this gallery, 'which has an almost terrifying air of permanence', may doubt whether the generation that produced it possessed any real understanding or appreciation of sculpture. 'What they will be forced to realize, however, is how splendid and opulent a man was Lord Duveen.'

Penelope Betjeman said that both Karen and she were less sociable than their husbands. Both by temperament and because of her poor health, Karen was never a great one for going out. Osbert, by contrast, was compulsively sociable. His friends were always astonished at his appetite for any kind of gathering. He would faithfully turn up at the very dullest of engagements, and by doing so disperse much of the dullness. It seems as though there was hardly a party, a first night, a private view throughout the thirties – and beyond – that he failed to attend. Then there were his clubs: Brooks's, Pratt's, the Beefsteak and the Garrick.

There were also visits to the Betjemans at Garrard's Farm, Uffington, where fellow-guests included at various times Maurice Bowra, Evelyn Waugh, Cyril Connolly and Peter Quennell. Betjeman was by now married to the redoubtable Penelope Chetwode, daughter of Field-Marshal Lord Chetwode, the Commander-in-Chief of India. Betjeman had been working at the *Architectural Review* when they met, and his courtship of Penelope was conducted in an unusually public manner which consisted of his shouting from the window of his office at the top of the building down to her as she stood in the street below. The Chetwodes evidently felt their daughter was marrying below herself. Lord Chetwode couldn't even get the hang of Betjeman's foreign-sounding name and used to call him Mr Bargeman. Betjeman was not daunted. Osbert recalled how, when John and Penelope were engaged, the Chetwodes gave a white-tie dinner at the Savoy to mark the event. 'John went to amazing pains to get a made-up tie sewn on elastic. Throughout the dinner, he plucked the bow forward six or seven inches and let it snap back – purely to annoy his future mother-in-law.'

Uffington is a delightful village in the Vale of the White Horse,

105

Berkshire. The Betjemans' house was a stone-walled cottage with William Morris wallpapers. Penelope, every bit as forceful and eccentric as her husband, threw her considerable energies into the Uffington Women's Institute, lecturing its members on Indian religions and Nepalese architecture, urging them to keep goats and instructing them in the mysteries of cooking. On one occasion, when demonstrating how to make mayonnaise, she suddenly and vehemently exclaimed, 'Oh f—, it's curdled.' Unable to suppress their giggles, Betjeman and Osbert had to run out of the hall.

There were musical evenings too. One that the Lancasters attended coincided with a prize-giving for the best home-made wine. They all joined in a performance of 'Summer is icumen in'. This was sung by Adrian Bishop, Maurice Bowra, Karen Lancaster and John Betjeman, accompanied by Lord Berners on the piano, Penelope Betjeman on a zither-like instrument, and Osbert on the flute. The cacophony was punctuated from time to time by exploding bottles of home-made wine which showered those who were unfortunate enough to have seats nearby with broken glass and elderberry juice.

Whatever the audience got out of the evening, the performers had a thoroughly enjoyable time. Osbert said that he never spent an evening of such continuous and unalloyed pleasure.

The Lancasters and Betjemans often visited William Morris's house at Kelmscott when May Morris still lived there. Outside there is an earth closet with three seats in a row. This prompted Osbert's drawing *After Breakfast at Kelmscott*, showing William Morris, Mrs Morris and Rossetti seated side by side at stool.

And there were house-parties and fancy-dress parties. A large and notable one was held at Whistler's house in Cheyne Row. Guests chose, or were allotted, roles. Arthur Barbosa was King; Nicolas Bentley was Prime Minister; Rex Harrison, Head of Household Cavalry; Frederick Ashton, Grand Duchess Maria Petrushka. Prinz Franz Wilhelm, in splendid uhlan uniform, was Osbert. Photographs of them all are to be found in Cecil Beaton's imaginary memoirs of a Balkan Princess which had their origins in these parties. Published by Batsford in 1939, it was called *My Royal Past* by Baroness von Bülop née Princess Theodora Louise Alexina Ludmilla Sophie von Eckermann-Waldstein, as told to Cecil Beaton. The erratum slip contains the memorable 'For "Mademoiselle" read "Meddlesome".'

106

V

BUSINESS AS USUAL

S HORTLY AFTER the demise of *Night and Day* Osbert found alternative employment at the *Daily Express*. 'Like so many other developments in my life,' Osbert wrote, 'my appearance in Fleet Street was in the first instance due to John Betjeman.' Betjeman had undertaken a series of articles on the theme of 'Man into Superman', tracing the rise of civilization. Having got stuck on the early period, and knowing of Osbert's interest in archaeology, he roped in his friend to help out. This led to Osbert's meeting the features editor, John Rayner, a book-lover and typographer who had recently re-designed the *Express* in a way which was soon to be copied by rival dailies. After dinner one evening Osbert commented to Rayner ('a great and good man') how much he admired the little column-width cartoons which featured in French newspapers, and wondered why the English press didn't do the same. 'Go ahead,' Rayner said. 'Give us some.' He did.

The pocket cartoon that appeared on 1 January 1939 was the first of roughly 10,000 that Osbert was to produce with only brief interruptions over the next forty years or so. It was called the pocket cartoon on the analogy of the pocket battleship which was much in the news at that time, being a small warship built to conform with treaty limitations on tonnage and armament. The pocket cartoon rapidly showed that it too combined a small size with considerable hitting power. Nowadays pocket cartoons are common enough. Trog, Michael Heath, Mel Calman, Bryan McAllister and others maintain a high standard of pithy comments on the events of the day in this form, but Osbert can be said (at least as far as this country is concerned) to be its inventor. No one has surpassed him, though Marc (the late Mark Boxer) was a worthy successor.

The pocket cartoons originally appeared in Tom Driberg's widely read William Hickey gossip column. Later they were transferred to the still more prominent front-page position. An additional benefit came with wartime paper rationing. While all the other cartoonists had their space cut down, Osbert's alone was not diminished.

Osbert was not the only cartoonist of the time who was making witty social comments. Indeed, apart from the actual line of the drawing, his cartoons had much in common with those of *Punch*'s Pont (Graham Laidler), the *Night and Day* cartoonist Paul Crum (Roger Pettiward) and Senep in France. (Sadly both Pont and Paul Crum died at an early age – Pont of polio at the age of thirty-two, Paul Crum killed leading a commando troop at Dieppe in 1942.) What was innovative about Osbert's pocket cartoons was not only their small size, but also the fact that instead of appearing in a weekly such as *Punch* they reached the mass audience of a national newspaper. Daily appearances meant that they could be up-to-the-minute with the news. It also meant that it was possible to develop a cast of characters who appeared regularly and were soon readily identifiable. Maudie Littlehampton and the rest of the pocket cartoon gallery of characters – such as Canon Fontwater, Mrs Rajagojollibarmi and Father O'Bubblegum – could otherwise never have come into existence. No subsequent pocket cartoonist has built up so rich a cast. Indeed, for a rival, one has to look to his fellow

'We do want to fight
But by Jingo if we don't!'
(11.6.40)

'Sometimes, Ulrich, I get so depressed that even thinking about the next war doesn't cheer me up.' (20.3.41)

Express contributor, the equally inventive and indefatigable Beach-comber (J. B. Morton).

The success of the *Express* cartoons was immediate and enormous. They suddenly gave Osbert the kind of national fame that today only television can bestow. They were the subject of conversations beginning 'Did you see . . .?' that you overhear on trains and buses, in pubs and offices.

Many of today's pocket cartoonists can make you chuckle in the morning with a comment on a news item that you have forgotten in the evening. Look at them a year later, even a month later, and they are often incomprehensible since you have forgotten what they were alluding to. Inevitably this has been the fate of some of Osbert's, but a remarkably high proportion have proved less ephemeral, less fugitive. In some ways they actually improve with time, for the collected volumes that have appeared over the years, or the compendium *The Life and Times of Maudie Littlehampton*, constitute a vivid and hilarious social history and running political commentary on the history of Britain from 1939 to the beginning of the eighties. If you want to know what was the issue of the day – any

(5.11.46)

'My subject this afternoon is "Some recent developments in high-tension molecular fission and their application to modern industry".' (8.2.47)

109

day – during that period, Osbert's pocket cartoon would be a good place to start your researches.

Osbert's characters developed over the years. Of Maudie, he said (in a radio interview with George Melly on the twenty-fifth anniversary of the pocket cartoons), 'Like most of us she has grown up. Having started as a slightly dotty class symbol she's been increasingly useful as a voice of straightforward comment which might be my own. I have a sort of feeling she's matured.'

In the same interview Melly suggested that Osbert's approach to foreigners 'verges on the sour, particularly towards the Germans'. Osbert replied: 'You must realize that most of them date from the early forties when it was not all that easy to set prejudice wholly aside with regard to either Germans, Italians or French. I don't think the attitude has really persisted except perhaps in the case of the Germans – whom I know well, and many of whom I like. I know the country – but I feel there are certain aspects of the German character which remain constant and it would be foolish to overlook.'

Some of George Melly's comments evidently needled Osbert, for he returned to them in his interview with Michael Bateman a couple

'I've just made the intewesting discovewy that Mr Bevan's national teeth aren't weally up to coping with Mr Stwachey's national beef.' (6.7.48)

'I suppose you're having to send all the No. 11's round by the Cape!' (29.11.56)

of years later: 'George Melly accused me of doing unworthy, upper-class characters instead of mods and spades. Well, I did the Notting Hill race riots. It's silly to say, as he did, that I don't understand foreigners. I was the first to realize the change in the US image. And duel-scars on Germans?' – a gruff cough – 'Yes, well, the Germans still are fundamentally duelling-scar people.'

The background of the pocket cartoons is unashamedly that of London, and especially the world of politics, publishing, the arts, the church, clubs and other institutions of the establishment. It is the world to which Osbert belonged and it would be fatuous to criticize him for not firing off his cartoons from some other vantage point. Indeed, consistent targets of his were those who cut their cloth to suit the fashion, both metaphorically (in their attitudes) and literally (in their attire). In yet another radio interview (*Quick on the Draw*, Derek Cooper, 24 March 1974) he said, 'What I really dislike, and try to attack – I'm not an attacking sort of person – is this tendency today, particularly among politicians, civil servants and even leader-writers, not only to write in clichés but to think in clichés.' He called this a very disturbing aspect of modern life,

'Is that the one we swopped for Burgess?' (19.3.63)

'Sure, Father, an' I thought it was just an aspirin.' (8.5.64)

instancing the then current phrase 'a meaningful dialogue' when 'worthwhile conversation' is just as good a description. This kind of pretentiousness and sloppy thinking was, he said, the kind of thing he disliked and hoped to laugh out of court.

'Never speak ill of a brother brush' was the formula which Osbert habitually used when people sought his opinion of a fellow cartoonist. Derek Cooper did, however, succeed in extracting from him some comments on two of his notable contemporaries. Osbert had said that his aim was not to preach or put over a particular political point of view. He saw this as a problem for the overtly political cartoonist, and it applied to both Low and Vicky.

> It's OK when you're in opposition. When you have to be *for* something then they all fall flat on their faces. Even Low – those splendid attacks on Hitler, Mussolini and Tories – then he occasionally had to do an idealistic picture of happy young workers marching into the dawn – like a soap ad. Same with Vicky. When Vicky turned on the sob stuff it became rather embarrassing. When he was attacking something he was absolutely first-rate. . . . If one looks through old copies of *Punch* the ones one gets the most pleasure from are the ones

'I bet whoever gets *your* liver won't wake up bright and smiling!' (7.5.68)

'Well, all we need now's some sackcloth!' (18.2.71)

with the most social document, what people were saying, what people were wearing, how people were behaving at that time. Whereas exactly what Lord Aberdeen said about Mr Gladstone – however brilliant the cartoonist's comment may have been at the time, it doesn't really evoke any very lively response fifty years later.

Given that the cartoons are quite openly directed from an elevated position, they are mostly even-handed in their attacks on both the high and mighty and the humble and meek. No one seems to object to his jokes about civil servants or bishops, but they do get very sensitive about coloured people or trade unionists. George Melly thought Osbert was cruel to Germans; Derek Cooper thought he was cruel to protesting students who were always presented as unwashed and with unkempt hair. Osbert's response to this latter criticism was: 'It's become a slight convention of course. They certainly look that way, the ones who are actually out demonstrating. It's not quite as simple as that . . . there are certain things one likes drawing. It's much more fun drawing hippies than civil servants.'

In fact the pocket cartoons most often poke fun at those in

'Dear Mrs Rajagojollibarmi, if it weren't for the Race Relations Board I'd say you've revoked!' (10.1.78)

'How do babies come? Quite honestly, darling, granny's no longer one hundred per cent certain.' (20.7.78)

positions of authority and privilege. One of the most celebrated was when the Duke of Edinburgh made his 'Pull your fingers out' speech about British industry: Maudie's elderly relative asks, 'Maud, my dear, pray explain what it is out of which dear Prince Philip is so eager that we should all take our fingers.'

Characteristically one of the very first pocket cartoons was aimed at town planners. Two of them are studying a map, and the caption reads, 'There's only one solution: we must by-pass the by-pass.' Thereafter for forty-odd years the social, cultural and political history of Britain and the world were to be sharply observed and pithily recorded day by day. In August 1939 we see Hitler and Stalin shaking hands under each other's flags: Hitler has Stalin's big curling moustache, Stalin has Hitler's absurdly small one (this is a rare example of one of Osbert's cartoons having no caption). During the war there are jokes about the Home Guard, ARPs, V1s (doodlebugs) and the blackout, evacuees, rationing, travel restrictions. In the post-war period we find spivs, nationalization, the New Look, the Cold War, King Farouk and power cuts. The fifties bring the Festival of Britain, the Coronation, commercial television, U and non-U, Suez, the anti-uglies, the Wolfenden Report, 3D horror films, the sack. Then the swinging sixties, with the space race, Cuba, spy scandals, the Profumo affair, colour supplements, pot, the pill, flower power, student power, the mini-skirt, the maxi-skirt, the topless look, and the Ronan Point tower block crashing down. Thence to the seventies and Mrs Mary Whitehouse, Watergate, decimal coinage, Mrs Thatcher, the N-bomb ('Just what we don't want – what we need is a bomb that wrecks the architecture and spares the inhabitants').

When Osbert joined the *Express* it was in its heyday. The editor, Arthur Christiansen, was enormously admired by all who worked for him. Osbert wrote that for more than twenty years he received from Christiansen 'nothing but kindness, encouragement and salutary criticism'. On the rare occasions when the editor rejected a drawing Osbert usually thought afterwards that he had been right.

> In appearance he was comfortable-looking, almost chubby, with an encouraging smile of which the sincerity was in no way qualified by the gleaming falsity of the teeth it revealed. Usually soberly dressed, he developed later in life a regrettable weakness for those hand-painted American ties so popular in the Truman era.[1]

[1] *With an Eye to the Future.*

Express colleagues included old acquaintances such as Sefton Delmer, and many new ones who became friends for life, such as Alan Moorehead, the women's editor Lucy Milner, the cartoonist (and later art dealer) Walter Goetz, and the chief leader-writer George Malcolm Thomson. The booming voice of J. B. Morton (Beachcomber) would resonate through the building – indeed from one end of Fleet Street to the other – and on Wednesdays the theatre critic James Agate would deliver his copy, 'looking, in his flat-brimmed bowler and horsey overcoat, more than ever like an absconding bookie with intellectual pretensions'. The *Express* at the time was the front-runner in popular journalism and must have provided a stimulating environment in which to work: other colleagues included such as Hannen Swaffer, Hugh Cudlipp, James Cameron, Michael Foot and Nathaniel Gubbins, as well as the cartoonists David Low, Strube, Cummings and Giles. Giles in particular became a close friend; Osbert both loved him and admired him hugely as an artist.

Osbert's closest colleague when he first worked on the paper was Tom Driberg, who was not much liked at the *Express*. The cry of 'Driberg, check your facts!' was constantly ringing in the corridors, but Driberg commanded professional respect as the creator of the leading gossip column in Fleet Street.

Osbert found his appearance 'subtly changed from the dadaist days of Oxford'. He had put on weight and his hair had receded, 'leaving a couple of curls stranded on his forehead like a misplaced moustache'. Committed Marxist and devout Anglo-Catholic, Beaverbrook columnist and Labour MP, compulsively and promiscuously homosexual, equally at ease in high life and low, a champion of the proletariat with the manners of a patrician, Driberg was a mass of contradictions. The word louche could have been invented for him. There were many who disliked him, but Osbert was not one of them. He respected Driberg's literary judgement (as did Betjeman, whose later poems were almost invariably vetted by Driberg before publication). Osbert thought Driberg was a kind man, and extremely good company.

The *Express*'s proprietor, Lord Beaverbrook, was a very different proposition. Though somewhat similar in size and shape to Osbert, the two of them were as unlike as could be in every other way. As far as Beaverbrook was concerned, Osbert was a complete enigma, and solving it was not easy for someone without a sense of humour.

From time to time the Beaver would go over the pages of his various newspapers, examining every item in detail. In due course he would come to the pocket cartoon. 'What', he would ask, 'is the point of Osbert Lancaster?' George Malcolm Thomson, Beaverbrook's mouthpiece at the *Express*, was also a great friend and admirer of Osbert's. He would reply to the proprietor's query that Osbert Lancaster appealed to perhaps a few hundred thousand readers, while to the rest he was completely meaningless. On the other hand Osbert Lancaster (like Beachcomber) was one of the things that made the *Express* distinctively different from its rival the *Daily Mail*.

Beaverbrook's other personal assistant was David Farrar, who put the matter slightly differently; he said that Beaverbrook saw the pocket cartoon as a sop to the intelligentsia. But whatever Beaverbrook's initial reservations, he evidently came round to Osbert, as is apparent from the congratulatory message he sent him (27 July 1948) on a particular cartoon: 'It was as brilliant a piece of work as anything I have seen in the *Daily Express*, and I have seen much that is good in that paper.'

For his part Osbert studiously avoided being sucked into Beaverbrook's inner circle of intimates and cronies. He had the rare distinction of being able never to accept a Beaverbrook invitation, and a Beaverbrook invitation was virtually a command. Whenever one was issued to Osbert, it turned out that unfortunately he had a prior engagement he couldn't get out of. George Malcolm Thomson says that no one but Osbert could have got away with this, and also regrets that Osbert never did attend a Beaverbrook gathering since he could have been so very funny about them. Probably, though, Osbert was shrewd in keeping himself at arm's length. Few who swam in the Beaver's brook emerged intact, and Osbert was always anxious that the proprietor should not, as he put it, 'interfere'. The extent to which he was successful may be gathered from the foreword to the pocket cartoon collection *Signs of the Times* (1961) acknowledging 'Lord Beaverbrook, who never in twenty years made any attempt by limit or pressure to curb the free expression of his cartoonist's opinions, no matter how manifestly they failed to coincide with his own'.

Osbert would habitually refer to Beaverbrook as 'the old brute', but at the same time he had a great respect for his abilities. 'He was a bastard,' Osbert would say, 'but by God he knew his journalism.'

When the time came for Beaverbrook's portrait to be painted it was Osbert who suggested that it should be by Graham Sutherland. He said that besides Sutherland being the best artist available he considered that it would be 'an interesting confrontation – an enthusiastic Roman Catholic convert and a lapsed Calvinist with a keen interest in theology'.

So far Osbert's social and professional life had remained fairly detached from the political ferment of the years between the wars. It would, of course, have required someone far less observant to fail to notice the huge demonstrations at Hyde Park Corner and Trafalgar Square with their banners reading 'Abolish the Means Test' or 'Antifascists Unite' or 'Hands Off Abyssinia'. In regard to the Spanish Civil War he registered its emotional impact on others – friendships and love affairs breaking up over it, people resigning from their clubs – but he personally remained uninvolved. He took the view that what was going on in Spain was part of a recurrent phenomenon in Spanish history rather than an isolated incident.

In the case of Germany, however, he could achieve no such 'lofty, pragmatic detachment'. He had been in Germany when Hitler became Chancellor. At night he had seen the torch-processions, heard the shouts of 'Sieg Heil' and the 'Heil Hitlers' of the 'beefy young thugs of the Hitlerjugend rattling collecting-boxes'. In a beer-garden in Hanover he had been revolted by the sight of a Sturm-bannführer, a plump, middle-aged homosexual in a tight brown uniform, with face powder and wet lips. Unusually but understand-ably Osbert wrote of this creature with less than his accustomed urbanity:

> The combination of homosexuality and arbitrary power has for me always been productive of an irrational disquiet – Tiberius, James I, Frederick the Great are none of them figures with whom I would greatly care to have been closely associated – and the spectacle of this arrogant queer, disdainfully acknowledging the sycophantic greet-ings of the other customers while playfully flicking the ears of the better-looking of his attendant storm-troopers with his shiny leather gloves, seemed quite suddenly indescribably sinister.[1]

His own experiences were reinforced by the testimony of friends.

[1] *With an Eye to the Future.*

Christopher Hobhouse, who had joined Oswald Mosley's New Party, had his views of the Nazis abruptly changed by a visit to Munich with Mosley and Robert Boothby. They had met Hitler, whom Hobhouse found to be a very second-rate little man. Hobhouse was indignant that Hitler had had the effrontery to lecture him about Cromwell, of whom he clearly knew nothing, and to be quite put out when Hobhouse pointed out one or two of his more glaring errors. Hobhouse was reading for the Bar and had installed himself with Harold Nicolson in his King's Bench Walk Chambers. If Hobhouse had any remaining illusions about Hitler he was soon disabused of them by Nicolson who, to his enduring credit, was the only member of the House of Commons to remain seated when Chamberlain returned from Munich announcing peace with honour.

Osbert came across Robert Byron one evening in the Crush Bar at Covent Garden. A tankard of champagne in hand, Byron was giving his views on Hitler, the Third Reich and Sir Horace Wilson to everyone in earshot with a 'venomous and uninhibited directness' which Osbert said he had never heard equalled. At the time of Munich, Byron caused a scene at the Beefsteak by publicly asking an appeasing ex-Ambassador supporter of Chamberlain whether or not he was in German pay. A ferocious opponent of the Nazi regime, he announced his intention to alter the passport description of his occupation to 'war-monger'.

At around the same time Osbert bumped into Ronald Cartland in St James's Park. He had scarcely met him after leaving Charterhouse. Since then Cartland had embarked on what all predicted would be a brilliant political career, having entered the House of Commons in 1935 at the age of twenty-seven. He had just made a speech in Parliament in which he not only attacked his party's policy of appeasement but also foretold the coming war, the possibility of his own death in it and the certainty that countless like him would be killed. Harold Nicolson said it was the most moving speech he had ever heard in the House of Commons.[1]

---

[1] Cartland's prophecies were of Cassandra-like accuracy. All three of Osbert's friends who made such an impression on him in that pre-war period were killed in the war. Christopher Hobhouse was killed by a bomb in Portsmouth. Byron was lost at sea in 1941 at the age of thirty-six when the destroyer in which he was travelling to Egypt (purportedly to take up a job for the BBC) went down with all hands. Ronald Cartland himself was killed fighting with the rearguard of the British Expeditionary Force during its retreat to Dunkirk. His brother was killed the same day.

In addition to the evidence of his own eyes and ears in Germany, and the witness of his friends, Osbert's new job as pocket cartoonist required him to follow national and international politics day by day much more closely than he had done previously. To him, and to almost everyone else except the Chamberlain Government and Fleet Street leader-writers, it was apparent that the outbreak of war was imminent. In anticipation of this dreaded event Osbert enrolled with the Officers Emergency Reserve. He subsequently never heard a word from them, probably because of his medical history. More concrete results came from his signing on with the ARP (Air-Raid Precautions), where his first job was fitting gas-masks (to, among others, the bald head of the actor Robertson Hare). The Air-Raid Warden's Post to which he was sent was, incongruously, Leighton House, a building 'conceived in a period of unbroken tranquillity and totally lacking any hint of prophetic menace'. Osbert was on his way to report for duty at Leighton House when, having a moment to spare, he dropped into the Holland Arms, where he learnt from the one o'clock news on the wireless that Germany had invaded Poland.

With the outbreak of war Osbert joined the section of the Ministry of Information that dealt with promoting British propaganda abroad. It was located in London University's Senate House in Malet Street and was headed by Duff Cooper's Parliamentary Secretary Harold Nicolson; the Deputy Director-General was Walter Monckton. Other colleagues included Charles Peake, Kenneth Clark and Guy Burgess. Osbert described Burgess as 'Disastrous, unadulterated hell. A fabulous drunk. Very intelligent until six in the evening. He had charm and had been very good-looking, but the booze had done its work. When he was in his cups he made no bones about working for the Russians.'

Betjeman also worked at the Ministry of Information for a while, as did an assistant canteen manageress called Joan Hunter Dunn. Struck by her name and robustly healthy outdoor looks, Betjeman told Osbert that she must surely be a doctor's daughter and live near Aldershot. This surmise turned out to be completely accurate, and Betjeman immortalized Joan Hunter Dunn in one of his best-known poems, 'A Subaltern's Love-song', which was first published in Cyril Connolly's magazine *Horizon* in February 1941.[1]

[1] The index of Bevis Hillier's *Young Betjeman* lists 'Dunn, Joan Hunter (imaginary figure)'. This is

The new Ministry of Information was from the start an unhappy place, riddled with intrigue. Its low level of morale reflected that of the country as a whole at this stage of the war. James Lees-Milne comments in his biography of Harold Nicolson that 'seldom have so many literary intellectuals been assembled under one roof. For them to pull in harness at such a time was a lot to expect. And they did not pull in harness.'

In July 1941 the Ministry of Information was reorganized. Duff Cooper was replaced by Brendan Bracken, and Harold Nicolson was sacked (Osbert gave a leaving lunch for Nicolson, who was greatly touched by the gesture). Osbert himself was doubtless relieved to be moved from this antagonistic atmosphere to the Foreign Office News Department, which had the job of providing the press with information on foreign affairs. He was well qualified for such a job. He knew France and Germany well and spoke their languages. He also knew Fleet Street. Furthermore he soon gave evidence of perhaps previously unexpected diplomatic skills. He had excellent relations with 'that great and good man' Charles Peake, Head of the Foreign Office News Department. This was just as well given Osbert's cordial dislike of the Foreign Secretary, Anthony Eden. 'I privately thought he was a shit.[1] If *ever* the word *wet* was deserved . . .' One night in five Osbert would be on night duty alone. Occasionally there would come a call from the Secretary of State, delivering his thoughts of the day. Sometimes Eden would be dictatorial. Other times he would speak in a 'soothing, awful, slimy voice: "Oh, Osbert, I made rather an interesting speech at Leamington Spa today. I wonder if you would bring it to the attention of the Diplomatic Correspondents."' Osbert's reluctance to do any such thing was firmly backed by Charles Peake. 'This is a public department,' he said, 'and it is no part of your duty to promote the personal esteem of the present Foreign Secretary.' Osbert con-

---

at odds with the text, which quotes Lady Mary Dunn as saying, 'I was rather cross when I found out that there was a real Miss Hunter Dunn, because I thought John's poem was based on me.' Not only was there a real Joan Hunter Dunn, but she is alive and well (now living in retirement under her married name) and was the subject of a short newspaper interview not so long ago.

[1] Osbert was fastidious in his use of language and anything but foul-mouthed. He chose his words carefully, and it always came as a slight shock when he chose this one. Evidently for him the word carried no more force than the expletive *merde* does for the French. Not that Osbert used 'shit' as an expletive. Rather, it was part of his typological vocabulary in which, fortunately, the 'shits' were outnumbered by the 'great and the good' and the 'saints'.

sidered Eden to be 'one of the nastiest, certainly the most unreliable', public figures he came across.

Nor, while recognizing the need for someone like Churchill as a wartime leader, did he warm to that 'old brute'. 'Winston was a shit out of hell. All Churchills are shits since Marlborough, including Marlborough. I was a minority of one who liked Randolph. He had an engaging personality, which I thought Winston never had. Winston was a bully to end bullies, an egocentric of *such* dimensions . . .'

On one occasion Osbert was summoned to meet Churchill and found him seated in a room where an assortment of admirals, generals and air marshals (some of fairly advanced years) were being kept standing. 'Sit down,' Churchill instructed him. Osbert demurred slightly in view of the fact that the elderly top brass were evidently not included in the invitation. '*Sit down*,' Churchill repeated. He sat down.

He contrasted this with the conduct of de Gaulle (whom Osbert greatly admired). He found the General punctiliously polite, always standing until his visitor was seated. On one occasion Eden sent Osbert along to a press conference to make sure that de Gaulle didn't go too far. 'What could I have done? In fact de Gaulle was as nice as could be.' However, de Gaulle did kick up a fuss over the pocket cartoons, some of which had slightly made fun of the over-free Free French Forces. One of them shows a French *poilu* in a beret and an officer with a *képi* shouting together: '*Vive le Général Giraud! Vive l'Amiral Darlan! Vive le Maréchal Petain! Vive le Général de Gaulle! Vive le Uncle Tom Cobbleigh!*' Another points out the brevity of de Gaulle's accords with other French top brass: the pocket cartoon shows de Gaulle and another moustached French general embracing, while the studio photographer recording this historic moment says, 'This time, *mes généraux*, could you please hold it just a moment longer?'

De Gaulle may not have had much of a sense of humour (he once said that Stalin was the funniest man he had ever met), but what he did have was an opinion of himself which was of vertiginous height. Britain and France were supposed to be allies, and (as far as he was concerned) he was France. Jokes about him were jokes about *la patrie* and jokes about *la patrie* were jokes about him. He was furious. The pocket cartoons were unsigned during the war, and he was even more incandescent when he caught whiff of a rumour that they were actually the work of someone in the Foreign Office, which doubly compounded the outrageous and scandalous affront to the General and to *la patrie*. The Foreign Office replied that it was very unlikely that a man at the Foreign Office would do such a thing; its spokesman was evidently being what Sir Robert Armstrong has taught us to call 'economical with the truth'. It was true that the pocket cartoons were not done by someone at the Foreign Office. They were done by someone at the *Express*. Same person, different buildings.

De Gaulle simmered down. There were things even more important than his *amour propre* to be dealing with.

Nearly half a century later it is all too easy to fail to understand just how real was the threat of a German invasion, an eventuality for which we were unprepared. While the invasion remained a threat, the nightly bombardment of the Blitz was a reality which caused a nightly destruction of cities and a substantial loss of life.

A job in a London that was bombarded nightly was far from being a wartime soft option. The chances of being blown up were greater than those of many who saw active service in uniform in faraway places. Yet Osbert was undoubtedly fortunate in finding a job that suited his un-military talents and at the same time enabled him largely to continue his peacetime way of life – going to his clubs, taking part in radio discussions, drawing cartoons, book jackets and illustrations, writing book reviews for the *Spectator* and art criticism for the *Observer*, dining with chums from the Foreign Office, Oxford or Fleet Street.

For Karen, and for Osbert when his work did not require him to be in London, escape from the bombs was for a time at Rose Cottage, Aldworth, Berkshire, which they rented along with fellow *Express* cartoonist Walter Goetz and his wife Toni.[1] The cottage belonged (and belongs) to Anne Scott-James.

Aldworth is a tiny village of thatched cottages on the Berkshire Downs, at the beginning of the Ridgeway, a few miles up from the Goring gap. For Walter and Toni Goetz it was ideally situated. She was working at an aircraft factory in Reading in one direction, while he was working (in the other direction) at Woburn Abbey in the

---

[1] Cara and William Lancaster had been evacuated to Washington.

Political Warfare Executive, with colleagues such as Sefton Delmer and R. H. S. Crossman. Goetz had been an *Express* cartoonist since 1934, producing a strip called 'Colonel Up and Mister Down'. His gift for languages and experience as a cartoonist combined to produce propaganda to be dropped from the air on Germany and occupied countries. *Luftpost* was a boldly designed leaflet which showed photographs of a ranting Hitler making some preposterous claim juxtaposed with photographs of the actuality. There were drawings by Goetz himself, and, among others, David Low and Osbert. Osbert also drew a number of anti-Nazi cartoons which were made up into two little booklets (the covers in primrose yellow), each consisting of thirty-two pages about the size of a playing-card. The captions were bilingual, in French and Dutch. These are two of Osbert's rarest publications (copies are kept by Lincoln College, Oxford).

Two houses away from Rose Cottage in Aldworth lived the novelist Rosamond Lehmann, who used to be visited there by her lover Cecil Day-Lewis, but there seems to have been little contact between these two, the Lancasters and the Goetzes. Also nearby lived a retired major who was in charge of the Home Guard. He was convinced that when the invasion came Hitler personally would land half a mile away at Pibworth (the family home of Tennyson's parents-in-law) and march down Chandler's Path to Parsonage Green. The Goetzes' bedroom in Rose Cottage overlooked this spot and, the mad major declared, 'commanded the crossroads'. He decided that this room should be made into a machine-gun nest. Fortunately this hare-brained scheme collapsed under the weight of its own absurdity.

Since Osbert and the Goetzes were all working, the job of running the household fell on Karen. She did the cooking and, Walter Goetz remembers, did so very well – though Osbert would rather ungratefully comment that her idea of French cooking consisted of pouring a whole bottle of Beaujolais in the sauce. She smoked ceaselessly and was immensely lethargic. Food used to be ordered in Pangbourne and put on the bus to be collected at Aldworth. On one occasion Karen failed to meet the bus and all the food went back to Reading. There was nothing to eat that weekend. 'We were very fond of Karen,' Goetz says, 'though she did drive one round the bend.'

In contrast to Karen's lethargy was Osbert's constant sprightliness and marvellous conversation, which did something to make up for his untidiness and aversion to domestic chores. It can't have been easy for the non-smoking Goetzes, who did all the housework, to share a small cottage with two heavy smokers who did none. The survival of the friendship is a tribute to its strength. Whether it would have survived if the arrangement had continued for more than a few months, however, is another question.

Aldworth is the other side of the Thames from Fawley Bottom, near Henley, the home of Myfanwy and John Piper. Betjeman and Piper had come to know one another well through working together on the *Shell Guides,* but Osbert and the Pipers had not met. Osbert decided to put this right, and some time early in the war he cycled over from Aldworth. He arrived totally unannounced, but Piper (who was playing table-tennis at the time) recognized him immediately.

They took to one another, and the Pipers and the Lancasters were soon firm friends. The Lancasters were regular weekend visitors and then, when the Blitz was at its very worst, they actually moved in for a while. Osbert used to draw his pocket cartoons on the kitchen table before setting off for Henley station, the Foreign Office and the *Express.*

In due course the Lancasters bought a place of their own in Henley. Leicester House was a mid-nineteenth-century stucco building with a fine garden and a conservatory. Many years later the garden was discussed by Osbert and Betjeman in a radio conversation which included the following exchange:

> BETJEMAN: Mr Piper said it was like a London park. You'd never know you were in the country.
> LANCASTER: That un*call*ed-for remark was in *fact* made *not* by Mr Piper but by *your wife.*
> BETJEMAN: Oh dear.

Osbert's multifarious activities did not impede his London social life in the war years. His name is always cropping up in the memoirs, letters and diaries of such figures as Harold Nicolson, Isaiah Berlin, Maurice Bowra, James Agate, Evelyn Waugh and James Lees-Milne. Since Osbert's autobiography goes only up to the beginning of the war it is on these that we must largely rely for glimpses of Osbert and Karen, and their way of life, at this time.

In March 1943 we find James Lees-Milne going on foot and by bus for miles in the blackout to the Lancasters' flat. He was the only guest for a dinner of chicken and rum jelly, 'deliciously cooked by Karen': 'Karen very affectionate and sweet. I admire her total indifference to the world's opinion. Whereas Osbert is incorrigibly social, she is a natural recluse.'

During the following month he dined again with the Lancasters twice. Karen's mother, Lady Harris, was there on the second occasion:

> ... very amusing, and very deaf. She speaks in a honeyed voice, slowly and distinctly, with raised eyebrows, and makes outrageous remarks with no emphasis. Osbert was bright gold like a guinea with jaundice, but feeling well, which annoyed Eddy (Sackville-West) who was present and bright green, and feeling ill as usual. Osbert turned to his mother-in-law and shouted in her ear, 'My pee was paler this morning.'

A description of Osbert at this time is provided by Sir Hugh Casson. They first met in a restaurant near the Ministry of Information. Osbert commanded, says Sir Hugh,

> not only the table at which he sat, but the whole room. The sonorous voice, the elaborate phraseology, the bristling moustache and staring eyes, the physical presentation – half Balkan bandit, half retired Brigadier – was at first terrifying and then almost immediately endearing. Osbert, it quickly became clear, was a performance, meticulously practised and hilariously inflated and at times disturbing.

What, he wondered, was behind this 'elaborately woven yashmak of subsidiary clauses, this defensive portcullis of anecdotes cranked into place at one's approach? Where was the real Osbert?' He thought it lay in Osbert's 'tough professionalism', as a cartoonist, as a theatre designer (they were later sometimes to meet backstage at Glyndebourne), and 'as a lover of architecture passionately defending in particular those buildings of unorthodox character which he foresaw would soon be under threat'. When after the war they were both on the GLC Historic Buildings Committee, he found Osbert's demeanour 'always sober and correct, and when called upon for his opinion it was given seriously in those episcopal tones that always invited stunned respect and was always concluded with a witty late-cut. To win, he knew, you had first to disarm.'

*   *   *

125

Osbert's untiring social life had to be fitted in with a mass of other activities. As well as working at the Foreign Office, he was art critic for the *Observer* from 1942 to 1944, wrote book reviews for the *Spectator*, an introduction to a book on *Tiepolo* (1943), was a panel member on radio discussion programmes, and gave talks and lectures. And day in, day out, the cartoons poured forth, for the *Daily Express* during the week and (under the name of Bunbury) for the *Sunday Express* on the day of rest.

His introduction to the 1940 collection *Pocket Cartoons* describes the small volume as 'a record of what struck me as funny or worthy of ridicule during the period between the occupation of Prague and the beginning of those nocturnal activities which we are still so much enjoying'. These nocturnal activities involved heavy loss of life as well as the destruction of many of the streets and houses that Osbert loved so much, and were not generally considered either enjoyable or funny. But the defiant message of the bombarded cities of Britain was the one that was displayed outside many a half-demolished little street-corner tradesman's shop: 'Business as Usual'. It was Osbert's business as a cartoonist to make jokes, and he made them.

One cartoon shows an old chap sipping his port while in the outer darkness all hell is breaking loose with bombs, ack-ack, tracer and searchlights. His comment is, 'Judging by the illuminations I fancy Mafeking must be relieved at last.'

Another cartoon shows firemen handing to a lady in a dressing-gown a small dog rescued from the smouldering remains of what used to be a house. She says, 'Thank you so much. And now would you please look for my husband.'

In another, a Messerschmidt, flying low over the English countryside with guns blazing, shoots a fox, thereby enraging an English huntsman who expostulates, 'You impossible cad, sir!'

The second collection, *New Pocket Cartoons* (1941) (dedicated to John Rayner), takes its epigraph from the Goncourt journals: '*Dans les grands dangers la bêtise augmente d'une manière formidable.*' In his foreword Osbert finds himself a bit stuck for people to acknowledge apart from the editor of the *Daily Express*, 'by whose kind permission . . . etc', but has to say that otherwise it is all his own work. 'Alone, in fact, I did it.' But then, reflecting on all that *bêtise* produced by the war, he thinks of the help given by those who provided him with daily comic material:

Too numerous to list in full, I can but acknowledge my indebtedness to a small selection. To Marshal Goering, whose never receding girth and sartorial enthusiasm have kept a hundred cartoonists from the workhouse; to the B.B.C., and in particular Mr Alvar Liddell, whose wide culture and high idealism have inspired so much of the best contemporary humour; to the War Office who have so readily placed so many models at my disposal; and above all to the Italians, without whose unflinching resolution and imaginative communiqués the war would be so much duller . . .

The pocket-cartoon Italians are stereotyped as unshaven cowards whose proper role in life is selling ice-cream. They are also lazy: a John Bullish farmer berates a recumbent Italian prisoner of war thus: 'I dessay it's different in the Isle of Capri, but in Shepton Mallet we don't 'ave no siesta hour.'

The other Axis nations, the Japanese and the Germans, are also stereotyped in a way which would now be considered xenophobic, but these people were, after all, the enemy against whom we were fighting for our lives.

On the domestic front there was rationing of food and clothes and practically everything else, while anything normally imported in peacetime was unavailable altogether. One cartoon shows two people at an exhibition looking at a still life of a bottle of wine, a fish and some lemons. One of the spectators says to the other, 'Extraordinary the way these painter fellows seem to be able to work entirely from memory.'

The pocket cartoons made Osbert a national figure. They caught the mood of the nation, defiantly facing adversity with good humour. In a time of peril they gave people something to laugh about. Though they were small in size, their contribution to national morale was enormous.

The war was approaching its end when Osbert was abruptly called upon to serve his country in a totally different and unexpected manner.

VI

ATTIC ATTITUDES

So revolutions broke out in city after city, and in places where the revolutions occurred late the knowledge of what had happened previously in other places caused still new extravagances of revolutionary zeal, expressed by an elaboration in the methods of seizing power and by unheard-of atrocities in revenge. To fit in with the change of events, words, too, had to change their usual meanings. What used to be described as a thoughtless act of aggression was now regarded as the courage one would expect in a party member; to think of the future and wait was merely another way of saying one was a coward; any idea of moderation was just an attempt to disguise one's unmanly character; ability to understand a question from all sides meant that one was totally unfitted for action. Fanatical enthusiasm was the mark of a real man, and to plot against an enemy behind his back was perfectly legitimate self-defence. Anyone who held violent opinions could always be trusted, and anyone who objected to them became a suspect . . .

Revenge was more important than self-preservation. And if pacts of mutual security were made, they were entered into only in order to meet some temporary difficulty, and remained in force only so long as there was no other weapon available.

Thucydides (c.460–395 BC) on the revolution in Corcyra
(translated by Rex Warner)

ALL THAT can be said with confidence about Greek politics is that there is nothing simple about it other than the truth of the adage about what happens when Greek meets Greek. Every self-respecting wall in Greece is a palimpsest, an alphabet soup of the acronyms and slogans of parties that go back for centuries. Perhaps that is an exaggeration, but it is only a slight one. C. M. Woodhouse's history of *modern* Greece starts in AD 324, and Thucydides's account of the politics of Greece nearly 2,500 years ago is a startlingly accurate description of the country's internecine politics and carnage in the mid-twentieth century, a subject which is

as controversial as it is complicated. A vast quantity has been written about it, and it is rare to find two authors who agree on the facts,
let alone the interpretation. However, some sort of background is
needed to explain Osbert's sudden arrival in Athens just before
Christmas in 1944. I am resigned to the fact that in what follows
experts of every persuasion will find something to quarrel with.

In most of the occupied countries the Allies supported whichever
Resistance group seemed most effective, irrespective of its political
colour. In Yugoslavia, for example, there were two guerrilla move-
ments: General Mikhailovich and the Chetniks, and the Communists under Tito. In Greece, likewise, there were Communist bands
(ELAS) and the non-Communist EDES and EKKA (Republican and
Monarchist respectively). In Yugoslavia Britain backed the Communists; in Greece we did not, either during the occupation or after the
liberation.

This policy was fiercely opposed in Britain in the House of
Commons by such eloquent and influential voices as those of
Aneurin Bevan and Emmanuel Shinwell, in the United States by the
Secretary of State Edward R. Stettinius, and by much of the press on
both sides of the Atlantic. In spite of this opposition, Churchill,
Eden, Macmillan and (crucially important) the Labour Party and
Trade Union leader Ernest Bevin remained passionately committed
to the Papandreou government.

To this day the issue is still hotly contested. One side will argue
that Britain's policy led directly to the Greek civil war and later to the
regime of the Colonels. The other side will make the counter-claim
that it saved Greece from being absorbed into the Soviet hegemony
after the war, and that without Britain's firm stand from 1944 to
1950 Greece would have shared the fate of Poland, Hungary,
Czechoslovakia and the other Soviet satellites.

During the Second World War the Greek political scene was
fragmented even by its own standards. There were collaborators,
there were Monarchists, there were Republicans, there were Communists, there were Fascists, there were priests, there was a Government in exile, and armed forces in exile, there were groups in the
mountains and groups in the cities. In short Greece was divided
every which way.

The predictable result was that resistance to the Germans was hopelessly and self-destructively split. The various factions even accused one another of collaborating with the Germans: these allegations were not always unfounded.

Greece was far from being a side-show in the Second World War, and its divided condition had international effects. It caused the first serious rift between the Allies; it jeopardized the unity of the British wartime Coalition Government; and it played a crucial role in determining the post-war relations between the West and the Soviet Union.

The death of the dictator Metaxas in January 1941 left Greece without a constitutional government. The position of George II was precarious. Like most Greek kings (including his father Constantine I), he had been deposed once already, but had been restored in 1935. Wartime emergencies freed him from the troublesome business of holding elections in order to find a successor to Metaxas. Anyway, the Republican opposition was in exile and most of the Communist leaders were behind bars. He simply appointed Alexander Koryzis as Prime Minister.

On 3 April 1941, Germany attacked Yugoslavia and Greece. Despite heroic resistance the Germans soon captured Salonika. The fall of Greece was imminent. On 18 April Koryzis killed himself. Shortly afterwards the King and his Government moved to Crete, the British Expeditionary Force left, the Germans moved in and appointed a Quisling Government. On 20 May the Germans attacked Crete, and the King and Government escaped to Cairo.

The Germans held the whole of Greece apart from the mountains, which were accessible only on foot. Like the Turks before them, the Germans reckoned that these areas were more trouble than they were worth. It was there that the Resistance groups survived, in little contact with the rest of the country, and even less with the Government-in-exile in Cairo, which consequently failed entirely to understand the strength of anti-Monarchist feeling in Greece.

Napoleon Zervas, a former Republican colonel, had come round to the view that Monarchism was a lesser evil than Communism and had founded the National Republican League (EDES). This was violently attacked by the Communist National Liberation Front (EAM) and the National Popular Liberation Front (ELAS).

In September 1942 British parachutists were dropped into Greece. Colonel C. M. (Monty) Woodhouse, head of the British Liaison Mission, had the tricky job of getting the opposing guerrilla groups to work together against the Germans rather than against one another. His success was dramatically demonstrated when the British and ELAS and EDES co-operated in the destruction of the Gorgopotamos viaduct, thereby cutting the German supply line to Athens (and thence to North Africa) and at the same time greatly raising Resistance morale. Regrettably, this incident did not make the Resistance groups less murderously inclined towards one another for long. In the struggle between ELAS and EDES atrocities were committed by both sides, as they were in the ensuing civil war. There is little point in attempting to draw up a balance sheet to decide whose behaviour was the more beastly.

Nor was British policy united. The British Military Mission on the spot reported that the Communist ELAS (like it or not) was clearly the most effective resistance, but Churchill and the Foreign Office unwaveringly supported the Greek king in Cairo. By 1942 it was clear that the outcome could only be civil war or an unopposed Communist takeover.

After a rapid turnover of Greek prime ministers-in-exile, George Papandreou emerged. He had the advantage of being supported by the British, but at the same time he was stuck with the problem that hardly anyone was prepared to serve in his government. Effectively – or rather not very effectively – he *was* the Government.

After the expulsion of the Germans, Papandreou returned to Athens. His arrival, with that of Harold Macmillan and the British Ambassador Reginald (Rex) Leeper, was planned for 17 October 1944. When Papandreou heard of this plan he insisted on a post-ponement of one day – 17 October was a Tuesday. Constantinople had fallen on a Tuesday, and it had been established ever since that nothing of importance could be initiated on that day of the week. In Greek politics 1453 is a recent date.

Accordingly, Macmillan and Leeper arrived on the Wednesday. They were welcomed by a street procession consisting mostly of Communists, whose banners bore the names of Stalin, Churchill and Roosevelt. In general they seemed to be strongly pro-Allies, and particularly pro-British.

At the time of the arrival of the Papandreou Government, Macmil-lan, Ambassador Leeper and the British forces under General Scobie, there was really nothing to stop the Communists (EAM) from simply taking over. Papandreou's pathetically weak Govern-ment controlled Athens, Patras and Salonika, but even in those parts of the country was able to do so only thanks to the British forces who maintained order and organized the landing and distribution of relief supplies. In the country as a whole the government had little power to gather taxes. Even in Athens itself there was little the Government could do. Food was in very short supply. Transport was so restricted that trade had almost come to a standstill. The Government was virtually under siege. EAM was armed. All that Papandreou had at his disposal was the city police and gendarmerie. The use of British troops had to be kept to an absolute minimum, partly because the demands of the Italian front meant that there weren't many of them, but also because any conflict between British and anti-Nazi groups would have been political catastrophe.

What stopped EAM taking over? The answer is almost certainly Joseph Stalin. In that same October of 1944 Churchill had visited Moscow and informally agreed on the distribution of the Allies' respective post-war influence in the Balkans. In Romania it would be ninety per cent Soviet Union, ten per cent the other allies; in Yugoslavia it would be fifty per cent each; in Greece it would be Soviet Union ten per cent, United Kingdom ninety per cent. Churchill jotted down the figures and Stalin ticked them.

Was it this scrap of paper that held back the Communist forces in Athens in October 1944? There seems to be no firm evidence as to whether or not direct orders were sent from Moscow to the Greek Communists, but it was certainly Churchill's view that Stalin had kept his word. He noted in his diary that during the whole six weeks of fighting in Athens not one word of reproach appeared in *Pravda* or *Izvestia*, and in conversation with Harold Nicolson (27 February 1945) he said that 'a single article in *Pravda* would have tipped the balance, but Stalin kept an obstinate silence which was of immense value to us'.

There was no such silence on the part of the English-speaking press. On 3 December there was a massive demonstration in Athens in Constitution Square. The demonstrators carried the flags of Greece, Britain, the Soviet Union and the United States. They sang Resistance songs, they chanted EAM slogans. And then something happened which caused the Greek police to open fire, killing twenty people and wounding many more.

Whether it was the police or the demonstrators who started the shooting is still disputed, but the carnage took place in full view of the correspondents of the foreign press in the Hôtel Grande Bretagne which overlooks the square. By definition this meant that they were *not* in a position to witness the events which had happened not far away some minutes earlier. The journalists may not have seen the whole story, but they reported what they had seen: the police firing into a crowd which appeared to be unarmed and which included women and children. 'They had their type-writers ready,' Ambassador Leeper wrote bitterly. 'They had seen the whole story themselves, and comments flowed quickly from their machines. In a few hours the whole world had the impression that the Fascist or neo-Fascist police of Athens had fired on an unarmed crowd. Those typewriters gave EAM a major victory that day.'

Later that same day Leeper met some of the correspondents and berated them for the way they had reported the event. He told them that he personally would have been sacked if he had reported to his government such sensational news without making sure of the facts. He told them that shortly before the police started firing on the crowd two hand-grenades had been thrown at Prime Minister Papandreou's near-by house, killing a civilian and a policeman. He added that he thought it was most unlikely that the crowd was unarmed.

There is no record of whether (and if so, how) Leeper checked his own facts before coming to this conclusion, but his opinion was taken up and repeated by such as C. M. Woodhouse and Harold Macmillan.

It was clear by now that the press both in Britain and in the United States was hostile to the British presence in Athens. It was also clear that Leeper had a tendency to antagonize the reporters on the spot. At this point the Foreign Office decided to send out a Press Attaché to Athens, and the man they chose was Osbert Lancaster.

Osbert himself was to write scathingly of the 'unarmed leftist who skilfully tossed a hand-grenade into Papandreou's flat as he marched by *en route* for the fatal demonstration', an incident which was 'tactfully overlooked by the majority of British correspondents, confidently assessing the blame for the subsequent bloodshed from the secure vantage-point of the Grande Bretagne Hotel'.

It is only fair to the journalists to point out that they were there and that Woodhouse, Leeper, Macmillan and Lancaster were not. The correspondents were no more able to see round corners than

133

anyone else. As for Osbert's gibe about the 'secure vantage-point' of the hotel, this really is unjust. Geoffrey Hoare of *The Times* risked his life carrying a wounded child from the Square to that cosy haven and secure vantage-point.

This is not to say that the press was blameless. Not all reports were factually accurate. A Chicago journalist filed a report to the effect that British tanks had joined in the shooting. In fact no British were involved until some time later, when their arrival was greeted with cheers. The next day this same journalist gave the military censor a correction, shamefacedly admitting that he had been misinformed. The censor handed back the correction with the suggestion that the paper could be put to better use in the lavatory; the correction was unnecessary since the original report had not been transmitted in the first place. The incident is revealing both about the quality of the journalistic reports coming out of Athens at the time and about the censorship to which it was subjected.

Whatever the truth about the events of 3 December, in terms of public opinion at home and abroad the day was, as Leeper observed, a victory for EAM. The reports of most of the American and British journalists on the spot presented British action in Greece in a bad light, and these reports were amplified in the comments of their newspapers' editorials.

It can be argued that the criticism in the press, in Parliament and from the State Department in the United States was justified. It can also be argued (as Harold Macmillan did) that there was a feeling that this was an opportunity to have a go at Churchill. By now it was clear that we were going to win the war. Perhaps it was also time for the alliances and coalitions to loosen up a little. Whatever the reason, the press (in particular *The Times*, the *News Chronicle* and the *Manchester Guardian*) were (in Macmillan's view) dangerous opponents throughout the Greek crisis. Their attitude reminded him of the pre-war days when it was considered bad form to criticize Herr Hitler or Signor Mussolini: 'Now it is apparently thought ill-mannered to show any lack of confidence in the Communists.' While the *News Chronicle*, the *Manchester Guardian*, *The Times* and most of the American press were behaving in this reprehensible manner, *Pravda* and *Izvestia* were conducting themselves in a fashion that was exemplary; a looking-glass world indeed.

*   *   *

When Osbert arrived in Athens on 12 December 1944 the British presence in Greece was in a very tight corner. The shootings in Constitution Square had been followed by a number of attacks on police stations in Athens, and the situation was dangerously near to becoming out of control. After the outbreak of fighting on 3 December Churchill had sent a strongly worded telegram to General Scobie in Athens, telling him to 'act as if you were in a conquered city where a local rebellion is in progress ... We have to hold and dominate Athens. It would be a great thing for you to succeed in this without bloodshed if possible, but also with bloodshed if necessary.'

This telegram, which Churchill subsequently admitted to have been 'somewhat strident in tone', was in cipher and marked 'Personal and Top Secret'. On 11 December, however, an American newspaper had published it almost word for word. A copy of Churchill's telegram had been sent to General Wilson in Italy. It seems that General Wilson showed the telegram to the American Ambassador in Rome, and the Ambassador had repeated its substance to the State Department, from which source the American journalist had somehow obtained it.

This episode did nothing to improve relations between Downing Street and the White House, between Whitehall and Washington, between the government and its opponents in the House of Commons, the trade unions and (most relevantly for Osbert) the press.

More immediately to the point the contents of the telegram were hardly likely to endear the British army and Embassy to the Greek 'rebels'. If any blood was going to be shed it looked as though it would be British.

Osbert was put up at the Embassy where he shared a bedroom with Harold (now Lord) Caccia, who was Minister at the Embassy and Macmillan's representative. His office was at General Scobie's GHQ; twice a day Osbert and Caccia made the journey there and back. On the main streets this meant going by tank or armoured car; the more usual method was to drive as fast as possible in a 'thin-skinned' car through the back streets. It must have been hair-raising.

Nor was the Embassy itself at all safe. It held some fifty people, including servants and guards. They lived there, worked there, slept there, and were not allowed out except to take exercise in a small part of the garden known as the prison yard. This was safe from the gunfire of the rebels who were only a couple of hundred yards away. The rest of the garden was covered by the snipers. To reach this safe area the procedure was to wait for a lull in the shooting and then make a dash for it. The Embassy was a particularly easy target, since on the whim of the wife of the previous Ambassador, Sir Michael Palairet, it had been painted a distinctive pink which (in Osbert's view) made it 'almost ostentatiously recognizable'.

The most seriously exposed side of the Embassy building was that which held the best bedrooms, the dining-room and the Ambassador's study. The bedrooms had to be abandoned, and the beds were put in the corridors. The Ambassador kept his study, since his desk in the corner was not in the line of fire. Nor was the opposite corner of the room. Passing from one haven to the other was something to be done briskly. Osbert remembered Leeper skipping nimbly from one corner of his study to the other to avoid the bullets that constantly whammed into the building with a sound (Leeper recorded) like a ball hitting a fives court. Though many bullets did enter the windows of the Embassy, none actually penetrated the Ambassador's study: later, however, when it was safe to do so, Leeper counted the hits to the sides of the window. There were fifty-two.

Primrose Leeper, the Ambassador's wife, remembers being somewhat dismayed on learning the identity of the new Press Attaché. She knew of him 'only as a name, as a caricaturist'. She imagined that he would be rather highbrow and precious. Looking back, she comments that 'I need not have worried. He fitted in wonderfully and was a great asset in keeping up morale. He was ready to do anything.'

Ambassador Leeper was equally impressed. He wrote of how Osbert 'with unfaltering touch could always convey the humorous side of any incident', and Harold Macmillan described the new arrival as 'a tower of strength, common sense and fun'. Macmillan's private secretary was John Wyndham (Lord Egremont). In *Wyndham and Children First* (for which Osbert was to draw the author's portrait on the book jacket) he writes that:

> With fanatical Greeks on rooftops taking pot-shots at one another wherever one went, not to speak of a rebel battery lobbing shells on us from outside the city, Osbert had quite a job keeping in touch with his flock, the press, and keeping them in touch with the truth. But, being Osbert, he managed.

Wyndham tells of an incident involving both pot-shots and Osbert's style of managing. As a healthy young man, cooped up in the Embassy, Wyndham felt the need for some exercise. He found a piece of rope and decided to do some skipping in the garden. Hardly had he started than a bullet landed at his feet, having been fired by a sniper on a near-by rooftop. As he ran about taking evasive action a window opened and Osbert looked out saying, 'What *are* you doing?' Wyndham explained that a man was trying to kill him. 'Hang on!' Osbert said, and disappeared. He shortly returned to the French windows where he told Wyndham, 'Keep him in play; we've summoned the military to come and pick him off.' The Ambassador, his wife, Macmillan and other members of the Embassy took it in turns to appear at the window and shout words of encouragement to keep him skipping. When finally he dived into the flower bed Primrose Leeper was heard to cry 'Oh, John, not the dahlias.' At last an armoured car turned up and the sniper was dealt with. Osbert said to Wyndham afterwards, 'That chap made you skip, didn't he?'

Given the obsession with protocol that is the stock-in-trade of diplomats everywhere, it would seem a recipe for disaster to have a Government Minister and an Ambassador under one roof, let alone in a building under siege. Even if those involved were not particularly touchy, it would be understandable in such a situation for the Minister or the Ambassador or their respective staffs to ask, 'Who's in charge round here?'

Fortunately Macmillan was sensitive to Leeper's invidious position. He also respected Leeper. He found him:

> attractive and sympathetic ... a brilliant classical scholar [with] a remarkably quick and accurate grasp of the changing kaleidoscope of Greek politics. He understood the Greeks, and they understood him. He had infinite patience as well as great personal charm ... Not only was he devoid of jealousy, but he had the supreme gift of being able to work in a team.

The admiration was mutual. Leeper wrote that:

> There can be few instances where a Cabinet Minister and an Ambassador have found themselves in such an unusual and delicate position and where the Ambassador was so wholly pleased with the way it developed. Macmillan was always careful to show my staff and the Greeks that he had not come to supplant me. He refused to share my

study with me and worked in some discomfort in half a room in the Chancery.

It would be unworthy to suggest that the Ambassador's study was made less desirable by the bullets smacking round the window, while the Chancery in the basement was theoretically safe from snipers. This comfortable illusion was shattered when Edward Warner, head of the Chancery, announced that as he sat at his desk a bullet had passed just over his head and embedded itself in the wainscot.

Relations between Leeper and his staff were also excellent. In his acknowledgements to *Classical Landscape with Figures* (1947) Osbert speaks of working on Leeper's 'indulged staff' and of his 'delightful company'. For his part Leeper wrote that he could not have desired a better staff and had never known a friendlier atmosphere at any Embassy.

From Macmillan and Leeper downwards, all played their part. Osbert kept spirits up by making everyone laugh, while Mrs Leeper devoted all her energy and ingenuity to keeping physical discomfort to a minimum in the face of severe privation. Since the rebels had the power station, there was no electricity except what was produced by a German generator inside the iron gates of the courtyard. This puffed away until the early hours when the last telegram to London had been dispatched, producing a great deal of noise but not much light. Since it didn't produce enough electricity to drive the heating apparatus there was no heat either, and Athens in December can be (as it was that year) bitterly cold. The rebels had drained the Hadrian's Reservoir, so there was not much water either. As for food, they were on army rations at a reduced level. The food all came from tins. Everyone ate together in the hall, twenty-five or so of them at a time, dining on army biscuits and bully beef or spam brought in a 'soft' car from an army dump half-way between Athens and the Piraeus.

Primrose Leeper was described by Macmillan in his diaries as 'a really splendid woman. She keeps all the staff, male and female, in a good temper, and with the slender resources available, she and the cook produce really remarkable results.'

Macmillan himself produced some pretty remarkable results on the catering side. He solved the drink shortage. Occasionally someone would be intrepid enough to sneak out and get hold of some ouzo or retsina, but nevertheless a serious lack of alcohol developed. It was known that the previous Ambassador, Sir Michael Palairet, had left a quantity of champagne behind him, but this was tantalizingly behind locked doors, and Foreign Office protocol is punctilious about leaving the possessions of a previous Ambassador alone. Macmillan acted with characteristic decisiveness and put his rank of Cabinet Minister to effective purpose.

'Damn it all,' he said. 'I think it's legitimate to break into the former Ambassador's cellar.' Action swiftly and enthusiastically followed the word, and a quantity of splendid bottles was soon liberated. 'Michael would like us to have had them,' Macmillan said firmly.

Whether or not Osbert's enduring admiration for Macmillan dated from this resolute solution to an urgent problem, it was certainly strengthened by it. 'Life was more bearable after that,' he recalled. As for Lord Stockton (as Harold Macmillan became), he said in a television interview in 1984 that his taking of the wine cellar was 'the only thing I'm really proud of in my career'.

Osbert found the boredom worse than the physical danger which they were all in. He himself did much to entertain others with his jokes and drawings. Macmillan's contribution to morale was a performance which made an indelible impression on his audience. More than thirty years later, when Osbert received his Hon.D.Litt. from Harold Macmillan, by then Chancellor of Oxford University, he referred to Macmillan in his acceptance speech as a man

> whom I was once privileged to hear reading aloud Thucydides's account of the revolt of Corcyra in a supposedly safe cellar in our Embassy in Athens, substituting the names of all the more prominent and infinitely untrustworthy members of the Politikos Kosmos for those in the text – against a background of machine-guns, mortars and mercifully incomprehensible abuse.[1]

Christmas was exceptionally eventful. Primrose Leeper, who was High Church, organized a midnight mass in the Embassy drawing-room. She improvised a Christmas tree out of a fir-branch from the garden, and used white shoe-cleaner to add snow to the little fir-cones. She said it was a pity there was no crib to put under the tree.

---

[1] This would have been from the same section of Thucydides that heads this chapter, but not in the Rex Warner translation, which came some years later. Probably it was Jowett's translation. Perhaps – who knows? – it was Macmillan's own.

Osbert went up to his room. He found some white index-cards, drew crib figures and painstakingly cut them out with a pair of nail-scissors. The silhouettes of St Joseph, the Virgin, the baby Jesus, the three Kings and the Shepherds were placed under the improvised Christmas tree, lit from behind; it was a charming and unusual début to what would prove such a distinguished career in stage design. The figures are still in Lady Leeper's possession.

An army padre arrived for the Christmas Eve service in an armoured car. He preached a sermon in which he described the Herald Angels as 'God's parachute brigade' – or so Lady Leeper remembers; in John Wyndham's version it was 'God's airborne division'. In either case, Osbert pronounced himself delighted with what he called 'a seasonable and apposite sermon'.

They sang carols and the little ceremony ended shortly after midnight. Outside, peace on earth and goodwill to all men were being celebrated by the sound of gunfire as a night attack was launched on a part of the town the other side of Mount Lycabettus which towered behind the Embassy.

Thus began Christmas Day 1944. It was still in its small hours when the Embassy received a telegram. This was swiftly deciphered and found to contain the news that important visitors would be arriving that very day. At eleven o'clock that morning Field Marshal Alexander turned up and announced, to general astonishment, the identity of the important visitors: Churchill and the Foreign Secretary, Anthony Eden.

It is a mark of the seriousness with which Churchill took the situation in Greece, and of his keen personal interest in it, that at a time when there were many and great problems all over the world needing his daily attention he should have made this spur-of-the-moment decision to fly to Athens, thereby not only disrupting his own and Eden's intended family Christmas festivities and risking his own health, which was fairly fragile at the time (he was then aged seventy), but also subjecting himself to considerable discomfort and danger.

The three-week pause following the shooting in Constitution Square had enabled the British to improve their military position.

Now that it looked as though the rebels had missed their chance to take over, the military problem began to give way to the political one. With the resignation of the six Communist ministers at the beginning of December, Papandreou's Government had almost ceased to have any effective existence. Leeper suggested that, in the absence of the King and of any real government, a regent should be appointed to fill the vacuum, and that the man for the job – indeed, the only man for the job – was Archbishop Damaskinos.

Churchill didn't like this idea. He continued to back the King, who not only objected to the idea of a regent in principle but also to the Archbishop in particular, of whom he had a personal distrust. As recently as 17 December Churchill had written to Alexander: 'I have heard mixed accounts of the Archbishop, who is said to be very much in touch with EAM and to have keen personal ambitions.' Churchill's visit to Athens would at least give him a chance to form his own first-hand impressions of Damaskinos.

Macmillan, Leeper and Alexander went to the aerodrome by armoured car to meet the plane that was bringing Churchill and Eden. The welcoming party[1] expected a difficult time: less than a week earlier Churchill had sent Macmillan an angry telegram berating him for pressing the idea of a regent.

To their relief they found the old man in a good mood in spite of nearly twenty-four hours' travel. Churchill stepped from the plane to be greeted by a bitterly cold wind blowing from the mountains.

'Very chilly, isn't it?' he said. 'A glass of brandy, I think.' He returned to the plane, where the atmosphere (in both senses) was warm. Macmillan was relieved to find the Prime Minister in a mellow mood. Doubtless the Christmas spirit (again in both senses) helped.

After two hours of reviewing the strategic, tactical and political problems of the situation, it was agreed that a conference should be held without delay, that very evening. It would be held on HMS *Ajax* with Papandreou present, and Archbishop Damaskinos would be in the chair.

By seven o'clock all concerned had assembled on HMS *Ajax* (the celebrated light-cruiser of the battle of the River Plate), which was to be the home of Churchill and Eden during their stay. Papandreou

[1] I have not been able to establish whether Osbert was a member of this party or at which meetings and events of Churchill's visit he was present. Most of them, I would guess, on the evidence of photographs and newsreels of the time. These usually show Churchill, Eden, Macmillan, Damaskinos (or any combination of these) in the foreground, with Osbert smiling genially just a step behind.

and Damaskinos had been astonished, delighted and flattered by the arrival of the distinguished visitors from Britain, and had willingly agreed to make the journey to the Piraeus for the impromptu meeting. It very nearly got off to a disastrous start.

Archbishop Damaskinos was a most imposing figure. He was an ex-wrestler, weighing about eighteen stone, well over six foot tall, to which could be added a foot or so for the chimney-like Orthodox headgear with the black hood draped over it. As a finishing touch he sported a long black ebony cane with a silver top.

It was still Christmas Day, and the crew of the *Ajax* were preparing for a jolly evening. Sailors had dressed up for a fancy-dress parade in every kind of motley – as Chinese, Red Indians, blacks, clowns, anything that was as different as possible from the uniforms they wore all the other days of the year. As the Archbishop boarded the ship he was met by such a party from the lower deck, most of them holding glasses of gin.

The Archbishop was astonished to find that one of His Majesty's ships had been taken over by a multi-racial crew of drunkards playing a discordant variety of musical instruments. For their part the sailors made the equally understandable mistake of thinking that the towering Archbishop with his massive beard and flowing robes was all part of the fun. They leapt about enthusiastically, whooping with joy and making mock obeisances.

The Archbishop now decided that the whole thing was a deliberate, calculated insult. He was only prevented from returning to shore in an archiepiscopal huff by the arrival of the acutely embarrassed captain of the *Ajax* who somehow managed to explain what was going on and smooth things over.

Fortunately the meeting went well. Whether because of the antics on deck, or because he was informed that Damaskinos had been a champion wrestler before becoming a priest of the Orthodox Church, Churchill took a tremendous shine to the Archbishop. For weeks he had been teasing Macmillan about his admiration for the 'pestilent priest, a survival from the Middle Ages'. All this changed in a matter of minutes. Whatever his views about the regency in principle, Churchill no longer had objections to the Archbishop. The Christmas visit had already achieved something.

By eight o'clock it was decided that there should be a conference the next day at four and that, in addition to those present at the *Ajax* meeting, delegates from ELAS would also be invited.

The next day Churchill was able to experience conditions at the Embassy. He met the staff who, he told his wife in a Christmas telegram, 'have been in continued danger and discomfort for so many weeks, but are in the gayest of moods. Mrs Leeper is an inspiration to them.' Since there was no electricity, lighting was by hurricane lamps. Macmillan was worried about the cold and its possible effect on the elderly Prime Minister and Archbishop. They sat together side by side with huge blankets over them, further warmed by stoves borrowed from the Army for the occasion.

The Embassy had been as worried about Churchill's danger from the cold as about sniper bullets. They had done their best about the former, but Churchill was determinedly oblivious to their attempts to avoid the latter. On one of Churchill's three days at the Embassy, he and Leeper retired after lunch (in overcoats) to the Ambassador's study. Churchill sat firmly in the middle of the room in the area directly at risk from snipers.

Neither Leeper nor Eden could persuade him to move. Fortunately the snipers were having their lunchtime break. Shortly before they resumed work, General Scobie turned up, and just as he and Churchill were entering their armoured car a volley swept down the street. 'Cheek!' said Churchill.

The conference was chaired by the Archbishop, with Churchill on his right and Alexander on his left. Also present were Eden, Macmillan, Leeper, the US Ambassador McVeagh, Colonel Popov (the Soviet Military Representative), the French Minister, Papandreou, various Greek politicians including the next Prime Minister Plastiras, and representatives of ELAS. It lasted for three hours. Predictably there were angry scenes but eventually it was agreed that there should be a regency and that the Regent should be Damaskinos.

Churchill and Damaskinos leave the British Embassy after talks. Popov is second from the left, Alexander in the centre with Macmillan and Eden behind him, and Lancaster on the far right.

Churchill returned to London with Eden on 29 December, and immediately had a meeting there with the Greek King. It was scarcely six days since Churchill had left for Greece. He had been travelling for many hours from Athens to London. After discussions late into the night the King finally agreed that Damaskinos should be appointed Regent and that he, the King, would not return to Greece without a plebiscite in his favour. It was by now half-past four in the morning. Churchill's physical stamina at the age of seventy is even more astounding when one thinks of the chain-smoked cigars and the bottle of brandy a day.

During the days of Churchill's visit Osbert was a close observer of the current Prime Minister and two future ones – Eden and Macmillan. He admired Macmillan not only for his administrative ability and political skill but also for his personal qualities. He had little affection for the other two Prime Ministers. Eden he had always disliked. Churchill he found 'beastly to subordinates, arrogant, ungrateful'. On the other hand, he said, 'In Athens Macmillan, that great and good man, was not carried away by enthusiasm. He realized possibilities, what he could do and couldn't do, which Churchill didn't, and Eden was too conceited to understand. It would have been a miracle if anything had got done without a character like Macmillan. He understood how people's minds worked, what they could be asked to do with some chance of success.' Osbert paused for a very long time, thinking about Macmillan, and then added judiciously, 'He didn't write well.'

Not everyone was equally impressed by Churchill's visit. Pierson Dixon asked in his diary, 'Was this journey strictly necessary?' He commented that Churchill and Eden were like two housemaids answering every bell, and that the visit had given ELAS a vastly increased sense of its own importance. Osbert was equally dismissive (at least in retrospect). He took the view that the visit had achieved no more than could have been brought about by a couple of telephone calls.

Others (including Leeper, Macmillan and Churchill himself) thought it was a great success. The visit had dramatically demonstrated to the Greeks the priority that the British government gave to their affairs, and conveyed the same message to our Allies in Washington and Moscow. It also scotched the view of much of the press on both sides of the Atlantic that Britain was backing the Monarchist (therefore reactionary) side against the freedom-loving revolutionaries. After all, Churchill had actually sat down at the table with the Communists and reached some kind of agreement.

The regency brought with it a change of government. Papandreou was replaced as Prime Minister by the titular head of EDES, General Plastiras – 'thin as string, fiercely moustachioed, with eyes like Kalamata olives', in Osbert's words; 'stupid, vain, pig-headed, arrogant' in Macmillan's.

In what was called the 'Second Liberation' a truce was negotiated. ELAS surrendered a surprisingly large quantity of arms; Plastiras agreed to liberal reforms, an amnesty for political crimes and a plebiscite on the monarchy. For the time being it was once more safe to walk the streets of Athens. Nevertheless, colossal problems remained; not least inflation, which was out of control. Figures became meaningless: 60,000,000 drachmas for a loaf of bread in August, 10,000,000,000,000 drachmas for a newspaper in October.

On the advice of the British Treasury's Sir David Waley a new rate was set at one drachma to 50,000,000,000 old ones, and 600 new drachmas to the pound sterling. This means that before revaluation the pound sterling was worth 30,000,000,000,000 drachmas.

Osbert's first months in Greece were ones of intense activity. He had to establish relations with the press, and improve them. He also had to improve relations between the press and the British armed forces, which were every bit as bad as those between the press and the Embassy. It was in effect his job to change the attitudes of the correspondents from being hostile to the British to being supportive. He had, as the jargon goes, to turn them round.

The Ambassador, Rex Leeper, was a clever man and had a distinguished career (among other things he was instrumental in setting up the British Council), but handling the press was not his strong card. While the British Embassy was in Cairo he had for tactical reasons been economical with the truth to reporters on the subject of the mutinies in the Greek forces in early 1944. If he actually lied, he would not have been the first ambassador to do so: lying for his country is what an ambassador is sent abroad to do. But it was not so much mendacity that soured relations between the Ambassador and the press; it was more Leeper's maladroitness, his tactlessness and the condescension with which he treated the correspondents, whom he visibly regarded as at best a necessary nuisance.

By the time of the move to Athens the American press (with the exception of Alexander 'Shan' Sedgwick of the *New York Times*) was fairly well disposed to the Communists, and was sometimes asking openly why British troops were there at all. For the Ambassador to antagonize the journalists was therefore diplomatically inept. It could mean a bad press not only in the United States but also in Britain, since at the time American correspondents were also writing for such British papers as the *Observer*, the *News Chronicle* and the *Daily Express*. The wigging Leeper gave the reporters after the Constitution Square demonstration only made things worse.

Censorship was at a level that the Americans found unacceptable, and that today even British journalists would find hard to tolerate. As usual it was far from impossible to circumvent. In order to send an uncensored report of the December events the American radio reporter Leland Stone flew from Athens to Rome. This must have been inconvenient, but at least it meant that he could say what he, rather than the British censor, wanted.

Osbert's first step was to make his assessment of the various journalists on the spot. He did so with extraordinary rapidity. After only a week in Athens he reported back to Ridsdale, head of the Foreign Office News Department. In his forthright manner Osbert declared the majority of the correspondents to be third-rate. Exceptions were the strongly anti-EAM, pro-British, right-wing Sedgwick, John Nixon of the BBC ('a good man willing to accept guidance'), Clare Hollingworth, and F. G. H. Salusbury of the *Daily Herald*, who was 'very good but soured by the attitude of his paper'.

Geoffrey Hoare of *The Times* was of particular interest to London, since his reports had been the basis of leaders (mostly written by Donald Tyerman) which sparked off an angry counter-attack on the then influential newspaper by Churchill in the House of Commons. Osbert reported that Hoare was a big disappointment, 'woolly-minded. . . invariably reflecting opinion of the last person he has spoken to . . . total inability to select from mass of facts few which are significant . . . very deaf . . .' Clare Hollingworth, whose stuff had 'not been bad', seemed to be able to 'exercise some influence on Geoffrey Hoare' (she later married him).

In short there were bouquets for those who took the British Embassy line, brickbats for those who didn't. On this report (F.O.371/48234 Public Record Office) Anthony Eden wrote the marginal comment: 'Mr Lancaster has done well – wise and far-seeing report. Mr Ridsdale to pass on Foreign Secretary's views.' Osbert did not remember these views ever having been passed on to him.

Osbert had been in Greece for far too short a time to form unaided such strong opinions about the professional abilities of a fair number of people. Either he had reached his conclusions before he arrived in Athens or else he was acting as Leeper's mouthpiece. In a message to the Foreign Office on 15 January Leeper talked about the 'very unintelligent foreign correspondents here', words which echo Osbert's remark.

At the beginning of 1945 the American press corps wrote a collective letter to their Ambassador McVeagh for transmission to Washington, complaining that Scobie was denying them facilities to gather news from the ELAS side, or interview EAM leaders even with British officers present. They said that Scobie had forbidden all contact with the 'enemy', and asked that the US government should make sure that American correspondents were freed from these restraints so that 'the deeply interested American public may be enabled rightfully and without any infringement of British military security to hear occasionally part of the EAM view of the present conflict'.

This letter was signed by all the American correspondents in Athens: all except Sedgwick. Writing to the Foreign Office (11 January 1945) Osbert made much of the fact that the *New York Times*'s correspondent had *not* signed, that Sedgwick was 'far the most experienced and balanced of all correspondents here both British and American', and that Sedgwick had sent his own separate letter to the Ambassador 'entirely dissociating himself from his colleagues and expressing complete approval of the British military authorities' action . . .' So, once more, everyone was out of step except Sedgwick.

As ever in this turmoil, two sides to the story emerge, and there were rights and wrongs on both. While for Sedgwick the British were beyond reproach, some of the other correspondents were equally credulous about reports from the other side. Marcel Fodor (writing both for the *Chicago Sun* and the *Daily Express*) passed on from the Communist newspaper *Rizspastis* an ELAS account accusing the RAF of killing and wounding a thousand men and women by bombing Athens. The RAF did not bomb Athens.

On 3 January 1945 Osbert sent another message to the Foreign Office. Salusbury of the *Daily Herald* had that morning shown him a cable from his office urging him to find out what 'official encouragement' had been put over British troops to persuade them to write letters to the papers criticizing the press treatment of Greek affairs. Osbert commented that 'Not only has absolutely no (repeat no) attempt been made to influence the troops here politically in any way but all news and views about Greek situation available to them are abstracts from the British press and the BBC.'

Clearly Osbert took a dim view of some, if not most, of the correspondents, but at the same time not all of them were totally enamoured of *him*. On 16 January 1945 Constantine Poulos of the Overseas News Agency reported that 'It is becoming increasingly difficult to tell the story of developments in Greece honestly and completely. To the carefully schooled British military censorship has been added the blue pencil of the British Embassy here.' He had discovered at the Censor's office a file of his stories in which there were deletions and what he called subtle changes of wording. At least one dispatch was marked 'OKayed by Osbert Lancaster'.

Perhaps it was OL who made the subtle changes of wording. Perhaps there were also other dispatches which OL did not OK. At any rate, in the tightly knit group of correspondents, Poulos's discovery must have got about very quickly. The implications were obvious. For the British Embassy's Press Attaché to be anti-Communist, pro-Embassy and pro-British Army was only to be expected. For the Press Attaché also to be a censor was another matter.

Under such circumstances Osbert was presented with an uphill task. Yet he did manage to build a working, and even friendly, relationship with the correspondents. He did so mainly through his press conferences. These were something of an innovation after those of Leeper, which were mostly non-existent. Whereas Leeper was inaccessible, unforthcoming, patronizing and hectoring, Osbert was humorous and disarmingly frank. His press conferences were conducted in an idiosyncratically Osbertian manner which successfully baffled most of the Americans. Richard Capell of the *Telegraph* described him as

> a delightful man, whose accent makes his English incomprehensible to many Americans and even the ruder kind of Briton. Merlin-wise, he begins his pronouncements at our conferences thus: 'Not to prevaricate, gentlemen, the honest truth is . . .' or: 'To speak with perfect frankness . . . little can be said beyond what already in your devious ways you have . . .'

An Australian journalist who was in Greece at the time remembers arriving in Athens and being told that there was to be a press briefing at the Embassy that afternoon. Her reflex response, like that of any decent journalist, was that she could cut that, and would. To her surprise her colleagues said, 'Oh, don't do that. They're hilarious. We wouldn't miss them for anything. They're held by a man called Osbert Lancaster, and we've never been to briefings like them.'

She went along. Osbert started: 'Well, I'm afraid I have absolutely no news today, so I'm wondering what *you* can tell *me*.' She remembers that on other occasions he would start drawing sketches of the situation on the blackboard; of evzones with muskets and so on.

149

Americans have always had problems coping with the English sense of humour and they were particularly confused to discover that the outrageously, incomprehensibly English man from the Foreign Office, with his bulging eyes and incongruous tweed jackets sporting checks that might have been envied by a bookmaker in those days – this bizarre figure was doing funny drawings of the press. When Geoffrey Hoare, Clare Hollingworth and Marcel Fodor had gone to the help of a woman in prison, he had done a drawing of Hoare as Don Quixote, Clare Hollingworth as page, and Fodor as Sancho Panza. They must have asked themselves, like Butch Cassidy, 'Who *is* this guy?'

In his handling of the press he used every ruse. At one moment he would make them laugh with a verbal joke or a cartoon. At the next he would deliver a rap over the knuckles.

Osbert had the unenviable task of dealing not only with the critics but with the actors as well. Primrose Leeper once witnessed his calming influence on Anthony Eden. The petulant Foreign Secretary was in a frightful bate after remarks which he had thought were off-the-cuff and unattributable had found their way into print. He can't have been the easiest man to calm down, but somehow Osbert, in spite of his strong dislike of Eden, managed to do so.

He was also able to exercise his influence on the military. General 'Ginger' Hawksworth was cast somewhat in the mould of Evelyn Waugh's Ritchie-Hook. This fire-eater thought up something called Operation Dumb-bell, the first stage of which would be to drop leaflets on the Communists threatening to biff them with RAF bombardment unless they gave up. Osbert was able to restrain Hawksworth by pointing out what a powerful propaganda tool the leaflets would be for the Communists, who would be able to show them to the international press and say, 'Look, the British are even worse than the Germans.' His arguments proved persuasive and Operation Dumb-bell was dropped.

There is no doubt that following Osbert's arrival in Greece relations between the press and the British authorities improved, and that both in Britain and the United States perceptions of what was going on changed. Osbert told me that the change in the tone and attitudes of the press was the result first of the change in the situation, and second of an improvement in the quality of the correspondents.

In understating his own contribution he was being modest. It is hard to imagine how anyone else could have played his role. His appointment must have seemed a trifle bizarre at the time, but with hindsight it was inspired. He was a very rare creature – one who could talk on equal terms with the Embassy, the Foreign Office, the military and the press. He was visibly in the thick of things. Since he was staying at the Embassy and working at GHQ he met Ambassador Leeper and General Scobie daily, and through his regular briefings and conferences he was in constant touch with the press. Not only did he rub shoulders with politicians, diplomats and military top brass, but (even if he did use the censor's pencil) the press corps knew that deep down he was one of them, a journalist.

Osbert's Athens colleague and room-mate Harold Caccia says, 'Osbert was a nationally known figure. He could be listened to by anyone, generals or journalists. He was an essential linch-pin. What a man could do, he did.'

After the establishment of the regency and the agreement to hold a plebiscite on the monarchy, the international press could no longer continue to maintain that the British were trying to foist the King on unwilling subjects. Nor could they continue to glamorize the Communists in the face of mounting public outrage at their refusal to release their civilian hostages. An estimated twenty thousand people had been dragged from their homes and treated with appalling brutality. Furthermore facts were coming to light about the atrocities committed in and around Athens during the ELAS occupation. The Trade Union delegation under Sir Walter (later Lord) Citrine, which visited from 22 January to 3 February 1945, saw at Peristeri 250 bodies laid out for identification, hands tied behind their backs, all shot at close range; victims, in the words of the delegation's report, of organized murder.

The Citrine delegation was affected (as who could not have been?) by such appalling scenes and also by meeting British troops and learning of the way in which Greek affairs had been reported in the press. In *What We Saw in Greece* the TUC delegation reported that 'We found great and universal resentment among the British troops at what they considered the inadequate and unfair manner in which recent events in Greece had been presented to the British public through the newspapers and by certain Members of Parliament.' Citrine (briefed by Osbert) addressed British paratroops and asked them leading questions to which they replied with denunciations of the British press and the left of the Labour Party. They heard of ELAS's abuse of the white flag and the red cross, of the shooting of stretcher-bearers, of women dressed as nurses throwing grenades from the windows of the Polyclinic hospital. In Citrine's parting press conference, for which he was again briefed by Osbert, he made no bones about his low opinion of the international press in Athens. He told the journalists bluntly that the world had been inadequately informed about the atrocities.

It would be going too far to say that the Citrine delegation was bamboozled. Atrocities are atrocities, murder is murder. At the same time civil war is civil war. The Citrine delegation's visit was carefully stage-managed, to the extent (in the opinion of Clare Hollingworth, who was an eyewitness, and an observant one) that they were shown the same corpses more than once in different locations.

One would have thought that the horror was sufficient, that nobody would go to the lengths of trying to exaggerate it, but it is certainly the case that the Citrine delegation heard and saw only one side of the story. It was Churchill in person who suggested that Citrine should not cross the demarcation line into ELAS territory, and Eden, in his feline way, told Leeper, 'If I may suggest it, I feel sure he – Citrine – will respond to any attention you can give him.' Osbert was one of those who attended to him. He played a key role in the stage-management, was always in the wings and acted not just as prompter but also as script-writer. Some of Citrine's speeches were virtually written by Osbert. And the Embassy found the ideal interpreter for Citrine: Shan Sedgwick's wife Roxane, née Sotiriadis, who came from an extremely conservative Greek banking family.

From the point of view of General Scobie, Ambassador Leeper, his Press Attaché and the Foreign Office, the TUC delegation visit was a great success. The delegation returned to Britain on 3 February and published its report on 9 February. *The Times* commented accurately, though somewhat laconically, that this corresponded exactly with the Foreign Office line.

Meanwhile, Churchill had delivered a mighty counterblast to the press in a House of Commons speech in mid-January. Anyone foolish enough to think they could attack Churchill and go unpunished was soundly disabused. In the course of one of his really thundering speeches he said:

There is no case in my experience, certainly not in my wartime experience, where a British government has been so maligned and its motives so traduced in our own country by organs of the Press or among our own people. That this should be done amid the perils of this war, now at its climax, has filled me with surprise and sorrow. How can we wonder at, still less how can we complain of, the attitude of hostile or indifferent newspapers in the United States when we have here in this country witnessed such melancholy exhibitions as are provided by some of our most time-honoured and responsible journals – and others to which such epithets would hardly apply? Our task, hard as it was, has been and is still being rendered vastly more difficult by a spirit of gay, reckless, unbridled partisanship which has been let loose on the Greek question . . . I have never been connected with any large enterprise of policy about which I was more sure in my mind and conscience of the rectitude of our motions, of the clarity of our principles and of the vigour, precision and success of our action than what we have done in Greece.

The motion was carried in Churchill's favour by 340 votes to 7.

A few days later (8 February 1945) Churchill was telling Stalin at the Yalta conference that 'The British had had rather a rough time [in Greece] and he was much obliged to Marshal Stalin for his attitude to this matter. Marshal Stalin repeated that all he wanted was information and that he did not wish to interfere' [Protocol of the fourth Plenary Session, 8 February 1945 (R 3460/4/190)].

On the way back from Yalta, Churchill paid another visit to Athens, accompanied by Eden and Alexander. His reception was one of overwhelming welcome. Harold Nicolson recorded that 'At the mention of Greece his whole face lit up, and he put his hand on my arm. "I have had great moments in my life," he said, "but never such a moment as when faced with that half-million crowd in Constitution Square." '

After Churchill's second visit, a new chapter in modern Greek politics opened. Though there was now something resembling peace, the country had been devastated by war, by German occupation and bloody civil strife. The task of reconstruction was immense. Towns, villages, ports, roads, bridges and railways had been blown apart. Throughout 1945 and into 1946 (Osbert's time in Greece) political crisis followed political crisis. In April Plastiras resigned and was replaced by Admiral Voulgaris who lasted till October. A

153

more than usually confused and confusing period included a brief premiership by the Archbishop himself. Finally, the aged Sophoulis took over, declaring a political amnesty, withdrawing some 60,000 prosecutions and announcing the first general election for ten years on 31 March 1946. In this the Populists won the majority, Tsadaris became Prime Minister, and (would you believe it?) after a decisive plebiscite the King himself returned. He soon died, in 1947, and was succeeded by his brother Paul, then in due course by his son Constantine (who was in turn kicked out himself).

Despite the privations of life in Athens during Osbert's time in Greece, he thoroughly enjoyed himself. 'I was busy, and doing things I enjoyed in wonderful surroundings.' He worked hard and there were results to show for it.

Once it was possible to move about the war-shattered country, Osbert did some travelling (largely in the company of the Leepers). He visited Attica, Boeotia, Euboea, the Peloponnese, Phocis, Missolonghi and the Childe Harold country, Thessaloniki and the islands.

He also found time to paint and draw, and (as always) to enjoy a busy and convivial social life. He had known not a word of Greek when he arrived, but found that in the circles in which he moved everyone spoke English or 'filthily bad' French. He met such writers as George Katsimbalis (the hero of Henry Miller's *The Colossus of Maroussi*), Nikos Kazantzakis (author of *Zorba the Greek, Christ Recrucified* and much else) and George Seferis, a 'charming and saintly man', a professional diplomat who later became Greek Ambassador in London, and a recipient of the Nobel Prize for literature. Seferis's poems were translated by Rex Warner, who was at that time Head of the British Institute in Athens. The deputy Head was Patrick Leigh Fermor, who in due course married Osbert's secretary Joan Rayner. She had known Osbert since pre-war days at Sezincote, and had been married to John Rayner, the features editor at the *Express*. (Barbara Mayor became Barbara Rothschild before marrying Rex Warner and then Niko Ghika, an excellent painter who was a friend of (and artistic influence on) Osbert. Rex Warner too was later to get married again – to his first wife . . .)

One popular entertainment was the composing of *bouts rimés* at which Osbert showed great adeptness. Patrick Leigh Fermor remembers playing this game with Joan, Osbert and Rex Warner. The results were usually most improper and highly slanderous.

Leigh Fermor also recalls Osbert imitating some famous tenor, breaking into whole arias of Italian opera, demonstrating a remarkable memory and a 'fine, robust voice'.

But with the end of the war Osbert was at liberty to return to civilian life. Leeper was leaving to take up another post; and then there were London, the family, Fleet Street and the clubs all beckoning his return. It was time to go.

For Osbert, both as artist and as writer, Greece was not only a revelation but came at just the right time. His first book to be published after the war was *Classical Landscape with Figures*. Based on his Greek experience, it was 'not a ramble, nor a travel book, nor yet a guide, but a *description* in the eighteenth-century meaning of the term'.

In *Progress at Pelvis Bay*, *Pillar to Post* and *Homes Sweet Homes* he had (at least for the time being) in a sense *done* European architecture in general and the landscapes and buildings of England in particular. It is hard to think what he might have gone on to next had not

The Holy Apostles, Thessaloniki

155

the accident of war presented him with a fresh landscape and fresh characters on which to turn those observant, bright blue eyes.

The introduction to *Classical Landscape* anticipates objections:

> It may be contended that in a work intended to give a picture of the Greek scene as it presents itself today so obvious a preoccupation with the past is entirely misplaced, or conversely, that in a landscape which at the present time can only be regarded as historic such contemporary elements as intrude are as uncalled for as the little boy in the cloth cap who invariably slips into the foreground of what would otherwise have been an exquisite camera study of the ruins of Sunium or the bay of Salamis.

It is for this reason that in his 'description' of Greece the fore-ground is 'cluttered up with a heterogeneous collection of human oddities whose generally unromantic aspects fit them only for appearance in a news-reel'.

Equally deliberately he ignored the advice of those who say that writers on foreign countries must avoid judging by British standards. By what other conceivable standards, he asks, is one to judge foreign people? He robustly declares that his criteria, political, architectural and scenic, remain 'firmly Anglo-Saxon, and the standards of judgment are always those of an Anglican graduate of Oxford with a taste for architecture, turned cartoonist, approaching middle age and living in Kensington'.

The book's generous and brilliant illustrations show the influence of an earlier painter of the Balkans, Edward Lear. Osbert greatly admired Lear (and collected his landscapes long before it was fashionable to do so, at a time when Lear was still popularly known only for his nonsense verse). He considered Lear to be 'the only artist who has successfully captured the peculiar quality of this landscape'. What makes Osbert's pictures very different from Lear's is that instead of merely adorning the scene with buildings and figures, Osbert used it as a setting for them. Compared with the illustrations in his earlier works, those in *Classical Landscape* are much more the work of an artist than of a cartoonist, if this distinction is not invidious. The originals of the colour plates would look very fine framed and hung on a wall. Of course they are full of wit, but you never feel, as you do when most cartoonists turn to what one might call (for want of a better word) 'straight' work, that there ought to be a caption below.

Nor, with some exceptions, are they caricatures. They do not have the distortions of a Gillray or Grosz. Osbert was an observer, not a polemicist, working in the tradition not of political caricature and satire, but of the records of infinitely variable humanity that crowd the pictures of Brueghel and Hogarth, the carvings of medieval buildings and the margins of illuminated manuscripts.

In *Classical Landscape* the countryside and streets are peopled by a cast as rich and diverse as that of the England of Osbert's childhood, and he regards them with the same directness – the seller of sponges, the policeman, the priests in their high hats and flowing robes, the peasants on donkeys, the erect old men with wobbly sticks, the wobbly old men with straight sticks, the generals and admirals and politicians, the unshaven newspaper-man in his festooned kiosk, the men at café tables heatedly discussing politics. These may be types, but they are shown as individuals.

In addition to the Greek figures prodigally scattered through the pages of *Classical Landscape*, the book contains many line drawings of buildings and eight full-pages in colour. These are not printed as

they would be today on glossy art paper but on a matt paper only slightly heavier than that of the rest of the book. Only a few colours are used, and they are the same from one plate to another, used in flat areas which only rarely overlap. Unprinted areas are used for white. There are no tints; the few tonal variations are achieved by fine cross-hatching.

This method of printing – with only a few blocks, no screen and relatively cheap paper – may have been dictated by post-war economies. Be that as it may, the plates give no impression of being restricted by the technical and financial requirements of printer and publisher. As with a good lino-cut, the artist turns the restrictions of the medium to advantage in order to produce clear, simple and direct images. The combination of the few colours – blue for the sky, ochre and sienna for buildings and bare earth, green for vegetation, grey for window-shutters, shadows on white walls, tree-trunks, rocks and mountains, black for deep shadows and silhouettes – is remarkably satisfying, almost mysteriously so, as with the still lifes of Braque. The few, rather muted colours are used for tonal effects as much as for describing local colour and dramatically depict a scenery

soaked in the powerful Mediterranean sunlight. The effect is nothing like Lear or any other English watercolourist. It may originally have owed something to Niko Ghika, but Osbert used it in an original way and developed it into a style that was unmistakably his own.

Usually architectural artists idealize buildings. When a firm of architects produces its 'artist's impression' of a planned building it usually makes at best a token gesture to indicate the parked cars and passing traffic and untidy humanity that will in reality clutter it up. Similarly, photographers of great buildings of the past go to great lengths to find a particular angle or time of day which excludes the

159

twentieth century's intrusive contributions. This was not the Lancaster way. There are identifiably modern people in front of his ancient buildings. If there are traffic-signs and telegraph poles, in they go. The road to the little French village is heralded by an advertisement for Dubonnet or San Rafael; the two men in front of the Mosque at Chalcis are engaged in heated argument, totally ignoring the magnificent building behind them.

Classical Landscape puts the twentieth-century figures in the foreground not only in the illustrations but also in the text. The first Greek figure encountered is not Pericles or Alexander or Sophocles or Socrates but a bearded warrior rolling in agony after being slugged through the stomach by a political opponent. The first chapter is not about ancient history or classical architecture but, as its title announces, 'The Figures' – not the Classics master's Homer and Demosthenes and Aristotle, but the people of Greece as observed in the cities, towns, villages and countryside of Greece between 1944 and 1946.

These twentieth-century Greeks have two passions. One is politics. The other is noise. This 'extraordinary trait in the national character', Osbert argues, comes not from insensitiveness or indifference but from actual preference. He claimed to have discovered by chance in a car park in the Piraeus a motor-bike on which the two exhausts were fitted not with silencers but with amplifiers. Likewise,

> Political demonstrations, in addition to the high-powered stream of oratory and the rhythmical chanting of slogans, are invariably enlivened by the presence of one, if not two brass bands, while sessions of Parliament, thanks to the high pitch of development to which the slamming of desk-lids and banging of despatch boxes has here attained, frequently astound even French observers brought up in the hard school of the Chambre des Deputés.

Radios, gramophones and internal-combustion engines were used for fullest acoustic effect. Even the cocks of Athens, unlike those of anywhere else, crowed (according to Osbert) at all hours of the day and night.

Osbert's amused, and amusing, approach was not best calculated to please those for whom Greece is a very serious subject indeed. Nor, indeed, did he make any effort to please them. He treated scholars and archaeologists with near-contempt. Not only did he accuse them of 'learned vandalism' but he also said that the average archaeologist of any nationality 'being almost invariably deficient in visual sense is about as safe a person to have around a well-conducted city as a bomber-pilot or a by-pass builder'.

Traditional Hellenophiles, devout in their belief that the history of Greece stops with the death of Byron at latest, if not with that of Alexander the Great, would be intensely irritated by those (for them) anachronistic motorcars and radios, Orthodox priests and uniformed men with large moustaches and side-arms, and references to the civil war – not that described by

Thucydides but the twentieth-century one, equal in horror and even greater in scale.

At the same time the politically committed, as represented by Kingsley Martin's *New Statesman*, were bound to be equally offended by anyone who could look so calmly, humorously and ironically on the politics of Greece, finding time to take an informed and enthusiastic interest in buildings rather than concentrating exclusively on how the Marxist dialectic was working out its ineluctable way. It can hardly have surprised Brian Howard (who indeed did attempt to savage the book in the *New Statesman*) that the former Press Attaché at the British Embassy in Athens did not take the Communist side: Osbert was fully aware that horrors were committed by both sides, but it is true that he shows a particular distaste for the Communist leader Ares.

In Osbert's work there are few really repulsive characters. Three that come to mind are the sergeant in charge of Physical Education at his first school, the 'fat and greasy' Nazi officer, and Ares. All three were sadistic homosexuals in military uniform.

The classical landscape, far from being obscured by the conditions of twentieth-century warfare, was often illuminated by them. The original function of the Acropolis was defensive, something which tends in normal times to be obscured by the beauty and interest of the temples. This was brought home to Osbert, the first time he climbed the 'celebrated crag', by the fact that the summit had been held for the previous week by a handful of British paratroops against repeated attacks. Only the previous day the arrival of reinforcements had enabled them to extend their perimeter to the edge of the Agora.

> Above us the skies were those one finds more in the Derbyshire landscapes of Mr. Piper than in the posters extolling the beauties of the eastern Mediterranean; below, the whole overgrown city sprawled across the plain of Attica to the foothills of Parnes and Penteli. The usual deafening hubbub of Athenian life . . . was stilled, and the prevailing quietness was emphasized rather than broken by the continuous machine-gun fire in the streets immediately below, the detonations from the direction of Patissia (where the proletariat were blowing up houses to form street barricades) and that peculiar sound, half-whistle, half-rending calico, which shells make as they pass immediately overhead . . . Over all towered the Parthenon, its

clear unequivocal statement in no way blurred by the barricades hastily erected from fragments of its pillars and caissons, its own internal rhythm uninterrupted by mortar fire or rockets.

The prose cadences may be classical, but they are also those of one who is fully aware of living in the 'atomic age', a phrase Osbert actually uses in his description of the Acropolis (written within months of Hiroshima and Nagasaki).

The tension created by combining a lapidary manner with unconventional matter can, as Gibbon demonstrated, constitute a deadly weapon, and Osbert wielded it to great effect. For example, he points out that since the auditorium of the theatre of Dionysus dates in its present form only from the third century, 'any Agate-like musing on the vanished glories of Aeschylean first-nights would be misplaced. The stage itself is later still and is chiefly remarkable for a supporting figure of a Triton in whose hirsute features a former generation of conservative tourists were gratified to detect a striking likeness to the late Marquess of Salisbury.'

The Theseion is treated with equal lack of awe:

> Why should this temple, the best preserved of its date in the world, built within a few years of the Parthenon and embodying all the same principles, remain by comparison so devastatingly boring? . . . however receptive one's mood, it produces less effect than many a Doric corn-exchange in an English provincial town.

Osbert did not hedge his aesthetic judgements, and it is this very certainty that is so invigorating. If you want to disagree, he leaves you in no doubt what it is that you are disagreeing with. The one area in which he betrays a lack of certainty is in his use of the Greek language; as many reviewers pointed out, the book is stuffed with errors in the use of Greek words and place-names. This apart, the book had a very favourable reception, and after forty years it remains a most agreeable and entertaining companion on a visit to Greece. It is also a record of what Osbert thought of as the happiest time of his life.

VII

SIGNS OF THE TIMES

WHEN he came back to England in 1946 after eighteen months in Greece, Osbert took up a way of life that was hardly to vary over the next thirty years, though it was one of astonishing activity and productivity.

Between the time of his return and that of his retirement, the major landmarks were his mother's death in 1957, the death of Karen in 1964, and his marriage to Anne Scott-James in 1967. Later came the gradual decline of his old age. During this period he also received public recognition to an extent that merited the sobriquet of 'time-honoured Lancaster': numerous honorary degrees, doctorates and a knighthood.

The biographer finds a somewhat dismaying dearth of rows, intrigues, scandals or scrapes to report. The compensation (in plenty) is the work that confirmed Osbert as a national figure – including what was perhaps his most brilliant creation, namely his own carefully produced persona.

Osbert was always a gift to photographers, and fortunately he sat for some of the best. The 1940 portrait in *Vogue* by Lee Miller shows him sitting on a chair back to front in impeccably cut double-breasted suit; a striped shirt with plain collar and the cuffs projecting precisely one inch; handkerchief neatly folded in breast pocket; cigarette (doubtless Turkish) in hand; moustache delicately curled and ready for twirling; the very deuce of a pose, as Max said of Beau Brummell.

Also in the 1940s Osbert was one of the subjects of a series of eight portraits by Bill Brandt for *Lilliput*. The caption (at least in *The Bedside Lilliput*, Hulton Press, 1950) is comically inaccurate: 'Harrow, Oxford, the Bar, the Diplomatic Service, the life of Osbert Lancaster has been like a smooth ripening process, culminating in the dandyish man of all worlds whom you see here. Fruity as Victorian plum cake or vintage port, witty as salt, Lancaster puts into everything he draws or writes a deliciously infectious, amateurish zest.'

164

Harrow should, of course, be Charterhouse, and (although he made some perfunctory studies of Law) Osbert never came within calling distance of the Bar. Though he was certainly a man of the world, he was not a man of all worlds: his social circle was strictly that of his own background. But 'dandyish' is right, as are 'witty' and 'zest'. 'Amateurish' is wrong, for as writer and artist Osbert was highly professional. *Lilliput* must have been deceived by the dandy's sleight of hand which conceals the solid hard work that goes on behind the scenes.

The names of the other seven in Bill Brandt's series of portraits are evidence of the high esteem in which Osbert was already held at this date: they are Henry Moore, Benjamin Britten, Graham Sutherland, Dylan Thomas, Carol Reed, Evelyn Waugh, and Dr Edith and

The very deuce of a pose

165

Older and rounder, but dapper as ever

Osbert Sitwell. Brandt shows Osbert in the kind of pose that was used by *Punch* between the wars to depict the Bertie Wooster-type lounge lizard. He is leaning against a mantelpiece, smartly suited as always. The moustache does not have the upward buffalo-horn curve of the Lee Miller photograph, but rather the fullness of a Greek politician's or a Balkan bandit's. He holds his cigarette in a backhand position, with little finger slightly raised, like the Duchess drinking China tea from a porcelain cup.

Jane Bown's photograph of 1960 shows Osbert twenty years later, older and rounder, but dapper as ever.

The dandy dislikes games. When someone at Oxford asked Max if he was going down to the river for the boat races, he replied, 'What river?' Osbert's childhood and schooldays showed an equally healthy lack of aptitude or enthusiasm for games. He admitted to croquet as an exception, and in his family he had the reputation of being a wily, ruthless and unscrupulous player. John Piper remembers him as an enthusiastic if erratic tennis-player. I saw him play a game of table tennis (in his seventies, and in far from the best of health) which suggested that in earlier and more agile days he may well have been quite a crafty player. His general attitude to games could be deduced from his remark that all of them, from bridge to cricket, were improved by a little light conversation.

When it came to his costume, Osbert did not quite go in for dandyism on the scale of Beau Brummell – who had two glove-makers, one for the thumbs, the other for the rest of the hand – but his suits were always hand-made. The firm entrusted with this high-precision work was always Thresher & Glenny. While fastidious in his choice of clothes and the way in which he wore them, Osbert never took much care of them when they were not in active and public use. At the end of the day they would be left scattered all over the house in a trail leading to his bedroom on the assumption (correct in practice) that the womenfolk of the household would gather them up.

On 23 June 1963, an article appeared in the *Observer* as part of a series called 'My Clothes and I'. The subject of sartorial scrutiny that day was Osbert Lancaster and the scrutineer was Anne Scott-James. The subject and writer had known each other well for some time. 'One icy day last March,' it begins,

Mr Osbert Lancaster tottered to his desk at the *Daily Express* to record the daily thoughts of Lady Littlehampton, but before he could get pen to paper, he slumped exhausted to the floor. He was wearing his father-in-law's overcoat, made about 1900, of heavy black cloth lined with sealskin and collared in astrakhan. The weight, just supportable in a carriage, had proved too great for the 200-yard walk from the No. 11 bus-stop to the office.

Not all Mr Lancaster's clothes go back so far, but his style is deeply traditional. He says that most people are fascinated by the period which lies just beyond their memory, and 'such glittering survivors of *La Belle Epoque* as came my way when young left a deep impression'.

His exquisitely cut suits, says Anne Scott-James, 'have the faintly horsy flavour which has distinguished the English gentleman throughout the centuries (checked cloth, hacking vents, and so on). It is revealed in his evening clothes; he has worn velvet smoking-jackets with quilted lapels for 30 years and chooses pleated evening shirts. But it appears most strongly in the accessories.' By these she means the hats (especially soft black ones), the walking-stick or umbrella, and the carnation.

The old-fashioned shoes had rounded toes, which she suggested were almost stubby. 'On the contrary,' he replied, 'this pair is tremendously pointed by my standards. As pointed as a gentleman can go.'

An important influence on Osbert's wardrobe was reaction against his clothes at school.

> I wear everything that I was not allowed to wear at Charterhouse. We were not allowed jackets with vents, shirts with attached collars, or less than three buttons to a jacket until one was a monitor. As soon as I left school, I had all my suits made with two-button jackets, and I stick to them today, with only one done up, of course. I claim to have set the fashion for shirts with attached collars, which is now universal. My shirtmaker was appalled. I discarded forever the vests insisted on by my mother and the boots which she said were so good for my ankles. And I grew a moustache. It was a compensation for something or other, but don't ask me what.

Osbert claimed that he had set a number of fashions:

> I have worn pink shirts since I was at Oxford, and I started the revival of smoking-jackets. And I was one of the first to wear white dinner-jackets. By the way, I like dinner-jackets for dinner-parties. I can't see the point of saying 'Don't dress, just put on a dark suit.' If you are going to change, you might as well do it properly.

The comments not only tell us plenty about Osbert's class, background, social circle and finances, but also show him to have been a stalwart survivor from the time when the first article in the English code was the prime importance of dressing for dinner even in the jungle (or, in Conrad's novels, especially in the jungle).

He also listed some of his dislikes:

> I cannot bear brown suits. I dislike mutton dressed as lamb. All those middle-aged intellectuals we both know looking boyish in tight jeans. I hate central heating. I am always too hot; but now that it is here, I have had to give up waistcoats ... I hate uniformity, in dress or anything else, and I despise the Man in the Grey Flannel Suit. I take a keen interest in social distinctions, and regard the classless society as a fortunately unattainable ideal which would reduce our civilisation to a transatlantic level.

Osbert's fascination with clothes can also be seen in the clothes worn by the characters in the pocket cartoons, and in the wonderful costume designs he did for the stage, historically meticulous and aesthetically ravishing.

He may have disliked uniformity but he certainly didn't dislike uniforms. He loved them, and was upset when they were not worn. Bricklayers should look like bricklayers, bankers like bankers. In *All Done from Memory* (1953) he wrote that:

> even so late as twenty years ago one was fairly safe in assuming that any bearded figure in corduroys reading the *New Statesman* was at very least a photographer or a museum official, whereas now he is just as likely to be a chartered accountant or a dry-salter. In a world where only Guards officers and bookmakers still maintain a sartorial standard, the social ideals of Murger are everywhere triumphant and even ordained ministers of the Established Church do not hesitate to advertise their broad-mindedness with soft collars and grey flannel 'bags'.

Thirty-five years later grey flannel bags are already historic, and I suspect that few bookmakers still maintain sartorial standards with loud check suits and brown bowler hats. This post-war decline was distressing for Osbert. In 1963 he made a speech at the Midsummer Banquet at the Mansion House. In proposing the toast of the Lord Mayor of London and Lady Mayoress he made some scathing remarks about the buildings going up in the City (many of the perpetrators were doubtless in the audience) and about the urban landscape being 'red in tooth and Clore'; then he changed in midstream to another hobby-horse. Cartoonists, he said, were finding life difficult

> owing to a growing deplorable reluctance on the part of those who should know better to dress in the way they are intended to dress. The stockbrokers who still wear silk hats can now be numbered on the fingers. Bishops of the established church are all too frequently seen without their gaiters and in some cases openly advocate abandonment of the dog-collar . . .

The next decade must have been full of anguish for Osbert. During that neophiliac period the bowler hat disappeared almost entirely. Suits and even ties were swept away in a flood of blue jeans and clothes which may have been sportive but did not derive from field sports. Not that this can really have made life so hard for the cartoonist who delighted in recording every tiny charge. As Anne Scott-James has said, the clothes of the Littlehamptons were as up to the minute as their opinions: 'Maudie's clothes are so up-to-date that they put even *Vogue* to shame.'

If we look at the pocket cartoons in the year of the Mansion House speech, we see patterned seams on the stockings. In 1963 there are

'Papa!!!' (23.6.64)

'But, mummy darling, it's me! Your daughter!! Jennifer!!!' (23.10.65)

girls in floppy jumpers, high heels and black stockings; hem-lines are moving up, but dons are still wearing gowns and mortar-boards. In 1964 stockings are patterned all over, girls' boots have high heels, and skirts are now above the knee; yet Willy is still wearing a bowler hat and the Bishop is in gaiters. The same year sees the topless swimsuit: beach scene with topless girl and Willy, facing away, bottomless. In the caption the young girl is saying in shocked tones, 'Papa!!!'

In 1965 a girl is outside a shop called Gear. She is wrapped in a strange scarf and has an even stranger peaked cap on her head; these garments conceal her almost completely. She is saying to Maudie, who has been wearing glasses for some time now, 'But, mummy darling, it's me! Your daughter!! Jennifer!!!'

By 1966 the skirts are so mini that Maudie at the races is saying to her daughter, 'Tell me, dear child, which particular horse did you put your skirt on?' In the same year Willy is wearing a striped shirt, we see bunny girls, and a girl borrowing a hairpin from her long-haired boyfriend. The next year skirts are so short that a Harley Street doctor looking out of his window comments, 'You mark my

'Tell me, dear child, which particular horse did you put your skirt on?' (16.6.66)

'You mark my words, Matron – it'll be cystitis that keeps the old pot boiling this winter!' (22.12.67)

words, Matron – it'll be cystitis that keeps the old pot boiling this winter.'

In any one year Osbert would not only produce a cartoon virtually every day but he would also publish at least one book, illustrate several others, perhaps hold an exhibition of paintings, give numerous lectures, broadcasts and after-dinner speeches (invariably witty, and often polemical, especially when on the subject of modern architecture, town-planning or property development), he would design sets and costumes for the stage, and fire off trenchant letters to *The Times* on subjects that ranged from Greek politics and architectural outrages to street music in towns or straw-burning in the country. He would also fit in at least one substantial trip abroad. And, of course, he continued to lead a highly gregarious social life.

Though he was proud of his Norfolk roots Osbert was above all a Londoner. He was born in London, spent most of his life in London and died in London, only about three miles from his birthplace. He loved the country, but it was with a Londoner's love. The country was for weekends: London was for living in.

He was, indeed, not only urbane but also urban. He travelled much and widely, at home and abroad, but nowhere other than London could possibly have been the point of departure and return. To the west lay Berkshire and Oxfordshire, in which counties he spent cumulatively many years. To the east and south-east was abroad – France, Italy, Greece and all the way on to Byzantium and the Nile. London was the centre.

Johnson said that the full tide of human experience was to be found at Charing Cross. Had Osbert demurred it would only have been to make a slight geographical extension to take in a London that was much bigger than it was in Johnson's time. To the west were Notting Hill, Kensington, Belgravia and Chelsea, in all of which Osbert lived at various times: it would be hard to imagine his ever having lived in, say, Hampstead (full of *New Statesman* readers and writers), let alone south of the river.

Proceeding eastwards he would come to Albemarle Street, where he could drop off some drawings at the office of his friend and publisher Jock Murray. Then on to clubland: Brooks's, Pratt's, the Beefsteak and (near to Charing Cross) the Garrick, a convenient staging-post before sauntering on to the Foreign Office in Whitehall, or the *Express* in Fleet Street.

Finally, heading further eastwards into the City, he might visit his tailor. Also here were the Worshipful Companies of this, that and the other, whose large dinners he frequently attended, and to whose work in the fields of education and charity he contributed year after year. He was even at one time Master of the Worshipful Company of Carpenters.

London met his need for company and socializing, and at the same time provided the constant flow of well-informed gossip and stimulating discussion which was essential fuel for the pocket cartoons. He seems to have known everyone.[1]

On 4 September 1946 James Lees-Milne records meeting Osbert (in *Caves of Ice*): 'He was rather grey, and pustular. Full of gossip about our surviving friends.' Four days later: 'Dined with the Lancasters. Drank whisky *and* red wine – a mistake. We ate in their kitchen. Karen is so good-hearted and Osbert very amusing and invigorating. Speaking of John Summerson's triplets he said they would of course always be known as "the Georgian Group".'

Osbert's upper-class social circle was not just that of the great, the good, the famous, the powerful and the aristocratic. It included royalty too. Harold Nicolson writes in his diary (28 May 1947): 'I go to Sybil's [Lady Colefax]. I come into the room to find Osbert Lancaster there and a young man with his back to the window. He says, "Not recognise an old friend?" It is the Duke of Windsor.' In November 1958 the Court Report includes the name of Mr Osbert Lancaster at the Queen's Dinner Party along with such other guests as the Duchess of Kent, the general manager of Reuter's, an ex-Governor of Hong Kong and the Astronomer Royal.

Not long after Osbert returned from Greece it became apparent that there weren't enough hours in the day to spend three of them commuting between Paddington and Henley in addition to those spent on his multifarious social and professional activities. Accordingly he took what he called 'a characterless little modern flat' in Chelsea, and spent weekends at Henley.

He may not have been very practical in day-to-day domestic matters, but he was always determinedly well organized and self-disciplined where his work was concerned. Over the years the London weekday routine developed into something of a ritual. It

[1] See Appendix C.

would start fairly late, about nine, with the newspapers (*Times* and *Daily Express*), a leisurely bath, a breakfast of coffee, toast and sometimes a boiled egg. His mood at this time of day was usually one of gloom; he glumly contemplated the news and thought of the horrors that the day had in store for him. Then he would start work, still wearing a dressing-gown. His dressing-gowns had been acquired in the Middle East and were elaborately decorated. Since he never allowed them to be cleaned, and since he drew and painted in them, they were filthy, yet they retained sufficient exotic gorgeousness for him to be known in the household at that time of day as the Pasha.

In this garb he worked all morning. When writing he would do a steady thousand words a day. He wrote fluently, especially when it was a speech that he was preparing, but the activity was accompanied by a good deal of huffing and puffing. By contrast, drawing or painting instantly dispelled any residual breakfast gloom, and he always appeared happy and relaxed. He worked with remarkable speed and certainty, standing at his desk in his shabby Eastern gown, with – says Anne Lancaster – 'a beatific smile on his Roman Emperor's face'. She would take him a cup of coffee, which as often as not he would leave untouched. The telephone would ring and he would be too absorbed to answer it. Only when around noon she suggested it might be time for a dry martini would he show that he might be ready for a break.

These mornings at home resulted in a quantity of books, articles, journalism, book reviews, speeches, illustrations and set designs which, apart from being of a consistently high quality, on their own constitute a more than respectable output in terms of quantity. However, the day's work had only begun.

The noon martini (or gin and French, as he always called it) accompanied the dandy's important task of getting dressed: striped shirt, a striking tie (often a bow-tie), immaculate suit, carnation in buttonhole, hat with the brim turned up all round and set slightly to the back of the head.

Thus attired, he was ready to go out and face the world, for unless there were guests, lunch was never at home. Nor was it in a restaurant. He disliked restaurants and loved clubs. 'A club is cosier and friendlier,' he said, 'though one may not love all one's fellow members equally.'

Osbert enjoyed good food, which London clubs are not famous

for providing, though their wines may be excellent. He was prepared to forgo the pleasure of eating well at lunchtime because he so much appreciated club atmosphere and conversation. Afterwards, he would take his only form of exercise, which was the walk to Fleet Street (or possibly to a taxi). He would arrive at the bleak, black *Express* building at around four o'clock.

He never had his own room at the *Express*, preferring to work at a desk among the hustle and bustle, the coming and going, the ringing of telephones and clacking of typewriters of the feature department's general office. And after the all-male company of lunchtime clubland, he loved to have pretty girls around him.

In the post-war years the *Express* was at its journalistic peak. The personnel changed over the years but Osbert's colleagues at various times would have included Anne Scott-James, Sefton Delmer, Leonard Mosely, Drusilla Beyfus, René MacColl, Anne Edwards, Eve Perrick, Denis Pitts, Herbert Kretzmer, Bernard Levin, Michael Parkinson, Nancy Banks-Smith, Sally Vincent, George Gale, Godfrey Smith, Mary Collins – the list could easily be extended.

George Malcolm Thomson says that Osbert treated the *Express* office like a playground. He certainly didn't think of it as an office. When, as he frequently did, he enquired 'What news at the office?' he did not mean the *Express* but the Foreign Office.

On his arrival he would light a Turkish cigarette and retail whatever good stories he had picked up during the day. His appetite for gossip was insatiable and he would quiz all and sundry about what he always called '*local* news'. At the *Express* this meant gossip about the latest state of play in the power struggles, expense accounts and amorous fusions and fissions that are the life-blood of a great national newspaper. As he chatted away he would at the same time be browsing through the evening papers and those dailies he had not already perused.

Like many people who have never had to worry unduly about money, Osbert was parsimonious, not to say tight-fisted. He would save money by making his telephone calls and posting his letters from the *Express* rather than from home. And the letters were written on *Express* paper with a Rupert Bear heading that he had somehow acquired.

When a colleague was leaving there would be the customary whip-round for a present. Osbert always declined to contribute, claiming that he didn't know the individual concerned. The story that, when the editor retired, Osbert claimed not to know Arthur Christiansen is probably apocryphal.

He was notorious for sharing taxis and choosing a route by which his destination came before that of his companion. On arrival he never seemed to have any cash on him. He was notorious for not buying drinks and it was always the good-looking girls in the office who bought him cups of tea.

But his meanness only applied to small matters. In others he was enormously generous. He was always giving away drawings and books, and he was prodigal with his time and his company.

After the editorships of Christiansen and Edward Pickering came that of Robert Edwards, who was not Osbert's cup of tea. Bob Edwards stamped his mark on the *Express* with a night of long knives, one of the victims of which was Denis Pitts, who remembers with gratitude and affection that Osbert publicly gave him a bottle of Teacher's whisky.

Drusilla Beyfus thought that the distractions and errand-running were a small price to pay in return for the gossip and anecdotes, the jokes and laughter. At that time she was twenty-one, and had only recently been promoted from secretary to features writer. She would agonize for hours over a few lines of a picture caption or write a first sentence over and over again. In the circumstances she was understandably awed by Osbert's relaxed attitude and the apparently miraculous speed with which he worked, and dazzled by his worldliness:

> He had lots of lives – opera, ballet, architecture, literature, the Foreign Office. He would come in like a bird bearing interesting bits of gossip in his mouth. He made everything he was doing more important and more interesting than anything you were doing yourself. He made no concessions to whoever he was talking with, assuming they belonged to the same circle and shared the same acquaintances.

Just as the listener had to translate 'the office' into the Foreign Office, so did she or he have to supply to such first names as Nancy, Evelyn, John, Randolph, Tony, and Jock the surnames (respectively) Mitford, Waugh, Betjeman or Sparrow, Churchill, Powell and Murray.

He was not showing off, nor was he being condescending. On the contrary, Osbert's assumption that whoever he was talking with was also on first-name terms with these celebrated figures was

177

always immensely flattering. He dropped names wholesale, but invariably there was an anecdote or observation that provided full justification.

The clock would be ticking and still he wouldn't have drawn a line. Another Turkish cigarette. There was at one time another pocket cartoonist at the *Express*, infinitely less well known than Osbert, called Artie Jackson. Osbert tended to tease him by going to his desk to ask what was the subject of his cartoon that day. Artie was convinced that Osbert was trying to pinch his ideas. In order to conceal his drawing, Artie would sprawl across it, head down, and invariably say that the subject of his cartoon was the weather.

Osbert was usually reluctant to discuss the work of other cartoonists. Consequently there is no record of his opinions about Artie's jokes about the weather.

Both Nancy Banks-Smith and Sally Vincent remember Osbert scratching his head and saying, 'Oh God, give me a joke.' Still not a line, graphic or verbal, would be on paper. Time to potter down the corridor to the room of George Malcolm Thomson. 'Tell me something,' he would say as he entered. 'What's going on?' They would chat briefly about the day's news. After a while Osbert would say, 'You've been no good to me,' and stalk out. As far as Thomson can remember he only once succeeded in providing an idea for a pocket cartoon that was actually used. However, in his introduction to the collection *Signs of the Times* Osbert suggests that even one may have been an over-estimate, for he expresses thanks to 'George Malcolm Thomson for never failing to arouse the hope that he would one day prove a source of inspiration'. In fact Osbert had great admiration and affection for Thomson. He always referred to him as 'a saint'. Thomson's copy of Osbert's last book is inscribed 'For my old friend and ever-constant standby George, with much love, admiration and deep gratitude for his friendship and bracing company for many exhausting and apprehensive years! Love, Osbert.'

The feeling was mutual. 'Osbert was such fun, so witty,' Thomson says. 'The annoying thing at the *Express* was that he was not only the only one who could draw; he could also *write* better than anyone in the building. It didn't seem fair that anyone should be so talented. He was regarded with a respect that was almost awe.'

At last Osbert would sit down with his drawing materials, shoot

his cuffs and start drawing. Occasionally an idea for a cartoon would
have come to him during his morning bath, or over lunch, but
usually it emerged in that hour or two of wandering about the
Express. He never had a stock of drawings to fall back on in case
inspiration should fail. Some cartoonists and columnists live in a
state of perpetual dread that one day they will sit down in front of
that blank piece of paper and find they have an equally blank mind.
It wasn't like that for Osbert. Ideas were teeming the whole time: it
was a matter of selecting the best one. He did have a slight problem
in later years, which came from having done the job for such a long
time. This was the worrying thought of 'My God, did I make that
joke in 1939?'

Usually the cartoon was finished in half an hour. In the early days
he would produce half a dozen roughs, of which the editor would
choose one to be worked up into finished form. Later he simply did
one, without a preliminary rough. Drusilla Beyfus remembers him
once having a disagreement with the assistant editor, Percy Eland.
A newspaper report had appeared about someone breeding an
oven-ready wingless chicken. Osbert did a drawing of such a bird
saying 'Look, no hands'. Eland objected that chickens don't have
hands.

He got on much better with the editor himself: in the acknowledgements to *Signs of the Times* he thanks 'the long-suffering Arthur
Christiansen for loyal support and a toleration of personal vagaries
which would have driven many editors round the bend'.

Having finished the drawing he would give it a long look, tap his
fingers and say, 'That's it.' With a rather self-consciously jaunty
demeanour he would then take it to Christiansen, shortly emerging
from the editor's office looking much more relaxed.

By about half-past six he would be ready for a drink, perhaps at El
Vino's on the opposite side of Fleet Street. Then home – unless, as
was almost always the case, there was a private view, or a
publisher's cocktail party, or a City dinner (for which he would
dress in tails), or some such function. His conviviality and wit, his
ability to set the table in a roar, meant that he was invited
everywhere, and he accepted all invitations – except, of course,
those of Lord Beaverbrook.

When he had done his Friday cartoon (that is, for Saturday's
newspaper) there would be an atmosphere like school breaking up
for the weekend. Osbert would sing rather risqué French songs or

do equally risqué impressions of George Robey. Picking up the *Financial Times*, he would study the stocks and shares and say, 'Just to be safe I'm going to put my little bit in rubber.'

While he did his Edwardian music-hall turns, with Maurice Chevalier's 'Louise' thrown in for good measure, the laughter in the office attracted the attention of people in other departments who, passing by, would be astonished to find that the source of this universal and often ribald hilarity was someone they had assumed to be unapproachable.

One day he shuffled into the office and sat down with a great groan. 'My dear,' he said to Mary Collins, 'I've just been to see the quack and he's told me I'm not to smoke. I'm absolutely heartbroken.'

Mary Collins, herself a smoker, tactfully took to puffing in other parts of the building. Osbert soon noticed this and told her, 'For God's sake *smoke* and blow some in my direction.'

Osbert's ordeal lasted for about three fractious months. Then one fine day he appeared beaming, whistling, cigarette in hand. He was berated for backsliding. Not at all, he said. He'd been to the quack again and the quack had said that he was putting on so much weight that he was in danger of having a heart attack. He had been *told* to go back on the cigarettes.

Mary Collins remembers Osbert's Dickensian ability to cross social borders. With a prose style based on Gibbon he delighted in the vernacular. One day she said 'Cobblers' in a moment of exasperation, and Osbert immediately asked what it meant. She explained that it was Cockney rhyming slang for a rude word (which rhymes with cobblers' awls), and the next day he reported that he had used it to great effect at the Garrick.

'I adored him,' Mary Collins says. 'Everyone did. If he saw you were a bit down he'd say "What's up?" And you'd say you were fed up and he'd say "Don't be fed up. I'll sing you a little song."'

VIII

PEOPLE AND PLACES

I N his later years, when he was in poor health, Osbert could become querulous, but for the most part his friendships, once made, were made for good. Inevitably there were some exceptions: some of his relationships did go through ups and downs.

Cecil Beaton was a friend of the Harris family. His younger sister Baba was Karen's bridesmaid (and a close friend of Lady Violet Packenham, who married Anthony Powell). Osbert attended Beaton's fancy-dress parties and figured prominently in his spoof *My Royal Past*.

In 1941 the *Spectator* carried a review by Osbert of a book by Peter Quennell with photographs by Cecil Beaton. Osbert whimsically described Beaton as 'an elusive figure about whom too little is known but who occupied in relation to his age much the same position as did the Comte d'Orsay in the preceding century'.

That went down all right, but years later Osbert reviewed Volume Four of Beaton's diaries in a manner which the vain photographer considered to be spiky. Beaton attributed Osbert's attitude to the fact that he (Beaton) had received a knighthood before Osbert did. This absurd rationalization is more of a comment on Beaton than on the reviewer. A more likely explanation is that Beaton was aware that Lancaster's stage designs were superior to his own.

Beaton, whose need for adulation was boundless, seems to have been thoroughly confused in his attitude to Osbert. More than once Beaton quoted in his letters the pocket cartoon about Andy Warhol captioned 'Andy What-hole?', but in his diary he noted that Osbert Lancaster was 'the greatest bore in private life'.

It was a somewhat similar story with Evelyn Waugh, an even touchier cove. Osbert reviewed Waugh's *Rossetti* for *The Isis* at Oxford; they met first at Kolkhorst's salon, then later when Osbert was at the Slade. Waugh used to reproach Osbert for drawing carelessly. Osbert took the view that Waugh would rather have been a visual artist than a writer and that he envied the drawing ability of others, as was evidenced by his constantly pointing out their deficiencies. Waugh's letters are indeed full of derogatory remarks about Picasso and any other living artist of genius or talent who came to his attention. Osbert considered that Waugh's appreciation of art was nil: 'He *loathed* all modern art. [Long pause.] His handwriting was beautiful.'

Osbert's relations with Waugh were as fraught as those of everyone else who knew the splenetic novelist. In September 1943 Waugh wrote his wife a letter saying that he had dined at 'what should have been a very gay bachelor dinner in honour of Maurice Bowra, given by Osbert Lancaster, Freddie (Earl of Birkenhead) and John Betjeman being the other guests. But there was not enough to drink.' When Waugh's letters were posthumously published, Osbert was not at all pleased at this implied criticism. His version of the story was that he had been working at the Foreign Office all that day, and that the person entrusted with the job of buying the drinks for dinner had been none other than Evelyn Waugh.

In 1947 Waugh was the subject of one of Osbert's portraits in *Strand* magazine (edited by Macdonald Hastings, then husband of Anne Scott-James). 'Mr Evelyn Waugh reacting strongly to the century of the Common Man' shows a pop-eyed, apoplectic figure in bowler hat and striped suit, holding cigar and umbrella like offensive weapons, standing furiously on the steps of his club. In a letter to Betjeman Waugh wrote, 'O. Lancaster's sketch good in conception but poor in execution.' This was high praise from Waugh. At any rate he acquired the original in order (it was said) to frighten his children.

In a letter to Nancy Mitford, dated 10 August 1948, Waugh wrote that 'a boring neighbour' had asked him to find a celebrity to judge the village fête's beauty competition. 'I couldn't think who to ask so I got Osbert Lancaster whom I don't particularly cherish because I thought anyway his name is in the *Daily Express* every day.' He said that the problem was that people who were famous in London, Paris and New York were unheard of in Stinchcombe. It turned out that no one in Stinchcombe had heard of Osbert either. It poured with rain, Waugh took to his bed, 'and poor Laura was left with O.L. for a week-end. Goodness how sad.'

Waugh was more complimentary in another letter he wrote to Nancy Mitford in 1950. He had met Osbert at Portofino where he was staying with Robert Graves's daughter Jenny Nicholson, who also had Osbert staying with her: 'Well say what you will I don't mind him a bit, in fact rather like him.'

On the same day, in a letter to his wife, Waugh went yet further in his compliments, not only recording an example of Osbert's repartee but actually commending it. In order to be understood, the story needs to be glossed with the information that Elizabeth Russell (von Arnim) had published in 1922 a novel set at the Castello Brown called *The Enchanted April*, and that A. E. W. Mason had written a hugely popular but now forgotten novel called *At the Villa Rose*. Waugh wrote to his wife:

> A damn fool English woman (protestant and middle-class) has taken the Castello Brown & thinks herself lady of the manor and goes round saying how important it is to keep the votive plaques out of the church. Well you can imagine the snubs she collects. She is trying very hard and unsuccessfully to eradicate the name 'Brown'. She said to Osbert Lancaster: 'I expect you know the wonderful novel that was written about this castle?' 'Do you mean A. E. W. Mason's *At the Villa Brown*?' Quick.

It was at around this time that Osbert went with Waugh to visit Max Beerbohm at Rapallo. The conversation turned to the subject of the way in which some caricaturists declined as they grew older. Beerbohm said it was impossible to be funny about your contemporaries after you were forty because you no longer respected anyone after that age, and therefore the whole point was gone. 'I remember,' Osbert said, 'Evelyn was frightfully pleased and turned to me and said, "How much longer does that give you, Osbert?" And then Max said, "You know, Mr Waugh, exactly the same happens to writers. Look at poor Aldous." I felt very grateful for that observation.'

The real row with Waugh came in 1950 over Waugh's book *Helena*. The author sent Osbert a privately printed copy, and the next time they met Osbert thanked him. Waugh told him that verbal thanks were no good: what was wanted was a proper letter of appreciation. 'Right,' Osbert replied, 'you'll get it.' He wrote to Waugh that it was an admirable book but that it seemed to be missing a middle; it started with Helena as a young girl, and ended with her as an old woman. Waugh seemed to have left out the change of life, the transition; it wasn't scant, it was missing. After this letter, he recalled, 'I wasn't spoken to afterwards. The row was deeply felt.'

*　　*　　*

Osbert's relationship with Max, by contrast, was always cordial. Osbert remembered that Max's conversations were 'extraordinarily elaborate', as well as always coming back sooner or later to Charterhouse.

In 1952 Osbert contributed to a celebratory volume for Max's eightieth birthday a number of drawings illustrating *Zuleika Dobson*. This was an enterprise that cannot have been without an element of risk. Certainly Osbert was better qualified than most for the task, but Max was himself a distinguished illustrator. There might have been those who thought that the text which he had felt to be self-sufficient and had left without illustrations should be allowed to remain in that state in which the mind's eye provides its own images of the haughty features of the Duke of Dorset (pronounced like the name of one of the greatest of dandies, D'Orsay) and the stupefying beauty of Zuleika herself. Are not such things best left to the imagination?

Evidently Max himself had thought so when he published the work. In fact he did illustrate *Zuleika*, though only for his own private purposes. It says something about him, and his regard for Osbert, that he did not reveal this fact. (The Folio Society published an edition of *Zuleika Dobson* with eight watercolours by Max Beerbohm in 1966.)

Osbert stepped boldly in and produced the *Zuleika* drawings for the eightieth-birthday volume. Any worries he might have had about Max's reaction to the drawings would have been instantly dispelled by a letter to him from Villino Chiaro, Rapallo, dated October 1952. It starts thus:

My dear Osbert Lancaster,
First of all, I want to tell you how immensely amused and pleased I have been by your monumental design in my great Birthday Album. And the more I look at it, the more do I marvel at the flawless skill of the draughtsmanship. . . .

These drawings led to a series of twelve *Zuleika* pictures for the ballroom of the Randolph Hotel in Oxford. Osbert had a collaborator on this project; he worked for two years with Judyth Simmonds, an ex-Ruskin student in her early twenties.

This time Max was more closely involved, albeit at a distance. He writes from Rapallo – it's 'Dear Osbert' now – 'Greatly delighted by the two photographs that you have sent to me'. He says that he hasn't 'a shade of a suggestion' to make, and then suggests that 'Mme. Sand might look a little more dominant, and M. Chopin a little less so. The other characters, the living ones, entirely tally with my preconceptions of them.' Then in a postscript he has another look at the scene in the Broad and wonders 'whether the horses shouldn't be going rather faster . . . whether you would agree with me that the left-hand fore-legs should be rather less perpendicular – in accordance to the flashing spokes of the landau's wheels?' A further 'benigglement' is that the stripes of the Bullingdon ribbon of blue and white should be horizontal rather than vertical.

The end result shows the extent to which Osbert did or did not take notice of these words. Anyway Max was delighted and the press gave the pictures a uniform welcome.

Apart from comic strips, narrative series of paintings are not all that common. The best known are Hogarth's, especially *Marriage à la mode* and *The Rake's Progress*. The Victorians usually tried to cram the whole story into one picture (*When did you last see your father?*, *The Last of England* and so on) or at most have a contrasting pair of Before and After pictures. The *Zuleika* series is one of very few such exercises in this century and, consisting as it does of no fewer than twelve paintings, is on a bigger scale than Hogarth's. Not only are the pictures wonderfully entertaining, brilliantly observed and a joy to look at, but they are also among the few surviving works of Osbert's in this genre. The early murals at Blandford Forum have been covered up. It is not easy for the general public to gain access to the Shell mural. Most of the stage sets survive only in the form of working sketches and photographs.

Even the Randolph series is not on public display, but it is usually possible for the visitor to see them on request.

The series had a further life as the basis for the sets of the stage version of *Zuleika* (Saville Theatre, 1957), and was also used to illustrate the Shakespeare Head Press's edition of *Zuleika Dobson*, 1975, with a foreword by Osbert Lancaster.

The Carthusian connection with the line of stylish cartoonist–caricaturist–social commentator artists and writers from Thackeray to Max Beerbohm was of immense importance to Osbert. *Vanity Fair* always remained his favourite novel. The influence of Max Beerbohm was apparent not only in his writing and drawing but also in his temperament, style, attitudes and even physical appearance. 'A demure, dandified figure, with a big round head and heavy-lidded

The influence of Max Beerbohm was apparent

protuberant eyes, amused by contemplating the world and from time to time letting fall a whimsical comment on it.' The description is Lord David Cecil's of Max Beerbohm, but it would fit Osbert pretty well, as do other of Lord David's comments on Max:

> His talk, for all its ease, is still less indiscreet; his art is designedly an art of the surface, disclosing little of its author's deeper feelings. Nor do the Edwardian social chronicles in which he makes a figure help us to elucidate him. They are full of anecdotes about his wit, his dress, his demeanour. But they say nothing to reveal the inner man, they never catch him making a confession or giving himself away ... At once reserved and extrovert, he shrank from confession and was bored by self-analysis. He never could understand, he said, how anyone managed to keep a diary: his private letters – with rare exceptions – are as discreet as his essays. The result of this is that the biographer, though he may permit himself to guess a little, can never be quite sure that he has found the key to his hero's mystery. Max contains for posterity a puzzle. Luckily the puzzle is a delightful one and a man of genius as well.[1]

Both Max and Osbert followed Charterhouse with Oxford, where their academic performances were equally undistinguished. Both were cartoonists, caricaturists and stylish writers. Both were generally known by their first names *tout court*. Both were dandies, both brilliant talkers and reluctant letter-writers, both very reticent about their inner selves. Osbert's autobiographies look outward, to the past and the future, but hardly inward at all. They belong with Gibbon rather than with the self-analytical autobiographies of Wordsworth, John Stuart Mill or Montaigne, or in his own time those of Evelyn Waugh or Graham Greene.

The caricatures that Osbert did for the *Strand* magazine after the war are explicitly in the Beerbohm style, as can be seen from such titles as 'Mr. John Betjeman awaiting inspiration and the 4.47 from Didcot', 'Mr. John Piper enjoying his usual luck with the weather', and 'Mr. Kingsley Martin, looking on the bright side'.

Another Beerbohmian work (now belonging to Anthony Powell) is 'A rough sketch for a gigantic mural to be placed in the coffee-room at White's by public subscription celebrating the theme "[Cyril] Connolly at Conossa"'. Evelyn Waugh, Pope Pius XII, Father D'Arcy, a Vatican official and a Swiss guard are in attendance in this improbable scheme for a work which was, alas, never realized.

---

[1] David Cecil, *Max: Sir Max Beerbohm*.

When I asked John Betjeman if he thought Osbert had consciously modelled himself on Max Beerbohm, he replied, 'Yes, and very wise of him.' To the same question Osbert himself replied, 'No, but I was a great admirer.'

Although he tended to avoid correspondence when it was a chore, Osbert took a great deal of trouble over letters to his friends, often adding illustrations. He also kept up an intense and witty exchange of postcards with John Betjeman, Jock Murray, Anthony and Violet Powell, and John Piper.

Osbert had two other correspondents who are worthy of mention. Shortly after the war he crossed the Atlantic on the SS *Caronia* in order to investigate American architecture. A fellow-traveller on the liner was on his way to Washington to take up a job at the British Embassy. Osbert took the man on one side to give him some kindly advice. He warned him that one of his colleagues would be a man called Guy Burgess and that Burgess was not *reliable*. The man he was talking to th-th-thanked Osbert for the warning. His name was Kim Philby. [1]

While having 'no idea what he was up to', Osbert liked Philby and kept up with him. From internal evidence it is possible to deduce that the following letter was written in 1955 when Philby was acting First Secretary in the Embassy in Turkey; he was also Head of Section in the Secret Intelligence Service.

It concerns what seems to be a pretty innocent subject, namely ecclesiastical architecture, but so ingrained was Philby's deviousness that he was unable to discuss even this straightforward matter without weaving an intricate web of deceit.

Characteristically, he gives no address at the top of his letter, which runs as follows:

Dec. 29

My dear Osbert,

Many thanks for your note enclosing the letter from the Armenian lady. It is indeed gratifying to receive notice from such a distinguished quarter.

[1] In *My Silent War* Kim Philby writes: 'I sailed on the SS *Caronia* towards the end of September. I had a memorable send-off. The first thing I saw on the foggy platform at Waterloo was an enormous pair of moustaches and behind them the head of Osbert Lancaster, an apparition which assured me of good company on the voyage.' He does not, of course, mention Osbert's warning.

I shall do my best with the enquiries regarding other Armenian churches in Eastern Turkey, but it is now the close season for travel, and I shall myself be back in England for a few weeks in January. So answers will have to wait until late in summer, unless I can find another enthusiast who has recently visited the sites.

As regards the very important question whether it can be mentioned that my photographs were taken recently, I think it can safely be said that the photographs were taken since the end of the war, but I would not be particularly keen to be much more precise than that. And, for obvious reasons (one of the most important being my desire to revisit those areas!), no hint should appear that they were taken by a foreigner. If it could be left to the imagination of the reader to infer that the photographer was a Turkish national, it would save my sponsors possible embarrassment, as well as disarm what might otherwise be ugly suspicion on the left bank of the Arpa Cay.

Forgive this hurried note, written half way between Xmas and New Year with all that that implies. Many thanks, incidentally, for your three men and the dog.

Yours,
KIM

The handwritten postscript reads, 'Incidentally, in case the lady is an ardent Armenian nationalist, I wonder whether she could refrain from voicing anti-Turkish views in her article.'

Who, one wonders, were Philby's 'sponsors'? While he was in Tehran, Philby apparently displayed on the wall of his office a photograph which anyone in the know would be able to work out was taken from the Soviet side of the border. Perhaps this was one of the photographs mentioned in the letter to Osbert.

They are also referred to in a letter to Osbert from Guy Burgess. Reversing Philby's procedure he gives his Moscow address but gives as the date 'Washing Day', the meaning of which (he explains) can be found in Purcell's *Life of Manning*. (Did these spies ever write *anything* that wasn't in some sort of code?) The letter must have been written between 1960 and 1962 because that is the period during which Frank Roberts (who is mentioned in the letter) was the Ambassador.

Evidently Burgess had written to Osbert asking for some cartoons. Osbert had replied with a chatty, gossipy letter, saying the cartoons were on their way. Burgess's thank-you letter is four closely written pages long. It is obvious that Burgess had time on his hands, for he wanders from Victorian theology to memories of the Foreign Office and country weekends in England.

He was clearly home-sick, though still clever, witty and mischievous. Naturally, he writes,

> I'm not, prima facie, persona grata *with* the Embassy, but the news spreads. It's not only Frank [Roberts] – by no means – his own marked personal charm and consideration for his colleagues is, if possible, exceeded by his Levantine Ambassadress's. She is now said to have banned all dogs but her own from exercise in the Embassy garden. I foresee a similar end to Her Dog to that which overtook Sir Robert Craigie's and his wife's on their return in wartime from Tokyo. *Murdered*, you remember, by the Embassy Staff on the boat, who, rightly, I think, resented reservation of the Boat Deck for Sir Robert, his wife, and DOG. The others remained under hatches. The murder was disguised as suicide by a clever arrangement which I am trying to circulate to the staff here (who I don't meet).

He doesn't say whether or not he meets Philby, but one revealing paragraph reads:

> Will you send me a bill for yr. cartoons when they come. I have plenty of pounds in England. Alternatively is there anything you'd like from here. Architectural books are not v. good – tho' for the study of Stalinist taste the photographs of Sanatoria need some beating. I seem to remember that you were grateful for and interested in photos of Churches at ANI (?) which Kim sent you when I was staying with him in Istanbul.

Osbert's trips abroad often combined business and pleasure. There were, for example, visits to Sweden, Germany and Bulgaria in connection with his stage sets. The updating of *Here, of All Places* took him to the United States. He gave lectures on guided tours of Italy and Greece.

In 1969 he visited France for *Queen*. Patrick Lichfield took the photographs, Anne Scott-James wrote the words and Osbert did the drawings. In Arles he was seated at his work when a small boy went by and was heard to remark, *'Tout de même, je crois qu'il a du talent.'*

He visited Malta to illustrate Nigel Dennis's book about the island; and for his own book *Sailing to Byzantium*, which is by way of being a sequel to *Classical Landscape with Figures*, he made trips to Yugoslavia, Italy, Bulgaria, France and Greece. Wherever he went he drew and painted, and explored architecture tirelessly, for the pleasure it gave him and, as often as not, to pick up material for his next book.

On these foreign trips he usually stayed with friends, or in rented houses, or whenever possible in the British Embassy (in Lisbon, Athens and Cairo in particular). He sailed up the Seine and around the Mediterranean on Lord Camrose's yacht. One holiday he hired a boat with Alan and Lucy Moorehead, and there were many visits to the Mooreheads' home at Porto Ercole, and to Venice, Florence and

'Tout de même, je crois qu'il a du talent'

Rome. A package coach tour of the Abruzzi doesn't sound at all his style but, surprisingly, he took one and enjoyed it enormously.

He set a cracking pace on his travels. Freya Stark, no lazy-bones herself, wrote in a letter of 1947, 'We reached Rome two days ago . . . Osbert has seen 85 churches since his arrival . . . Osbert is very tough.'

Cara Lancaster remembers a holiday in France in 1950. She had just taken her O-level exams but term had not ended when her

191

father turned up at her boarding-school completely out of the blue. Most children find their parents acutely embarrassing when they visit school, but Osbert's appearance on this occasion was unexpected in more than one sense. He was wearing a white linen jacket with aggressively bold buttons, a pink shirt, a bow tie and co-respondent shoes. This attire was clearly in flagrant breach of the First Rule for Visiting Parents, which is that they should be dressed as conventionally and inconspicuously as possible.

Osbert promptly announced to the headmistress that he had come to take Cara away. Cara and the headmistress were equally startled since it was the first that either of them had heard about it. 'What about her trunk?' was all the headmistress could think of to say. 'I don't mind a bit about Cara's trunk,' he replied. 'I'm taking her on a cultural tour of France.' Thus sweeping aside trivial objections, take her away he did. He explained to her that he had rented a house – nay, a windmill – in the South of France for the summer, at Sanary-sur-mer, a charming little fishing village a few miles from Toulon. Osbert and Cara were going to spend a fortnight driving through France, some of the way with Jock Murray, and then they would be meeting Karen and William, who would be flying out after William's Eton term ended. (Eton would doubtless have put up a stouter resistance than Cara's school to the idea of a pupil being untimely ripped from the establishment.)

Osbert, who was very much in charge of the expedition, laid down his broad strategy for the cultural tour of France. It would not be possible, he declared, to see and do all the things they wanted. Therefore, the sensible thing would be to concentrate on one or two things and do them properly. He had already decided what these cultural objects would be: Romanesque churches and food.

For much of the time Osbert drove. That simple sentence could strike terror into the breasts of those who had shared the experience. There were many things that Osbert could do supremely well. There were some, such as playing the flute, on which opinion was divided. When it came to driving, however, the consensus was solid. 'He was the worst driver in the world,' his daughter states disloyally but truthfully. Behind the wheel he not only looked like Mr Toad. He drove like Mr Toad.

One of his personal rules of driving was that if he put out his indicator then there was no need to look in the mirror before moving into the middle of the road. This was a sufficiently hazardous

The Lancaster family in 1949

manœuvre in England, but it was far more so in France where not only do a higher proportion of motorists take this uninhibited attitude to road-use but they also have a different highway code and drive on the wrong (that is to say, right) side of the road. The background music to their journey through France was the hooting protests of other drivers, causing Osbert's constant comment: 'Extraordinary bad manners. I mean, I *had* indicated.'

They spent one night in an excellent hotel in Cognac. The meal was first-rate and Cara was allowed a small glass of cognac before being sent to bed. Jock Murray and Osbert stayed up and had more than one small glass of the local drink. The next morning they wore the stunned expressions of those suffering from what in Cognac would be called a *gueule de bois*. During the morning drive there were many little stops for a drop of Pernod to make the men feel better. Whether or not frequent *petits verres de pastis* are an advisable antidote to a surfeit of cognac is a matter of opinion. Evidently Osbert was of the hair-of-the-dog school of thought.

Osbert remembered this Katzenjammer as the last really great

hangover he had. Although he was always a steady drinker (after all, the motto of the Littlehampton family was *'Mon Dieu, Ma Soif'*)[1] the Cognac incident is one of the rare occasions on which the effects were evident. An anonymous profile of him in the *New Statesman* in December 1961 (probably by Tom Driberg) said that a friend who knew Osbert extremely well (probably Tom Driberg again) had recently remarked that it was odd that 'though he likes going to parties and drinking a few glasses of wine, no one has ever, ever seen him even slightly drunk'.

So Jock Murray, Osbert and Cara made their hungover way south, with stops for Pernod, stops for Romanesque churches and frequent stops on behalf of the puncture-prone tyres. Osbert didn't know how to change a wheel and didn't intend to learn, but Cara soon mastered the art out of necessity.

Finally, they arrived at Sanary, which did not entirely live up to expectations. The charming little fishing village, like so many on the Côte d'Azur, had become a built-up tourist spot, and the quaint windmill was a pebble-dash concrete job of only vaguely windmill shape, alongside numerous others just the same. Then, when the

[1] It was originally *'Mon Dieu, Mon Soif'*. The howler was corrected in later editions.

time came for meeting Karen and William, Osbert had lost his
traveller's cheques, and the car had finally packed up altogether. He
arrived at the airport in a break-down truck. Karen was not best
pleased.

When travelling abroad Osbert would usually take with him large,
specially made, landscape-shaped sketchbooks (fourteen inches by
nine) bound in green, for use as travel journals. These vividly
convey his energy as a traveller, artist and writer. In the drawings
(far too finished to be called sketches) there are hardly any false
starts or pages torn out; likewise in the writing there are never
second thoughts, very rarely a word crossed out to substitute a
better one or to clean up the syntax.

The green books record a punishingly active rate of sightseeing
and social rounds. Every minute seems to have been packed. How,
one wonders, could he have found the time not only to do so much
but also to record the events of the day in words and pictures? Here
is an example from the Nile trip he took with Lucy and Alan
Moorehead in November–December 1960. He had not visited Egypt

195

since the end of the war and the first entry (11 November) finds:

> *Cairo.* Town much changed. Smell fainter, fewer beggars, no pashas. Sorry to see that the army have abandoned fez for beret. A marked change for the worse, as the beret does not, by and large, suit the Egyptian face. Skyscrapers everywhere, none very distinguished, some awful. Streets cleaner. Practically no camels. Very few women veiled. Children look much healthier and as a result even more tiresome. Germans all over the place; all the taxis Mercedes. Quantities of Americans, mostly middle-aged. Saw one elderly woman whom for a moment I thought was Prof. Goodhart *en travesti.* Hotel brand new, ten storeys, none of the atmosphere of the old Shepheard's. Décor lush but no worse, in fact possibly better, than comparable hotel in England.

The same day he visited the palace of Mahomet Ali, lunched at the Canadian Embassy and dined with the British Chargé, then after dinner went on to a desert nightclub with some Canadians. The account of all this was presumably written on 12 November, which is also the date of a full-page detailed drawing of Cairo seen from Shepheard's Hotel, with the Pyramids in the background, then the river with dhows and paddle-steamer, and palm trees and sky-scrapers in the foreground.

At one cocktail party he met a notable woman whom he found very beautiful, 'with the most splendid bosom I've seen in years'. She seemed to know his name but he failed to catch hers. They had a long talk. It was only afterwards that he was told by Lucy Moore-head that in the first place the lovely lady was the Queen of Jordan, and that in the second place his flies had been undone throughout.

Most people who have taken the trouble to travel from Kensing-ton to the Nile feel impelled to admire what they have come to see. Osbert had no such inhibitions. At Luxor on 21 November he saw three tombs:

each duller than the last . . . all incredibly bad. Same old themes on walls. Did the ancient Egyptians *never* feel any urge to experiment? When one thinks of the variety of Christian iconography – Fra Angelico, Van Eyck, El Greco all within the space of 300 years – seems almost incredible that for 3,000 years they could remain content with the same old formulae!

Karnak he enjoyed as landscape but found it:

> As architecture very qualified success. All these enormous columns ill-proportioned and far too close together; did they *never* realise how much they were over-compensating? That columns half the size would have done the work just as well? If architecture is the organisation of space the Egyptians never got beyond lower Shell . . . spectacular sunset and crescent moon rising over the sacred lake unbeatable in a romantic, Mid-Victorian water colour way.

Which is rather the way of his drawings in the journal at this point. In fact they sometimes look more like the work of Edward Lear than of Osbert Lancaster, and reflect a lack of sympathy, if not actual antipathy, towards the unfamiliar landscape and architecture. Still, there is almost always a distinctly Lancaster touch, usually a comic detail, a black-robed female figure with a large water-pot balanced precariously on her head, or public statues of moustached politicians wearing fezes.

He found his fellow-passengers a source of 'abiding delight'. Favourites were Mr and Mrs Bliss who, in spite of being aged eighty-four and eighty-six respectively, took some strenuous travelling in their stride. There was a good deal of walking and three-hour train journeys in 'hard-arsed' trains with the temperature in the nineties. They impressed him by climbing up the 300-foot ascent to Ibrim at half-past two in the afternoon under a grilling sun.

Mrs Bliss impressed Osbert still further by telling him that she had had the unenviable task of breaking the news of Kitchener's death to his devoted sister, Mr Bliss having been at that time Counsellor in the United States Embassy in Paris where Miss Kitchener happened to be. He was captivated by her remark that:

> she had always had very romantic feelings about Khartoum ever since reading about Gordon as a child. Suddenly realised she did not mean in books but in the newspapers – as a contemporary event! Feel it very odd thing to have gone up Nasser's Nile with someone who was reading the papers when Gordon was killed and was a grown woman at the time of Omdurman.

With all this sightseeing and travelling he still managed to continue writing and drawing, sometimes producing architectural drawings of remarkable detail considering such marginal notes as 'Drawn thro' field-glasses while steaming at 8 knots. V. difficult.'

And he was reading too. At Aswan, 'Finished Stravinsky's reminiscences – no false modesty about him but despite (or because of?) egomania fascinating reading; started on Diana's [Lady Diana Cooper's], an egomaniac of a different kind.' Even Stravinsky and Lady Diana Cooper's egos were to be dwarfed at Abou-Simbel which contained 'what must be the supreme expression of absorbed egocentricity. A relief in which Rameses as Pharaoh is making a sacrifice to himself as God.'

Abou-Simbel on 30 November roused something closer to enthusiasm. 'The reliefs on the whole well-preserved. Thought, for the first time in Egypt, one could possibly detect a faint hint of an individual personality.'

At the Sudanese frontier the travellers encountered guards with tribal scars on their cheeks. 'One knew a little English, very chatty. Alan [Moorehead] said to him, "Are you a corporal?" Indignant reply, "No, I am a Christian." '

On 5 December they reached Khartoum, and attended rather tedious cocktail parties and buffet suppers at the British Embassy and British Council. But even in those surroundings Osbert was able to pick up interesting information. A Sudanese professor of art told him that owing to strong Islamic objections to life classes he had to send his students sketching in the brothels.

The last day of the trip was spent bird-watching and visiting the zoo. 'Never realised before how very different African elephant is from Indian.' Characteristically the journal ends on an architectural note: 'The windows in the Anglican cathedral all triangular-headed Anglo-Saxon. Why?'

IX

SET BOOKS

DRAYNEFLETE CASTLE had been in the de Cowgumber family since the Conquest, but after the execution on Tower Hill of Sir Thomas de Cowgumber and his five brothers in 1593 the family was extinguished in the male line. The castle then passed by marriage into the Littlehampton family, but it was not until 1672 that a Lord Littlehampton (the 'Wicked Lord') actually left the draughty castle of Courantsdair and took up residence at Drayneflete.

Drayneflete Revealed (1949) brings together various themes from the earlier books and introduces new ones. It contains parodies of archaeology, social and architectural history, painting and poetry, all carried off with the erudition, elegance and wit that had by now become the hallmark of a Lancaster production.

One notable figure in the history of Drayneflete is Dr Palinurus, Bishop of Horizon and the Isles. Cyril Connolly, 'Palinurus' and editor of *Horizon*, was a recurrent butt of Osbert's, for reasons that are not clear. When asked if he had fallen out with Connolly Osbert replied rather huffily that he had never fallen in, but denied disliking him.

Whereas *Pelvis Bay* took the form of a local guide, *Drayneflete* is a local history. It starts (as history books should) with the mammoths and sabre-toothed tigers which once prowled 'through the tropical undergrowth where now stands Marks and Spencers'. Drayneflete has moved with the times every bit as much as Pelvis Bay.

The most recent representative of the family is also the best known, Maud, Countess of Littlehampton, who is mentioned in the preface as one of those without whose assistance the work could never have been brought to a successful conclusion. Another acknowledgement is to 'Mr John Piper for his advice on syntax'.

From early days Drayneflete was rich in literary associations. When the young Richard II visited Drayneflete he heard the first performance of the delightful 'Drayneflete Carol', reproduced in the book in heavy Gothic typeface:

> Alle littel childer syng
> Prayses to our younge Kyng
> Some syng sherpe and some syng flat
> Alma Mater Exeat.

> Alle engles in ye skie
> Maken loude melodie
> With sackbut, organ, pipe and drum
> Ad Terrorum Omnium.

> Ye poure beastes in ye stalle,
> Alack, they cannot syng at alle
> Ne cock ne henne of either sexe
> De Minimis Non Curat Lex.

Clearly Osbert's studies of Middle English and the Law had not been entirely in vain.

His achievements in other fields have overshadowed his reputation as a versifier. This is a pity, for he was an outstanding writer of light verse, and a parodist in the Beerbohm class. *Drayneflete* contains some of his best work in this vein. A few of the parodies are so deadly accurate that they could easily escape detection in any university English Department's Practical Criticism seminar on 1 April:

> Deep in some crystal pool th'enamoured trout
> Frolics and wantons up a lichened spout
> By which the stream, in many a sparkling rill,
> Is made by art to turn a water-mill.
>
> > Jeremy Tipple, *The Contemplative Shepherd*
> > (eighteenth century)

In 1927, Guillaume de Vere-Tipple published *Feux d'artifice*, which includes the remarkably T. S. Eliotic 'Aeneas on the Saxophone'.

> ... Delenda est Carthago!
> (ses bains de mer, ses plâges fleuries,
> And Dido on her lilo à sa proie attachée)
>   And shall we stroll along the front
> Chatting of this and that and listening to the band?

That Guillaume de Vere-Tipple could keep up with the times was shown in his next volume *the liftshaft* (Faber & Faber, 1937), published under the name of Bill Tipple.

crackup in barcelona

among the bleached skeletons of the olive-trees
stirs a bitter wind
and maxi my friend from the mariahilfer strasse
importunately questions a steely sky
his eyes are two holes made by a dirty finger
in the damp blotting paper of his face
the muscular tissues stretched tautly across the scaffolding of
     bone
are no longer responsive to the factory siren
and never again will the glandular secretions react
to the ragtime promptings of the palais-de-danse
and I am left balanced on capricorn
the knife-edge tropic between anxiety and regret
while the racing editions are sold at the gates of football
     grounds
and maxi lies on a bare catalan hillside
knocked off the tram by a fascist conductor
who misinterpreted a casual glance.

There is nothing in Auden, Isherwood, MacNeice or Spender that so completely sums up the era. The poem also makes clear that leftist objections to capitals are as strongly held in typography as in architecture.

Considering the variety and quantity of Osbert's creative work in other media it is perhaps not surprising that he did not write more verse. Since the following example was never published in hard covers, it is quoted here in full. The lines were written on the occasion of the wedding of Tom Driberg (the very idea of which is comic) to Mrs Ena Mary Binfield in 1954.

Ode on the Wedding of Thomas Driberg, Esq., M.P.

Hark! The joyous nuptial tune
Cleaves the jocund skies of June,
Triumphant anthems rend the air
All the way to Eaton Square.
In Pimlico the strains are heard
Of Palestrina and of Byrd,
And marshalled crowds in patience wait
The due arrival of the Great.

Within the Church a tight-packed throng
Hope the Service won't be long,
A hope that I at once surmised
Unlikely to be realised;
For all experience has taught
The Very High are seldom short.
Flanked by chattering M.P.s,
BETJEMAN's down upon his knees.

Come to kindle Hymen's torch,
Yet still lingering in the porch,
Aneurin BEVAN and his wife,
Pose, with easy grace, for *Life*.
Ushers with extremist views
Show the Leftists to their pews,
But I, reactionary and grand,
Although on time, am left to stand.

Te laudamus Domine,
Chiefly in the key of A,
From CUDLIPP comes an angry belch,
For he can only sing in Welsh.
But look, they turn on every side
To see the coming of the bride,
Radiant, demure and neat,
She almost trips on BETJEMAN's feet.

But hark, the Bishop's on his toes
To ask if anybody knows
'Just impediment or cause . . .'
There follows then an awkward pause.

In every heart an anxious fear
Of what we half expect to hear.
Strike the organ! Beat the bell!
The Past is silent! All is well!

High up aloft the Happy Pair
Each seated on a golden chair
Their troth now plighted, sealed and blessed,
Are confidentially Addressed.
We cannot hear, we wish we could,
The homely words of Father HOOD
Because the choir, some thirty strong,
Are launched upon a sacred song.

Swing the censer! Wave the stole!
Let the mighty organ roll!
No length to which the priest may go
Will here be ritually *de trop*.
Counter-tenor, tenor, bass
All are purple in the face
And praise the Lord *fortissime*
As DRIBERG bears his bride away.

Friends of yours and friends of mine,
Friends who toe the party line,
Labour friends who're gratified
At being allowed to kiss the bride.
Artistic friends, a few of whom
Are rather keen to kiss the groom.
Friends from Oxford, friends from pubs
And even friends from Wormwood Scrubs.

Friends we always thought were dead
Friends we know are off their head,
Girl-friends, boy-friends, friends ambiguous
Coloured friends from the Antiguas,
Friends ordained and friends unfrocked,
Friends who leave us slightly shocked,
All determined not to miss
So rare a spectacle as this!

Façades and Faces (1950) moves away from parody and has Osbert writing *in propria persona* light verse of a quality that has been recognized in such anthologies as Kingsley Amis's *Oxford Book of Light Verse*. As well as bringing together pocket cartoons showing the efforts of the Littlehamptons to cope with the rigours of post-war life, the book contains eight 'Afternoons with Baedeker'. The Afternoons are spent in European and Middle Eastern townscapes. The illustrations are drawn in black-and-white, with the text written in verse 'due to a desperate and, from the author's point of view, entirely successful, attempt to relieve the tedium of caption writing'.

As was his way, he showed past and present, ancient and modern, cheek by jowl. The Italian Afternoon shows a sunbaked Piazza dominated by a flamboyant equestrian statue. The first verse reads:

> In yonder marble hero's shade
> Aunt Drusilla used to sit
> With her memories of the Slade
> And her water-colour kit.

Equally deflating are the Eireann Afternoon (a lifeless Dublin square), and the Bavarian Afternoon at a megalomaniac rococo *Schloss* whose façade the tourists greet with pious jeers.

Things cheer up on the Aegean Afternoon, illustrated with a particularly splendid drawing of a Greek fishing-village starkly depicted by the chiaroscuro of the white walls and the black shadows thrown by the soporific Mediterranean sun.

> In the spongeshop Vassilias
> Gives a deep, responsive snore
> As the steamer from Piraeus,
> Hooting loudly, nears the shore.

Façades and Faces is an accurate barometer of the way in which various parts of the world affected Osbert's imagination, but the tone of the book does sometimes seem a little weary. Perhaps it is because for once human beings are absent from the drawings of the Afternoons, which are the Façades. The Faces refer to the part of the book devoted to the Earl and Countess of Littlehampton. Nevertheless, it is an extremely entertaining book, and even more elegant than its predecessors.

A discordant note in the chorus of critical welcome was struck by the reviewer in the *Tablet*. He found the verses 'extremely neat and witty' with many memorable lines. However, for all their smartness and competence, he found that they fell far below the high standard of Betjeman, with whose verse he said they invited comparison. Inaccuracies were pointed out, but the reviewer conceded that 'the buildings themselves are in all cases brilliantly conceived and executed, and the Irish and Greek scenes make as pretty pictures as one could want'. Of the Littlehampton cartoons the reviewer shrewdly commented that:

> I should imagine that 'Beachcomber' and Mr. Lancaster between them are more responsible for the *Express*'s huge popularity than any political views it may profess. 'Lady Littlehampton' is a national figure and it is greatly to the credit of the public that a wit so sharp and a humour so unpopular, should be recognised. That could not happen in America.

The last sentence gives away the identity of the reviewer as Evelyn Waugh, together with the disparaging 'pretty pictures' and the belittling comparison with Betjeman. Still, by Waugh's standards the review was mild, especially as it came only a few months after the row over *Helena*.

In 1973 the Earl of Littlehampton presented to the nation (in lieu of death duty) the great Drayneflete collection of ancestral portraits. This was (all too briefly) displayed at the National Portrait Gallery, whose Director, Dr Roy Strong, acclaimed the Littlehampton Bequest as a collection representative of the whole history of English portraiture which was almost without rival and one which constituted, 'in one magnificent gesture, the most significant addition to the National Portrait Gallery's holdings since the last war'. It later appeared in book form as *The Littlehampton Bequest* (1973), which, following *The Saracen's Head* and *Drayneflete Revealed*, completed the Littlehampton trilogy.

It is indeed a collection of extraordinary richness (the death duty must have been colossal). Between such early works as *Cleopatra* (by Lucas Cranach the Elder) and *Dame Agnes de Courantsdair* (attributed to the Master of the Foolish Virgins) and the most recent (*Basil Cantilever Esq. and the Lady Patricia Cantilever*, by David Hockney) come stunning portraits that include work by Hilliard, Van Dyck, Bernini (*Monsignor de Courantsdair*), Lely, Stubbs, Reynolds, Gainsborough, Winterhalter, Landseer, Sargent, Augustus John and John Bratby. As well as constituting a history of English portraiture, the Littlehampton pictures make up a social history: through them we can trace the waxing and waning of the Little-hampton fortunes as one generation fritters away the wealth

Dame Agnes de Courantsdair
Master of the Foolish Virgins[?]

The Countess of Littlehampton
Thomas Gainsborough, R.A.

207

The Reverend the Hon. Dr Lancelot de Courantsdair
George Stubbs

The 5th Earl of Littlehampton
F. X. Winterhalter

'Jennifer'
John Bratby

accumulated by the previous one. This recurring situation is repeatedly remedied by marriage into families whose members, though perhaps of a lower social level than that of the Courantsdairs and the Littlehamptons, have not only the acumen to stem the financial haemorrhage but also the hard cash to replenish the family coffers.

The Littlehampton Bequest is one of Osbert's most pleasing works. The images and the text work in splendidly harmonious harness. Surely Stubbs never painted a horsier horse than the one which bears the Reverend the Hon. Dr Lancelot de Courantsdair, author of the 2,000-line poem in heroic couplets *Hengist and Horsa*, of which Dr Johnson said: 'Sir, a man who can make so prodigious a brick with such a scant quantity of straw has a just claim to the amazed consideration of his fellows.' Never did Landseer stuff a portrait with more members of the animal kingdom (including the Monarch of the Glen himself) than he did in the portrait of the kilted and hirsute 6th Earl of Littlehampton, a 'child of nature' who was 'never happier than when in the company of dumb animals'. Never did Millais paint a more stomach-churningly sentimental picture than *Pussy's Going Bye-byes*, a 'charming study of childhood' in the person of Ethel, youngest child of the 6th Earl. Nor was a packet of soap powder ever so prominent in a work by John Bratby as in his portrait of Jennifer, eldest daughter of the 8th Earl, founder of The Theatre of the Totally Absurd, winner of the Vanessa Redgrave Memorial Award, briefly fashion editor of *Private Eye* and 'though still unmarried, a devoted mother'.

The Littlehampton portraits are not simply like the originals: nor do they exaggerate very much. It is rather that they are more typical of the artist than anything the artist himself ever got round to producing. This goes for the writing as well as for the pictures. Where in the diaries of Evelyn Waugh is there a more characteristic entry than the one recording his meeting with the 7th Earl's daughter Amethyst?

> After dinner went on to a party of *****. Everyone beastly drunk, Bruno Hat and some filthy dago sodomizing on the sofa. Found myself next to a Lesbian friend of Hamish, who I at once suspected of being a flagellant, who bored me to death talking about people in Paris I don't know. However, when Hamish told me she was Willy Drayneflete's half-sister, decided to accept her offer of a lift home. Discovered in the cab that she was not a Lesbian but was a whipper.

Woke up sore and exhausted and had to go straight round to White's
for a couple of brandies-and-crème-de-menthes.

In 1978 Dr Roy Strong and Marcus Binney (then Architectural Editor
of *Country Life*) organized an exhibition under the title 'The Destruction of the Country House' at the Victoria and Albert Museum.
Osbert contributed a self-contained section called 'Great Houses of
Fiction Revisited'. Like *Pelvis Bay* and *Drayneflete*, this is an account
of 'progress', but if the theme was by now familiar there was no
sense of repetition. In this case 'progress' refers not to town
architecture but to country houses, fictional ones in which change
has come about as the result of the heirs of the original owners no
longer being able to afford to keep them up in the way that their
authors had originally conceived them.

Thus Jane Austen's Mansfield Park has become a School for Girls.
The Georgian house has been extended to cope with an increasing
population of hockey-playing St Trinian's characters. The conservatory has been converted into a Memorial Chapel designed by
Sir Edward Maufe, and the stables (now the Jane Austen
gymnasium) have been balanced by Sir Basil Spence's dormitory
wing, 'a forthright and welcome expression of twentieth-century
ideals in a contemporary idiom'. The new science block, 'the work of
a distinguished Danish architect . . . carefully sited just off the main
axis of the old façade, provides a discreet and agreeable contrast to
the pilastered splendours of a bygone era.'

Disraeli's Brentham, requisitioned by the War Office in 1939 and
never relinquished, is now either an atomic warfare centre or else
has to do with army catering or something equally secret and
essential to national security.

The 'bold round-surfaced lawn' of Thomas Love Peacock's
Crotchet Castle has been excavated by the Pang Valley Grit and
Gravel Company. At Dickens's Chesney Wold a motorway now
cuts its swathe between the splendid entrance gates and Sir Lester
Dedlock, Bt.'s stately home, which is surrounded by a network of
roads and flyovers down which thunder vehicles of every description from motor-bikes to fume-belching lorries, a car with a pram
strapped to the top, and a monstrously large juggernaut from Lille
bearing the name of the Société Anonyme des Camions Enormes.
Tennyson's Locksley Hall, in total disrepair, now has a marina

which (it is hoped) will check the further advance of the sea's erosion, while Trollope's Gatherum Castle fares scarcely better with a safari park. As for P. G. Wodehouse's Blandings Castle, perhaps Lord Emsworth would not have been totally displeased to know that it is now the headquarters of the Ministry of Agriculture's National Pig Board's breeding research centre.

The drawings and commentary of 'Great Houses of Fiction Revisited' are to be found in *Scene Changes* (1978) which also includes the 'Afternoons with Baedeker' (including two new ones) and a series (done for the Coronation issue of the *Ambassador*) on the subject of 'The Englishman's Profound Horror of any Sartorial Ostentation', which is, of course, full of exotic-looking uniformed schoolboys, undergraduates in extravagantly coloured blazers and scarves, dons in mortar boards and gowns, beefeaters, diplomats with cocked hats, Guards officers in scarlet jackets and bear-skins, Lord Mayors with chains of office, huntsmen in riding pink, and every other kind of English sartorial self-effacement.

Though fourteen years separated the original publication of *All Done from Memory* (1953) from that of *With an Eye to the Future* (1967), the two books are so intimately connected that even after repeated reading of them I still sometimes find it difficult to remember which volume contains a particular description, character or incident. In fact they comprise a single work, and one with a structure of considerable intricacy.[1]

In a radio conversation with Osbert in 1964 John Betjeman described *All Done from Memory* as 'profound, moving and curvilinear'. The narrative does indeed loop backwards and forwards on itself like one of those Celtic designs which form an endless knot.

Both books start geographically in the part of London where the author was born; not (as is the usual autobiographical method) at the time of his birth but more than thirty years later, in the very different London of the Second World War; the London of barrage balloons, black-outs and air raids. Then with a regard for chronological order that can only be called relaxed, the author tracks his course backwards and forwards through the period *entre deux guerres* to the First World War, and ends at the starting point, Kensington and the Blitz. Curvilinear indeed.

[1] They were published in a single volume in 1986. See p. 22 n.

211

Parts of *All Done from Memory* first appeared in the *Cornhill Magazine*, copies of which were passed from hand to hand by admirers. It first appeared in book form in a limited edition of forty-five copies in 1953, and was not published in a trade edition for another ten years. This gap was out of respect for the feelings of Osbert's mother, who was still alive when the book was written.

It would be going too far to say that Osbert was obsessed with bombs, but first-hand experience of being on the receiving end of them had given him more than a passing interest in the subject, as the opening words of *All Done from Memory* clearly show: 'I cannot honestly say that my attitude to flying-bombs was ever one of gay insouciance. Nevertheless as they grew more frequent I developed a paper-thin tolerance which I had never achieved during the earlier, more orthodox, bombardment.'

Bombs are also prominent in the first pages of *With an Eye to the Future*, as the author drops in for a quick one at the Holland Arms on the way to his Air Raid Warden's Post. The first drawing of the book shows searchlights against the night sky, while over the townscape of the last drawing barrage balloons are floating.

Osbert detested bombs, whether they were dropped by the Germans or the Allies. He was very much against the bombing of insurgents in Greece, and he never forgave Sir Arthur 'Bomber' Harris for the destruction of Dresden. Harris spent his retirement in

Goring-on-Thames, only a few miles from Aldworth. It was inevitable that sooner or later he and Osbert would find themselves at the
same social occasion, and indeed this happened more than once.
However, he somehow always managed to avoid being introduced
to Bomber. 'I've got a lot of time for Lady Bomber,' I heard him once
say, 'but Bomber . . . I am happy to say that I have never shaken his
hand.' Nor did Osbert care a great deal for the late Sir Douglas
Bader, the celebrated legless aviator. Osbert once happened to be at
a party where Bader was a fellow-guest; it happened to be Bader's
birthday. Osbert showed considerable reluctance to produce the on-
the-spot birthday card he was being pestered for. Finally, he gave a
great sigh and produced his pen, with which he drew a pair of legs
being borne heavenwards by the wings attached to them. The
drawing was received with some puzzlement but, as far as I
remember, good humour.

All Done from Memory is perhaps the most vivid of all accounts of
the Wind-in-the-Willows England that perished in the First World
War: 'not a monument but a small memorial plaque to a vanished
world'. *With an Eye to the Future* is an equally sharp, informative and
witty picture of what has come to be known as the Brideshead
Oxford of the 1920s and the London society of the 1930s. Both books
reveal as little as possible about the author's private self. Osbert
described people in external terms: their personalities, opinions and

circumstances are expressed by their clothes, their houses, their style. He adopts the same approach to himself, having little to say about his inner feelings, his intimate personal relations, griefs, hopes and ambitions.

It would be facile to assume that Osbert's sense of privacy and careful construction of a public persona were a self-protective device. There may be an element of truth in that, but it is hard not to think of the happy hypocrite in Max Beerbohm's story of that name. When Lord George Hell's mask is finally removed it turns out that the face it has so long concealed has become exactly like it.

It is quite possible to deduce all we need to know from what Osbert himself tells us without invading his privacy. It is not hard to tell, for example, that financially he was always well off: we do not need to see his bank statements and tax returns to know that. In the same way we do not need an explicit declaration of his political views to make out where he stood. He was clearly opposed to any kind of totalitarianism, whether of the left or right; indeed to any form of extremism. In the Greek civil war he opposed the Communists. Then during the extreme right-wing regime of the Colonels he expressed his distaste by writing letters to the papers and denying himself the joy afforded to him by visiting that country.

Obviously he was not a revolutionary, and equally obviously he was a conservative, but he was not necessarily a Conservative. Where architecture and town-planning were concerned he was even-handed in his opposition to the destruction wrought both by socialist town-planners and by capitalist developers. In his poem on Tom Driberg's wedding he calls himself a reactionary but that is in self-mocking contrast with Driberg's more left-wing friends and members of the congregation. (Nor did differences in their political beliefs ever disturb their friendship.) Osbert was far too much of an aesthete to nail his colours to any doctrine or -ism or political party. He used to say that his voting policy in general elections was to reduce the majority of the sitting member. In politics as elsewhere he valued independence above obedience, and greatly regretted the abolition of the non-party University seats. It is a pity he never held one himself. Had he done so, as he probably would have liked, the House of Commons would have been every bit as enlivened as it was by A. P. Herbert. *Faute de mieux* he made full use of the letters column of *The Times*.

The casual assumptions in his autobiographies are what reveal his political and social stance. His description of the street characters of his pre-1914 childhood – the organ-grinder, the muffin-man, the lamplighter, the chimney-sweeper and so on – has already been quoted. He comments about them: 'Doubtless their disappearance should be welcomed, and yet they did not appear to be either downtrodden or exploited.' As so often the Gibbonian balance of the prose makes the sentence seem utterly and judiciously reasonable. In fact it is highly tendentious. The thundering 'Doubtless' at the beginning is immediately undermined by doubt. The observation from the pram by the infant analyst of society is properly qualified by 'they did not appear to be . . .'

At his best, though, he does not purport to be objective, and this is one of his strengths. He does not claim to write from anywhere other than his own viewpoint.

Accusations of élitism, that he looks down on lower classes and foreigners, are not baseless, but they miss the point. He is a cartoonist, a caricaturist, even a satirist. The comic vision is a reductionist one. For Osbert, as for any comic artist, it is not just those who belong to another class or another nation who are laughable. Everyone is laughable. It would be pointless to pretend that a diligent researcher would not be able to find a few remarks or drawings or cartoon captions of his which went unremarked at the time but would offend the sensibilities of some of the *bien-pensants* of today. The same is true of far greater talents, from Shakespeare downwards. But for the most part his characters are presented with good-natured amusement and affection.

When people speak of Britain as being two nations they usually mean north and south, or poor and rich. In an essay on the Festival of Britain,[1] Michael Frayn made a different distinction between the two nations which inhabit the country. There was the Britain of the *Guardian*, the *Observer* and the *News Chronicle*, which was inhabited by what he called the Herbivores, the 'gentle ruminants who looked out from the lush pastures which are their natural station in life with eyes full of sorrow for less fortunate creatures, guiltily conscious of their advantages, though not usually ceasing to eat the grass'. The Hervibores are despised by the Carnivores, who are the *Express*

[1] In *Age of Austerity 1945–51*, edited by Michael Sissons and Philip French.

readers, the Evelyn Waughs, the *Directory of Directors*, 'the members of the upper- and middle-classes who believe that if God had not wished them to prey on all smaller and weaker creatures without scruple he would not have made them as they are'.

The Beaverbrook press was particularly hostile to the Festival of Britain, even though Beaverbrook might have been expected to be enthusiastic about a patriotic celebration of British achievements in industry and art. As Michael Frayn comments, it could easily have struck him as being almost as admirable as the *Daily Express* Boat Show. But Beaverbrook's likes and dislikes were never consistent, and he unleashed the full wrath of his newspapers on what they called Herbert Morrison's 'multi-million-pound baby', 'Mr Morrison's monument', 'Morrison's Folly'.

The readers, however, did not share the Beaver's sentiments. A Gallup Poll showed widespread support for a bit of fun and frivolity to celebrate the nation's survival of six years of war and five years of post-war hardship, shortages, rationing, drabness and austerity. The Festival received the highest seal of respectability when the King and Queen became patrons in 1950, and by the time it opened the next year the *Express* had been forced to come round to something like reluctant support.

Evelyn Waugh did not give up so easily. In the epilogue to *Unconditional Surrender* he wrote that in 1951 the government had decreed a Festival to celebrate the opening of a happier decade. 'Monstrous constructions appeared on the South bank of the Thames, the foundation was solemnly laid for a National Theatre, but there was little popular exuberance among the straitened people, and dollar-bearing tourists curtailed their visits and sped to the countries of the Continent where, however precarious their condition, they ordered things better.'

Waugh loathed everything that had been done since 1945 by a Labour government which appeared to him to be building a socialist state while at the same time destroying the upper-class world of himself, his friends and acquaintances and the characters of his novels. He felt as though he was living in a country occupied by an enemy power. He was deeply and gloomily nostalgic about Britain's past, and even more pessimistic about the present and future.

Osbert's outlook was very different. In the Levin television interview (June 1967), for example, he described himself as a commentator with more affection for the clergy than for politicians.

When asked his political affiliation he replied, 'I would describe myself as a pragmatist had it not become a dirty word.'

During the miners' dispute of January 1974, when the nation was reduced to working a three-day week, he wrote a letter to *The Times* in which he spoke of, on the one hand, 'ill-considered legislation unimaginatively presented and, on the other, cleverly manipulated obstinacy'. In short there were, as a Herbivore leader-writer would say, faults on both sides.

It is also worth noting that he joined the National Union of Journalists at the age of seventy as a gesture of support in its dispute with the Newspaper Society (the proprietors' union).

His was an independent voice. In his own area of special interest (architecture and town-planning) he was perfectly well aware that the instruments of destruction were not just Labour ministries and Town Councils but also the Tory ones and the big business concerns which finance the Conservative Party.

Just how devastating he could be when on top epistolary form was demonstrated in July 1972 when there was a controversy bubbling away about the new Queen Anne's Mansions, on which subject *The Times* had published a critical leader. The affronted architect, Sir Basil Spence, OM, RA, wrote a letter of reply. *The Times* had complained that among other things the new building would spoil the view from the park:

> You use several times the phrase 'view from the park'. But when our photographer visited the park to take pictures from important points like the bridge it was impossible to see anything of the new building – not even the crane was visible . . . The fact is this building would only be seen properly from Bridge Walk, in summer, and through a dense net-work of branches and twigs in winter from the park.

He concluded his letter with a wonderfully pompous flourish. 'I would like to correct you', said Sir Basil, 'when you suggest that I find criticism from non-architects unacceptable. I welcome broad-based, objective, constructive criticism from any source.'

Well, he did ask for it. Retribution, in the form of Osbert's letter, followed swiftly:

> Sir, Lady Littlehampton, to whom in your columns I have recently been advised to stick, has put to me an interesting question which I hasten to pass on. She asks if any architect in recorded history from Vitruvius to Colonel Seifert, engaged on an important public building on a prominent site, has ever before put forward the claim (one hopes

justified) made by Sir Basil Spence in his letter today that his masterpiece will, when finished, be to all intents and purposes, invisible?

His views of party politics were pretty much those expressed in a pocket cartoon drawn at the time of the 1950 General Election. A mother holding a baby says cheerfully: 'Oh, we're enjoying every minute of it – he's bitten the Tory, been sick over the Socialist, and now I can hardly wait to see what he's going to do to the Liberal!'

Dim Little Island, a short film made in 1949 for the Central Office of Information and beautifully directed by Humphrey Jennings, set out to re-create some of the 'glories' of Britain and to wonder about the country's future. The subject was seen through the eyes of four men: Ralph Vaughan Williams, the ornithologist James Fisher, the Vickers industrialist John Ormston, and Osbert.

The comic artist's job, Osbert said in the film, is to expose illusions and to be the guardian of reality. His view was very un-Waughlike. Far from sentimentalizing the past, he showed the dark side of the good old days. Ford Madox Ford's picture of an emigrant couple, *The Last of England*, is often shown as an example of regret at parting from the homeland. But what was there to regret? Osbert pointed out that what they were leaving was a world of urban squalor, oppression, disease, poverty and a twelve-hour working day. They were not miserable because they were leaving: they were leaving because they were miserable.

As for the present, it would be an illusion (he said) to see the Great Britain of 1949 as a 'dim little island'. It would be a mistake to see the country as being on a downward slope and to moan 'Ichabod, Ichabod, our glory is departed.' If we were a rational race, he said, we would doubtless be overwhelmed by our position, but we were deaf to the rational.

This optimistic faith in the future of Britain was as different as could be from Waugh's assessment of the state of the nation, and pretty close to that of the Herbivorous editor of the *News Chronicle*, Gerald Barry, the original proposer of the idea of a Festival and the driving force behind the project. Almost echoing Osbert's words in *Dim Little Island*, Barry wrote in *Picture Post* that 'The Festival will demonstrate to those of our friends who have somewhat prematurely wiped us off the world-map, the strength of a nation still determined to play its full part as a virile and adaptable people.'

'Don't make fun of the Festival,' warbled Noël Coward. Of

course, Osbert did make fun of it: it was just as much fair game as any of the other front-page stories on which the pocket cartoons made their daily comments. At the same time he yet again showed his independence from the Beaverbrook line by making practical contributions to the Festival. In 1950 he wrote an introduction for a new edition of his late friend Christopher Hobhouse's *1851 and the Great Exhibition*, published by Murray with an eye on the Festival of Britain. He also illustrated Ruth McKenney's and Richard Bransten's *Here's England* (1951), a book by two Americans (published by Rupert Hart-Davis) and 'aimed squarely at the American visitor to the Festival of Britain'. It is a feebly jocular, cliché-ridden book, only redeemed by some excellent illustrations by Osbert. Another Festival book was *This Britain* (Macmillan), edited by Newton Branch, with a foreword by Compton Mackenzie and containing contributions by, among others, L. A. G. Strong, Ivor Brown, Nigel Balchin and Osbert Lancaster. (In the same year, incidentally, Osbert also illustrated *London Night and Day*, an admirable guide-book, and Alan Moorehead's *The Villa Diana*.)

His major Festival contribution, though, was his collaboration with John Piper on the 'Main Vista of Battersea Park's Festival Pleasure Gardens' – a 250-yard succession of pavilions, arcades, towers, pagodas, terraces, gardens, lakes and fountains in styles that included Brighton Regency, Gothic and Chinese, in a setting intended to recall the glories and fantasies of the eighteenth-century pleasure gardens of Vauxhall, Ranelagh and Cremorne.

Even more than the South Bank site, the Battersea Gardens were beset with problems in which filthy weather was exacerbated by a shortage of materials and recurrent strikes and go-slows. A pocket cartoon of that year shows a well-wrapped artist telling his shivering model: 'Allow me to remind you, Miss Maltravers, that if Michelangelo had knocked off work every time there was a trifling power-cut the Sistine Chapel would never have been finished!' The Minister of Works, Richard Stokes, visited the Battersea Gardens to harangue the workers during one industrial dispute. Informed of yet another stoppage he is said to have asked despairingly, 'What is it this time?' A shortage of shovels, he was told. 'Well,' said Stokes, 'tell the men they'll just have to lean against one another.'

On the Battersea site things went from bad to worse. Overspending rose from £1,100,000 in 1950 to £2,400,000 in March 1951, after which Parliament had to vote an extra £1,000,000. Harold Macmillan denounced the project as 'a little gem of mismanagement, a cameo of incompetence, a perfect little miniature of muddle'. Only five weeks before the opening was due, *Harper's Bazaar* said that 'Still sunk in primeval slime, it seems that the Pleasure Gardens can never be more than a lovely mirage in the minds of Piper, Lancaster and the other artists who imagined them.' Prospects of the Pleasure Gardens' financial success were further reduced when a free vote in the Commons decided that the amusement section of the Pleasure Gardens should not be open on Sundays. In the event the Gardens opened three weeks late. The fountains, which had been Osbert's idea, lasted for only the first day, because stall-holders complained that the spray was falling on their goods.

The problems of the Festival reflected the grim national and political scene. The Korean war was breaking out, the pound was devalued, and the Attlee Government was tearing itself apart. Ernest Bevin died on 14 April, and a week later Aneurin Bevan, Harold Wilson and John Freeman resigned from the Government. The diplomats Donald Maclean and Osbert's ex-colleague Guy Burgess defected to the Soviet Union. And it rained, and rained, and rained.

Against all the odds, and contrary to Evelyn Waugh's account, the Festival was a huge success. So great were the crowds swarming to the South Bank that the streets round the Embankment had to be closed to traffic. The *Manchester Guardian* wrote that 'People making for the South Bank begin to smile as they come close to it', and suggested that 'On bright sunny days it seems that a trip across the Thames to the South Bank will be as invigorating as a trip across the Channel, for in its final form the scene is quite as unfamiliar as any foreign seaside resort.' Foreign visitors *did* come, spending some eighteen million pounds more than they had the previous year (the total expenditure of the Festival was some £8,000,000, apart from loans for the Festival Gardens: so much for profligate socialist mis-spending). A Gallup Poll showed 58 per cent as having a favourable impression of the South Bank, against 15 per cent unfavourable. 8,500,000 people visited the South Bank, and almost as many the Pleasure Gardens.

When it was all over, the Carnivores of the new Conservative Government lost no time in eradicating all traces of the Festival, apart from the Festival Hall itself. The 27-acre site on the South Bank was cleared and in due course the Dome of Discovery and the delightful Skylon were replaced by a car park for 700 cars and the hideous Shell building.

The collaboration with John Piper on the Festival Gardens was not Osbert's first experience of working on a large scale. There had been the pre-war murals at Blandford Forum, and in 1947 he executed a large backcloth, entitled *The Railway Bookstall*, for the National Book League. These works, however, were not widely known, any more than were his easel paintings or his book illustrations in colour. To the general public he was a cartoonist who worked in black-and-white in a small space. The Battersea project with Piper had now shown to a wide audience what he could do with colour and on a big scale.

That same year (1951 was something of an *annus mirabilis* for Osbert) Sadler's Wells put on *Pineapple Poll* for the Sadler's Wells Ballet Theatre, based on W. S. Gilbert's *Bab Ballads*. John Piper suggested Osbert as designer. The result was an enormous success. More than four decades later the sets still look as fresh, as witty, as bright, as light, as inventive and as joyful as they did on the first night when they were so roundly applauded as the curtain rose.[1]

Someone once asked Osbert how stage design compared with drawing pocket cartoons. 'Bigger,' he replied. 'Definitely bigger.' To Moran Caplat, Glyndebourne's general manager, he said, 'The theatre holds no terrifying mysteries for me.' His confidence in his own abilities was entirely justified, and some of the very best work he did was for the stage.

He was by now in his early forties, which might be thought a late start, but in fact it was a perfectly natural development from everything he had done before. It was one that brought together his varied talents and gave them full scope. Whether consciously or not he had been preparing himself for this all his life. He was, in fact, formidably well qualified. Music, architecture, landscape, paintings, these were his passions. Add dashing young men, beautiful young women, talented people of all shapes, sizes and nationalities, and what you have is theatre, ballet, opera. What more could he want?

---

[1] Regrettably *Pineapple Poll* and *La Fille Mal Gardée* are the only stage designs of Osbert's that are still extant and in use.

A couple of years before his own first works for the stage, Osbert was praising Diaghilev for reintroducing the painter to the theatre (*Spectator*, 25 March 1949), and in his introduction to Hobhouse's book on the Great Exhibition he went so far as to say that the greatest single influence on the arts between the wars had been exercised by 'that scintillating chip of [*sic*] the old block, Serge Diaghileff'. In addition to all that, of course, he had studied at the Slade under Diaghilev's scene-painter Vladimir Polunin, and had married a fellow-student of his (Karen was to prove an enormous help in making models for the sets).

The Lancaster family background was a good one for nurturing musical interest, and one of the redeeming features of Charterhouse had been its strong musical tradition. Not only had it produced Vaughan Williams; it also invited musicians as distinguished as Alfred Cortot to school concerts. During vacations from Oxford Osbert had been to concerts in Germany and Austria and to the Salzburg Festival, and since then he had been a regular visitor to the ballet and opera. In short, though he had had no formal musical education he had a knowledge and appreciation that were more than adequate for a stage designer for ballet or opera.

In his visual art he had by now fully developed his distinctive way of placing tones and colours side by side with telling effect. His preferred medium, gouache, lends itself to the use of flat areas of colour with the minimum of visible brush-strokes – ideal, in fact, for translation into theatre sets. Similarly, his lifelong fascination with clothes and encyclopaedic knowledge of period costumes and uniforms dated back to those childhood hours spent poring over Mrs Ullathorne's scrapbook, and with so many outstanding books on architecture and interior design behind him no one should have been surprised that he made such a triumphant début with *Pineapple Poll*.

For the next two decades he produced costumes and sets for plays, ballets and operas at the rate of more than one a year: one each for the Hippodrome, the Festival Ballet, the Winter Garden, D'Oyly Carte and the Bulgarian National Opera, Sofia; two each for Sadler's Wells, the English Opera Group and the Old Vic; three each for the Saville and Covent Garden; and no fewer than six for Glyndebourne. In the late 1960s he also designed sets for two plays by Anthony Powell, a project which unfortunately never reached the stage.

Pineapple Poll was followed by another ballet, John Cranko's *Bonne Bouche* at Covent Garden. Reviewers of stage productions usually devote most of their space to the playwright or composer, the producer, the actors, singers or dancers, and tag on at the end a brief mention of the sets and costumes. All the more remarkable, then, that the *Observer*'s distinguished ballet critic Alexander Bland started his review the other way round: 'The ranks of Kensington (of which there were undoubtedly many at Covent Garden on Friday) could scarce forbear to cheer when the curtain rose on *Bonne Bouche* to show Osbert Lancaster's charming vision of their homeland.'

With these two successes behind him, Osbert was well launched. The next year he designed *Love in a Village* for the English Opera Group, and in 1953 (the year in which he was awarded the CBE) no fewer than three productions: *High Spirits* at the Hippodrome, *All's*

La Fille Mal Gardée: on the paint frame at the Royal Opera House

Well at the Old Vic (with a cast that included Fay Compton, Claire Bloom and Michael Hordern) and *The Rake's Progress* in Edinburgh for Glyndebourne.

Two years earlier Desmond Shaw-Taylor had commented in *Opera* that décor had been Glyndebourne's weak spot. Moran Caplat, general manager at Glyndebourne since 1948, remedied this by bringing in Oliver Messel, Leslie Hurry, John Piper, Hugh Casson and Osbert Lancaster. Stravinsky's *The Rake's Progress*, with libretto by W. H. Auden and Chester Kallman, was Glyndebourne's first ever production of an opera by a living composer. Its world première at the Teatro Fenice in Venice in 1951 had not been a great success, in spite of having a cast that included Elisabeth Schwartzkopf and being conducted by Stravinsky himself. The producer, Carl Ebert, attributed much of the blame to the décor of the Italian designer, who had simply rehashed Hogarth. When Ebert came to direct it again, this time for Glyndebourne, it was decided that a *modern* satirical cartoonist and artist should design the sets: Osbert.

This time *The Rake's Progress* proved a triumph. It has been one of Glyndebourne's most popular operas, and the company has given

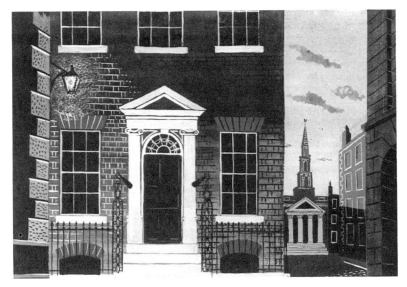

Backcloth design for Stravinsky's *The Rake's Progress*, Glyndebourne, 1953

far more performances of it than any other company in the world. Its initial success and continuing popularity owed a great deal to Osbert's contribution. Without disparaging David Hockney's 1975 set, it is hard not to feel that it is a pity Glyndebourne chose to replace Osbert's.

Year after year reviews of his sets were, very nearly without exception, not just favourable but almost extravagantly admiring. A *Sunday Times* profile in 1954 said his *Bonne Bouche* and *Coppelia* were 'among the gayest and most captivating ballet sets ever designed by an English artist'. When Lillian Hellman and Leonard Bernstein's *Candide* opened in 1959 it was panned by the press, but most of the reviews picked out the Lancaster set designs as a redeeming feature. *The Times*'s review of Rossini's *La Pietra del Paragone* in 1964 was another that *started* with the décor:

> When the history of Glyndebourne comes to be written a century hence, the names of composers and producers and conductors will abound, and high in the roll of honour will stand the name of Mr. Osbert Lancaster who has the great gift of designing décors that invigorate every opera with which he is connected. Much of his best work has been done for Glyndebourne, and his settings for *La Pietra del Paragone*, the latest Rossini comic opera to enter the Glyndebourne repertory, are some of his most life-enhancing.

Spike Hughes, the historian of Glyndebourne, says that a great deal of the huge success of the 1955 production of Verdi's *Falstaff* resulted from Osbert's contribution. Some critics did object that the architecture of the set looked too bright and new, more like modern Slough than Tudor Windsor. This was obtuse of them. Osbert had had the wit to realize that in Falstaff's time Tudor buildings *were* new, not Olde Worlde. Ford was a *nouveau riche* merchant and therefore his desirable residence in suburban Windsor would have been akin in spirit to Stockbroker Tudor. The Garter Inn, however, was an old pub, a century earlier in style, and would look old. As for Windsor Forest and the Thames, their natural beauty would be today much as it was in Falstaff's time. In fact Osbert's sense of period was as usual impeccable. The sets, Moran Caplat comments, came out just right, 'never too heavy, never too frivolous, and always romantic when required. Indeed the last scene, with Herne's oak and the river glinting in the background, had a real magic. There were no gimmicks.'

There were jokes, though. The ancestral portraits that hung on

Costume design for Alice in Verdi's
Falstaff, Glyndebourne, 1955

Costume design for Von Zastrow in
Maw's *The Rising of the Moon*,
Glyndebourne, 1970

the walls of Ford's house were of Caplat and other members of the Glyndebourne company. Osbert also proposed at one point to introduce a ridiculous Lady Godiva on a hobby-horse, wearing a mask of John Christie, the proprietor and creator of Glyndebourne. Christie quashed this idea on the grounds that he was (he claimed) a direct descendant of Lady Godiva and would not have her made fun of. Another version of this story has it that the idea was Christie's own, but that he forgot to tell Osbert about it.

Christie was famed for his eccentricity. He once went to a party with a clip-on moustache in imitation of Osbert, and wore it all evening. On another occasion Osbert was driving down the Mall in the rush hour when he saw Christie standing in the middle of the road. He stopped and Christie got in, saying 'I knew I'd see someone I knew who was going to Victoria station.' In fact Osbert wasn't going to Victoria station at all, but he did.

Opera people have a reputation for their rows and temperamental behaviour. Osbert got on well with everyone, staff, stage crews, chorus and singers, keeping people laughing all the time. He invented names for the critics: Philip Hope-Wallace was Abandon Hope-Wallace, Martin Cooper was Martin Carper, Stanley Sadie was Stanley Sadist. In the wardrobe room he drew cartoons and caricatures on the walls. Unfortunately these have gone, with the wardrobe itself, in the course of rebuilding. Even more unfortunate is the loss of almost all of his sets and costumes. What do survive are photographs, and Osbert's drawings and designs from which the stage carpenters, painters and wardrobe worked; the splendid programme covers he did for Glyndebourne; and the Folio Society's 1963 edition of *All's Well That Ends Well*, which is illustrated with his designs for the Old Vic production ten years earlier.

In 1963 Cecil Beaton designed the basement theatre of the Shell centre on London's South Bank. The mural in the foyer is by Osbert. It is an enormous work, measuring more than thirty feet wide and sixteen feet nine inches high.

Because of its size it had to be prepared in eight vertical panels. Osbert did the drawings at home, and then spent six weeks in a scene-designer's studio, assisted by two students from the Royal College of Art. After various experiments, he chose the medium of Indian ink on fibre-glass. The main problem was making sure the drawings on the panels joined up precisely, but the result showed that this technical challenge was successfully met – perhaps more so than in Picasso's huge mural at the UNESCO building in Paris.

The title of the mural, *Progress in Transport*, is as ironical as that of *Progress at Pelvis Bay*, and perhaps more so than may have been expected by the oil company that commissioned it, for it is an eloquent account of the damaging impact of the internal combustion engine on the twentieth century. It is also an autobiographical work, showing the social and architectural changes that occurred in London over a period of half a century as seen through the eyes of one whose life coincided with the Age of the Car. The mural's chronological narrative moves (like the Bayeux Tapestry, or a comic strip) from left to right. In the first panel, a nanny is pushing a pram while in front of it a small boy in a sailor suit runs along with stick and hoop. In the road the only traffic apart from a cyclist is an open car occupied by a lady in a large hat who is speaking through a tube to her chauffeur in the front. There is a gas lamp, a bright-red pillar box (the one splash of strong colour in the panel). The buildings behind are solidly Georgian or Victorian and in the sky there is a monoplane.

In the next panel the sky is dark, but a Zeppelin is picked out by searchlights and flashes of explosion. From a wall poster Kitchener's admonishing finger puts over the message that Your Country Needs YOU. The open-topped bus in the street advertises *Chu Chin Chow*. Going eastwards through a composite London boldly punctuated by the black exclamation mark of Nelson's Column roughly in the middle, the chronology continues to be established by the names of the shows and plays of the day – from *No No Nanette*, to Charles Laughton in *Mutiny on the Bounty*, to The Crazy Gang at the London Palladium, to *Oklahoma!* at Drury Lane.

The progress from peace to war to peace, and then to war and peace again, is marked mainly by destruction, from aerial bombardment in two wars and, yet more devastatingly, by post-Second World War property development. The last building on the right is a monolithic glass-and-concrete rectangle not unlike Shell's own great lump on the South Bank, a point that is emphasized by a sign reading GARAGE and a row of three Shell petrol pumps. Above the skyline cranes threaten worse to come, and in the sky drones a helicopter, the latest successor in the line from monoplane to zeppelin, bombers and fighter planes. Below in the street the traffic has become chock-a-block. There is a huge coach owned by Olde Worlde Tours Ltd, a long American car with white-walled tyres, a huge British Railways lorry and a motor-scooter. In the very bottom corner we see Maudie Littlehampton driving back to Knightsbridge in a bubble-car. Hers is a very different world from that of her chauffeur-driven grandmother at the other end of the mural, in social terms as well as those of transport and architecture.

Osbert said that he disliked the Shell building so much that he was almost ashamed to have done the mural for the company. In that case, why did he do so? One possible answer is residual gratitude to Jack Beddington who had given him work all those years ago. Another is that it gave him an opportunity to express forcibly his views and observations on the effect of the petrol engine on the century of Mr Toad.

In the mid-1960s Anne Scott-James was staying in Paris at the flat of her friend the novelist Romain Gary, then living with Jean Seberg whom he later married. One day he reported that an Englishman had come round looking for her. He was, Gary said, 'in a very emotional state – as far, that is, as an Englishman is capable of emotion'. The Englishman was Osbert.

Anne Scott-James had won a scholarship to Somerville College, Oxford, where she read Classics just a few years after Osbert's time at the university. She then went on to a distinguished career as a journalist, author, broadcaster and authority on the practice and history of gardening. She was on the staff of *Vogue*, women's editor of *Picture Post*, editor of *Harper's Bazaar* for six years, women's editor of the *Sunday Express* and women's adviser to the Beaverbrook Press from 1959 to 1960, a *Daily Mail* columnist from 1960 to 1968. Had Fleet Street not been so male-dominated, there can be little doubt that she would have become the editor of a national newspaper. Her books include *In the Mink*, *Down to Earth* (illustrated by Osbert), *Sissinghurst: The Making of a Garden*, and *The Pleasure Garden* (again illustrated by Osbert).

Anne and Osbert had known one another long before the day he turned up in an excited state at Romain Gary's flat. When they first met in Fleet Street before the war, Osbert was already a celebrity and everyone's favourite guest. But Anne's first impressions of him, like those of quite a few people, were not particularly favourable. It was not just his disconcerting physical appearance. She found his manner to be what used to be called 'stagey': he struck her as supercilious.

Anne didn't really get to like Osbert until she started to see more of him after the war, on his return from Greece to Fleet Street. They got to know one another better partly as a result of the full-page frontispieces that Osbert contributed to the *Strand* magazine under the editorship of Anne's then husband Macdonald Hastings.

In the 1950s they were both working for Lord Beaverbrook in the same building. They would bump into one another frequently, and sometimes have a drink at El Vino's, though still not getting on particularly well. Then came what Anne remembers as an appalling cocktail party given by the *Express* editor Arthur Christiansen. Anne found herself looking round the room and thinking that there wasn't a single person she knew there except Osbert. At the same moment Osbert was looking around and thinking that there wasn't a single person he knew there except Anne. After they had chatted for a while and the party had shown no sign of becoming any less dull, Anne said to Osbert, 'What are you doing after this? How about you buying me dinner?' She doubts if Osbert would ever have

suggested it himself, but he agreed willingly. 'That's all right,' he said. 'We'll go to the Ritz. I've got an account there.' From that dinner there developed a close friendship.

In the years following Karen's death Anne and Osbert continued to spend a great deal of time together. They went on holidays abroad, often with Anne's daughter Clare.

In 1967 they married. They kept one flat in Chelsea, while Osbert gave up Henley: from now on, until only a couple of months before he died, weekends were spent in Aldworth.

Anne and Osbert made a most unusual-looking couple – she was tall and beautiful; he was not. There were many ways other than looks and stature in which A and O[1] were different from one another. Anne's idea of a pleasant evening is one spent at home either with one or two friends or (perhaps even better) reading a nineteenth-century novel. Osbert didn't care much for novels (apart from those of Proust and Stendhal and *Vanity Fair*) and for him an evening was wasted if it didn't involve at least one social gathering – usually an all-male affair, at a club or City dinner.

---

[1] John Betjeman used to call Anne Alpha – though apparently Osbert was never Omega.

Anne is immensely practical and well organized in everything from planning a journey or a meal to paying the bills on time. This was just as well, since Osbert was not. It would not be strictly accurate to say that he never raised a finger in the kitchen: sometimes he would pine for Greece and cook keftalies. Very good they were too. The trouble was that he made such a performance out of it that the keftalies took up more time and space than the rest of the meal put together. The kitchen would be left in a state of chaos. Cleaning up was a major task. There was also a period when he prided himself on his omelettes, which had the texture of leather.

Anne was in charge of the business of providing a comfortable home and good food – cooked by the Lancasters' German house-keeper Martha, who became a valued friend – and of organizing hotels when they went abroad. But it was Osbert who directed their travels – an expedition to Greece to search for Byzantine churches, or a trip up the Seine in the Camrose yacht. Until his very last years, he was the leader in their joint lives.

'The suburban garden is the most important garden of the 20th century and there is no excuse other than ignorance for using the word "suburban" in a derogatory sense.' This sentence is taken at

Industrial Revolution Gardenesque: 'The gardenesque is not a crowded style.'

random from *The Pleasure Garden*, a hugely enjoyable and informative book which resulted from Anne and Osbert's collaboration. You don't need to be told that Anne penned that sentence. Osbert might well have had the same thought, but his expression of it would have been ornate, elaborate, circumlocutory. Anne, by contrast, is no-nonsense, to the point (down to earth, indeed), brisk, almost brusque, and with a slight air of pull-your-socks-up. One thing Osbert and Anne very much had in common was that they didn't suffer fools gladly. They also shared a high degree of intelligence, and where their fields of interest differed they complemented one another. In the 'Apologia' to *The Pleasure Garden* Anne is writing about their collaboration on the book, but she could easily be writing about their marriage. She says:

> This marital partnership has not been wholly easy. Each of us has been accustomed to plough a lone furrow, and in double harness we often pulled in different ways. While I was sweating over Pliny, he tended to be musing on his youth in a London square. When I was studying Canon Raven on the mediaeval naturalists, he would demand a list of plants suitable for the Dutch garden to be delivered in ten minutes, and then most of my solutions would prove unsuitable for illustration. Sometimes the only plant he felt like drawing was a yucca, with its strong architectural outlines, and I am surprised that there is not a yucca in every sketch, from the Romano-British period onward.

Not the least of Anne's achievements was her ability to tease Osbert and get away with it.

X

CODA

ONE Saturday morning I answered a knock at the door and found Osbert standing outside. This surprised me for two reasons. One was that at Aldworth he rarely ventured forth without Anne. The other was that visits between us were usually pre-arranged either by a few words spoken (in the manner of Pyramus and Thisbe) through the yew-hedge which separated their lovely and impeccably cared for garden from my jungle of docks and bindweed, or else on the phone with Anne, to whom all social arrangements were delegated. If I phoned and Osbert should answer, his reply would usually be on the lines of 'Dear *boy*, how good to hear from you. What are you *up* to?' He would ask this even if we had seen one another the previous evening. 'Why don't you come round and . . .? Hold on, I'll pass you to Anne . . . *Dar*ling, it's er . . .'

This helplessness was to a large extent illusory. He could not abide solitude, and on the rare occasions when he was left on his own for a brief period he proved quite capable of picking up the phone and making it clear that company was needed. I accepted such invitations eagerly, partly because I always enjoyed his company, but also because it was fun to see him in the unfamiliar domestic role of being in charge. Not that this involved more than mixing and pouring the martinis, which in Anne's absence always seemed somehow different. Bigger. Stronger.

So there he was, that Saturday morning, on my doorstep, unannounced. I invited him in and he compounded my surprise by asking if he could look at my cat.

I had found Watkins in a hedge, an abandoned kitten, miaowing piteously. As she grew up, her grey hair had become longer and longer and she sported a tail like a feather boa which suggested some Persian ancestry. At the same time her behaviour indicated that the other side of the family was less aristocratic and had spent a great deal of time in farmyard barns. At any rate she was a ferocious hunter.

On this particular morning she had given the local rodents a day off, and was taking her nap in the best armchair. Osbert bent over her and for a long time gazed with his bulging blue eyes. 'Yes, yes,' he said. 'I thought so.' I offered to lend him the cat; or (better still)

why didn't he stay and do a drawing? But no, without even a sketch he had what he wanted.

The result is to be seen in the Folio Society's edition of Saki's stories (1976) where Tobermory is actually Watkins. It's a most peculiar-looking cat, but then so was Watkins. Even so, I think it is true to say that when it came to animals, Osbert's drawing was not always at its best. He could do a very good Mediterranean donkey,

236

preferably bearing a bearded Greek Orthodox priest. There are some fine steeds in *The Littlehampton Bequest*, and he executed impressive representations of equestrian statuary from time to time. He loved birds and was expert at identifying them, but in his drawings they are usually little more than marks in the sky. Landscapes, buildings and people, yes, but animals were not his forte, particularly (I suggest) when it came to cats.

Another surprise visit, some years later, also involved a drawing. One day the conversation had turned to the subject of lost masterpieces and we had agreed that it was a tragedy that Byron's autobiography had not survived. After Byron's death the manuscript was burnt in John Murray's Albemarle Street office in the fireplace over which Byron's portrait now hangs. The incendiaries were John Murray II, Tom Moore and Byron's friend Hobhouse (an ancestor of Osbert's friend Christopher). I said it was a pity that we lacked a proper record of this dastardly deed of literary destruction.

One morning, a couple of weeks later, the phone rang. It was Osbert, saying that he had something for me and would it be convenient if . . .? I offered to come round but he preferred to deliver it in person. By now I was living at the other end of the village, a good quarter of an hour's walk, mostly uphill, and by this time Osbert's health was not good (this was in about 1980). He was not to be deterred.

The 'something' turned out to be a pen-and-ink drawing of the scene we had talked about. It showed Murray, Moore and Hobhouse holding the sheets of Byron's manuscript with expressions of horror on their faces as they perused the pages before throwing them on the fire, while Byron glowered down at them from his portrait. Osbert had made no preparatory sketches for this drawing – as usual it was all done from memory – but comparison with the original portrait and fireplace shows that they have been recorded with considerable accuracy. Whatever the state of his other faculties by this time, his visual memory was unimpaired.

So was his cartooning skill. Long after the time when in conversation he often seemed to be out of touch with the public events of the day, the front page of the *Daily Express* would produce a pocket cartoon that was spot on. The last one of all appeared in May 1981.

By this time his hearing was poor. He used an ear-trumpet, which would have been more effective if he had not tended to put it to his ear when he was speaking and put it down when someone else was talking. When he did get the combination right, as often as not he would point it at the wrong person. His memory too had become very selective. He would quote faultlessly, in German, Heine's *Lorelei*:

> *Ich weiss nicht, was soll es bedeuten*
> *Dass ich so traurig bin;*
> *Ein Märchen aus alten Zeiten,*
> *Das kommt mir nicht aus dem Sinn.*

(I don't know why I should feel so sad but there's an old fairy-tale that I can't get out of my head.)

But he suffered from nominal aphasia; he was unable to remember even extremely well-known names. He might mention – 'What's his name? The one who did so much in the war?' One would tentatively offer Alanbrooke, Slim, Alexander – 'No, no, though mind you Alex was . . . no, you know perfectly well who I'm talking about.' Macmillan? Monty? 'No, no.' With some trepidation one would eventually offer Churchill, which was indeed the name he had been striving for.

'Did you know Asquith?' he once asked me. He was often astonished to find that I was not of his generation, or possibly even a previous one. Some time after I had embarked on writing this book, he enquired as to its progress. 'Tell me, er, Richard,' he said, eyes bright with interest, 'How are you getting *on* with . . . (long pause) . . . that book you're writing about . . . (very long pause) . . . that chap?'

Sometimes we would make expeditions. One I particularly remember was to Bradford-on-Avon. It was quite a job getting Osbert out of the house, since he was in extremely low spirits. It is a commonplace to say that people whose job it is to make others laugh are themselves all too well acquainted with gloom; a commonplace, but nevertheless often true. It certainly was so in Osbert's case. Old age and the deterioration of his faculties made the depressive side of his character ever more apparent.

He was sunk in gloom throughout the morning's drive. On arrival at about noon we immediately headed for the nearest inn for lunch. Osbert's martini had the kind of transforming effect that spinach had on Popeye. By the end of the meal he was in sparkling form. We

238

stepped out to visit the tiny Saxon church and the contrastingly vast fourteenth-century tithe barn; these two buildings consolidated the effect of the martini, gloom was banished, and Osbert became a wonderfully informative, observant, erudite and stimulating guide.

But when I think of him now, the image that comes to my mind is of him sitting in his deep armchair by the fireside at Rose Cottage with Maud the dachshund on his lap. It is a longish room with a low ceiling, well lit, bright and warm. There are always flowers from the garden, and the walls are covered with pictures. There are landscapes and townscapes of his own, and drawings, paintings and engravings that include work by Edward Bawden, John Piper, John Craxton and a lithograph by Patrick Procktor (among other younger artists he admired David Hockney, but he owned nothing by him).

He is reading one of the weeklies, or one of the books with which Anne keeps him provided. On the side-table to his right is a pile of more books which almost invariably includes Thackeray's *Vanity Fair*. There is also a glass of martini, the first of the evening, and a heavy cut-glass ashtray containing several cigarette ends – Silk Cut nowadays; only rarely Turkish. As I come into the room Maud jumps down, wagging her tail dreamily, her long nails tick-tacking on the wooden floor. This sound alerts Osbert to my presence. He looks up and says 'Dear boy', and makes a token getting-up gesture which consists of putting his hands on the arms of the chair before sinking back into the cushions. 'Find yourself a drink. Anne is . . . *some*where.'

On one occasion I brought him a copy of Alan Bell's biography of Sidney Smith, for whom I had often heard him express great admiration. He asked if the book was any good. I said I thought it was very pedantic and that the author was nothing like so well matched to the subject as his predecessor Hesketh Pearson, though undoubtedly far more scholarly, since he had worked on it for about ten years and found about two thousand new letters.

'Ah, *letters*,' Osbert said. 'The telephone has put an end to *that*. If anyone was unfortunate enough to write *my* biography they'd find about twelve letters.'

Anne and I were both saddened and amused; Osbert had apparently forgotten that he was talking to his unfortunate biographer.

We sat down to dinner, and by the time we were about to go on to the cheese it was apparent that Osbert was, if not exactly incoherent, at least extremely sleepy. Anne suggested that he should sit in the armchair by the fire. He was a bit grumpy about this, but finally agreed. He refused offers of help, saying that he wasn't so geriatric that he couldn't walk across the room on his own.

Unfortunately he was wrong. He had walked only a few steps when out of the corner of my eye I saw him stumble. It is extraordinary how quickly the mind works in such circumstances. A lightning calculation of angles and distances came up with the answer that he was going to fall and hit his head on the doorjamb. I shot from my chair and half caught him, but I was off-balance and he was surprisingly heavy. The polished floor was slippery and the two of us crashed down together, Osbert embraced in my arms.

Though I hadn't stopped him falling I had at least cushioned his impact and prevented him from hitting his head on the doorjamb. (Instead I hit *my* head on the doorjamb.)

Osbert lay on the floor and we put a cushion under his head. He went to sleep, and Anne and I returned to the table – Anne calmer than I was. When it was time for coffee we were faced with a problem: the door that leads to the kitchen is the door that Osbert's head was propped against. This meant that I had to go out by the front door, round the house to the back door, and bring the coffee back by the same route.

Anne and I talked for a quarter of an hour or so, and eventually our conversation took a literary turn, in the course of which I confessed that so far as I was aware I had never read a word by George Meredith. 'Do you mean you haven't read *Modern Love*?' queried a disbelieving voice from the floor.

He was amazingly resilient. Over and over again he bounced back. Though the wit was now sporadic, when it came it flashed as brilliantly as ever. In his last years it could require effort and some patience (of which Anne evidently had a limitless supply) to keep things going, but I can't remember an occasion when I didn't enjoy his company. He was not only a very clever chap: he was a lovely person, and it was a joy and a privilege to know him.

Sir Osbert Lancaster died at his home in Chelsea on 27 July 1986, eight days before his seventy-eighth birthday. He is buried in the churchyard at West Winch in Norfolk, among the tombs of his eighteenth-century ancestors.

Appendix A

LANCASTER, Sir Osbert, Kt 1975; CBE 1953; RDI 1979; Artist and Writer; *b* 4 Aug, 1908; *o s* of late Robert Lancaster and Clare Bracebridge Manger; *m* 1933, Karen (*d* 1964), 2nd *d* of late Sir Austin Harris, KBE; one *s* one *d*; *m* 1967, Anne Scott-James *qv*. *Educ*: Charterhouse; Lincoln Coll., Oxford (Hon. Fellow, 1979); Slade Sch. Hon. FRIBA. Cartoonist *Daily Express* since 1939; Foreign Office (News Dept), 1940. Attached to HM Embassy, Athens, 1944 – 46; Sydney Jones Lecturer in Art, Liverpool Univ., 1947. Adviser to GLC Historic Building Bd., 1969. Governor King Edward VII Sch., King's Lynn. Hon. D.Litt. Birmingham Univ., 1964; Newcastle-upon-Tyne, 1970; St. Andrews, 1974; Oxon., 1975. Fellow, University College, London, 1967. Theatre Decors: *Pineapple Poll*, Sadler's Wells, 1951; *Bonne Bouche*, Covent Garden, 1952; *Love in a Village*, English Opera Group, 1952; *High Spirits*, Hippodrome, 1953; *Rake's Progress*, Edinburgh (for Glyndebourne), 1953; *All's Well That Ends Well*, Old Vic, 1953; *Don Pasquale*, Sadler's Wells, 1954; *Coppelia*, Covent Garden, 1954; *Napoli*, Festival Ballet, 1954; *Falstaff*, Edinburgh (for Glyndebourne), 1955; *Hotel Paradiso*, Winter Garden, 1956; *Zuleika*, Saville, 1957; *L'Italiana in Algeri*, Glyndebourne, 1957; *Tiresias*, English Opera Group, 1958; *Candide*, Saville, 1959; *La Fille Mal Gardée*, Covent Garden, 1960; *She Stoops to Conquer*, Old Vic, 1960; *Le Pietra del Paragone*, Glyndebourne, 1964; *Peter Grimes*, Bulgarian National Opera, Sofia, 1964; *L'Heure Espagnole*, Glyndebourne, 1966; *The Rising of the Moon*, Glyndebourne, 1970; *The Sorcerer*, D'Oyly-Carte, 1971. Publications: *Progress at Pelvis Bay*, 1936; *Our Sovereigns*, 1936; *Pillar to Post*, 1938; *Homes Sweet Homes*, 1939; *Classical Landscape with Figures*, 1947; *The Saracen's Head*, 1948; *Drayneflete Revealed*, 1949; *Façades and Faces*, 1950; *Private Views*, 1956; *The Year of the Comet*, 1957; *Etudes*, 1958; *Here, of All Places*, 1959, reissued as *A Cartoon History of Architecture*, 1976; *Signs of the Times*, 1961; *All Done from Memory* (Autobiog.), 1953; *With an Eye to the Future* (Autobiog.), 1967; *Temporary Diversions*, 1968; *Sailing to Byzantium*, 1969; *Recorded Live*, 1970; *Meaningful Confrontations*, 1971; *Theatre in the Flat*, 1972; *The Littlehampton Bequest*, 1973; (with Anne Scott-James) *The Pleasure Garden*, 1977; *Scene Changes*, 1978; *Ominous Cracks*, 1979; *The Life and Times of Maudie Littlehampton*, 1982; *The Littlehampton Saga*, 1984. *Recreation:* topography. *Address:* 78 Cheyne Court, Royal Hospital Road, SW3. *Clubs:* Brooks's, Pratt's, Beefsteak, Garrick.

(*Who's Who*)

Appendix B

Osbert was one of the select few who have twice been guests on the BBC radio programme *Desert Island Discs*. On the first occasion (17 February 1955) his selected gramophone records with which to be cast away were: *'Papa peint dans les bois'* (Les Frères Jacques); Donizetti's *Don Pasquale* (Act 2 quintet); 'Any Old Iron' (Harry Champion); Mozart's *'Il mio tesoro'* (from *Don Giovanni*), sung by Richard Tauber; 'Drum, Drum' (Danae and T. Maroudas); Mozart's Piano Concerto in B flat major (K.595); 'Bridge Game' (from the revue *Nine Sharp*); Stravinsky's *Apollon Musagète* (Boston Symphony, Koussevitsky). His chosen luxury was the Venus de Milo.

He was abandoned for the second time on a desert island on 22 December 1979, when he chose: Gluck's *'Che faro senza Euridice?'* from *Orfeo ed Euridice*, sung by Kathleen Ferrier; Weill and Brecht's 'Alabama Song' from *The Rise and Fall of the City of Mahagonny*, sung by Lotte Lenya; 'Spring', sung by Douglas Byng; Verdi's *'Va pensiero, sull'ali dorate'* from *Nabucco*; the love scene from Noël Coward's *Private Lives* (Act 1), played by Noël Coward and Gertrude Lawrence; Poulenc's *Les mamelles de Tiresias*; Stravinsky's *Apollon Musagète* (Ansermet conducting the Orchestre de la Suisse Romande) – the only survivor from the list of a quarter of a century earlier; Bach's *'Ein' feste burg ist unser Gott'*. The luxury this time was a live sturgeon to provide caviare. By now the programme also allowed its castaways to take a book other than the Bible and Shakespeare. Osbert chose Gibbon's *History of the Decline and Fall of the Roman Empire*. (Osbert was never able to get the cottage wireless to work, so he went out on a cold winter's day and listened to this broadcast on the car radio.)

Appendix C

Osbert and Karen's address book at Henley includes among others the names of (in alphabetical order): Edward Ardizzone, Frederick Ashton, Lord and Lady Astor, Mr and Mrs Michael Astor, the Betjemans, Cecil Beaton, Maurice Bowra, Lady Bonham-Carter, Max Beerbohm (crossed out, after his death), Sidney Bernstein, Earl Birkenhead, Nicolas Bentley, Elizabeth Bowen, Lionel Brett, Bernhard Berenson (crossed out), Sir Gerald Barry, Sir John and Lady Balfour, the Duke and Duchess of Buccleuch, Sir Harold Caccia, Arthur Christiansen, John and Ernestine Carter, John Cranko, Hugh Casson, Moran Caplat, Lord and Lady David Cecil. And so it goes on: Roger Fulford, Peter Fleming, Sir Henry d'Avigdor Goldsmid, M. and Mme Ghika, Walter Goetz, Carl Giles (the *Express* cartoonist), Roger Hinks, H. de C. Hastings, Sir Roy and Lady Harrod, Lord Horder, Sir William Hayter, Rupert Hart-Davis, John Hayward, Philip Hope-Wallace, Lord Gladwyn, Lord Kinross, Ludovic Kennedy, James Lees-Milne, Sir Reginald and Lady Leeper, Patrick Leigh Fermor, John Murray, Raymond Mortimer, Alan Moorehead (Port Ercole, Prov. di Grossetto), Harold Macmillan, Angus Malcolm, Fitzroy Maclean, Malcolm Muggeridge, Harold Nicolson, Alan Pryce-Jones, John and Myfanwy Piper, Anthony and Lady Violet Powell, Lord and Lady Pakenham (now Longford), the Hon. Mrs Rodd (Nancy Mitford), J. M. Richards, Sir Steven Runciman, Roger Senhouse, Christopher Sykes, Reynolds Stone, Saul Steinberg, Sir John Summerson, John Sparrow, Ronald Searle, Sir Osbert Sitwell, Sacheverell Sitwell, C. M. Woodhouse, Rex Warner, Mr and Mrs Gerald de Winton, Evelyn Waugh, John Wyndham, Sir John Wheeler-Bennett.

Since most of these names must have been in *Who's Who* one half-wonders why the Lancasters bothered to have an address book, though *Who's Who* would not have included the homely and practical telephone numbers of doctors (a huge number), dentists, taxis and the local rat-catcher which jostle with these celebrated names from the world of art, architecture, cartooning, ballet, opera, literature, publishing, politics, the aristocracy, Fleet Street and Oxford.

Appendix D

Proust's questionnaire is so-called because Marcel Proust completed it twice, once at the age of thirteen and again when he was twenty. Its origins, however, are in Victorian England, where it was a parlour game, and Proust certainly read the questions in English. I put them to Osbert in May 1981.

What is for you the height of misery?
I can think of many.

Where would you like to live?
London. I've always lived in London.

What is your idea of happiness on earth?
Being pushed in a pram through a London which no longer exists.

What faults do you find most forgivable?
Idleness.

Which fictional heroes do you prefer?
The hero of *Vanity Fair*. Of course it's a book without heroes. They're all shits, or utter fools. That's why it's such a good book. Dobbin is an admirable character, the only admirable character in the book, but by God he's a bore.

Who is your favourite historical character?
Somebody very lazy. Disraeli.

Who are your favourite heroines in real life?
I don't know. The ones who did most good were so bossy you'd be driven mad by them.

Who are your favourite heroines in fiction?
I suppose Becky Sharp. The heroine of *La Chartreuse de Parme* – what's her name? – the Duchessa.

Your favourite painter?
Vermeer. My favourite picture now is *The View of Delft*, but it changes all the time.

Your favourite musician?
That also changes so quickly. Handel or Mozart, but perhaps Haydn. There's such a hell of a lot of Haydn I don't know. He lived such a long time. But I always come back to Handel.

What quality do you admire most in a man?
Of course one likes generosity. Yes, generosity in the widest sense – generosity of judgement and behaviour.
In a woman?
Devotion.
The virtue you admire most?
Imagination.
Your favourite occupation?
At my age, remembrance of things past.
Who would you like to have been?
Who did have a really happy life? Who was that character who fell dead finishing his last work? Perhaps Verdi.
What is the main trait of your character?
Gregariousness – I like my fellow men.
What do you appreciate most in your friends?
Their company.
Your main fault?
Procrastination.
Your dream of happiness?
A total absence of anxiety.
What would be your greatest unhappiness?
Deprivation – of friends, loved ones, faculties.
What would you like to be?
I'm content with my lot. I've been very fortunate.
Your favourite colour?
That's an idiotic question to ask anyone who's an artist. Colours only have any reality in conjunction with other colours.
Your favourite flower?
I can never think of their names. I must ask Anne. I suppose roses.
Favourite bird?
A very interesting question. The golden oriole I've only seen twice, and I don't think it's my favourite. I'm very fond of nuthatches.
Favourite prose writers?
I could read Boswell till the cows come home. Donne. Henry James.
Favourite poets?
Again Donne. And the incumbent Laureate (John Betjeman). I've been reading Matthew Arnold, but he's so gloomy. But I'm not constant in my loyalties.
Heroes in real life?
Not Winston . . . I must come back to this one.
Heroines?
I suppose Elizabeth I.
Favourite names?
What do you mean? That's a funny question. I like Osbert.

What do you dislike most?

Pain. Let's have no nonsense about being brave. Deprivation, in which I include one's memory, one's family.

The historical characters you despise most?

That list is as long as your arm. Chamberlain comes very high. I suppose Louis XV. Rosebery was very despicable – so many missed opportunities, so lazy and always shifting the blame on to others.

The military achievement you admire most?

One of the great retreats. There were several brilliant ones in the last war. On the whole I would say quite firmly those which achieved the maximum effect with the minimum casualties.

The reform you admire most?

I can't think of one at the moment.

A natural gift you would like to have?

Ability to play the piano.

How would you like to die?

Swiftly, suddenly, painlessly. But with a short time for reflection – to confess my sins and think of all the things I have left undone and ought to have done. I would like to die shriven.

Your present mood?

Dilapidation.

Your motto?

My family motto is so shaming. *Ornat fortem prudentia.* Prudence adorns the brave. It was thought up by my grandfather for the Prudential Insurance Company. If I had to think of one for myself it would be 'If you can't forgive, forget'.

Notes to the Illustrations

The publishers would like to thank the following for permission to reproduce drawings, paintings and photographs for this book: John Murray, Anne Lancaster, Cara Lancaster, Lee Miller (© Lee Miller Archives 1985), Jane Bown, Patrick Lichfield, Robert Tobin, Keith Cattell, Paul Cannon. Grateful acknowledgements are also due to Glyndebourne Festival Opera and Chatto & Windus for their help.

Index

Illustrations are not indexed. See Notes to the Illustrations *on p. 247*